PRAISE FOR CH

"A gritty, compelling, and altogether engrossing novel that reads as if ripped from the headlines. I couldn't turn the pages fast enough. Chad Zunker is the real deal."

—Christopher Reich, *New York Times* bestselling author of *Numbered Account* and *Rules of Deception*

"*Good Will Hunting* meets *The Bourne Identity*."

—Fred Burton, *New York Times* bestselling author of *Under Fire*

SHADOW
SHEPHERD

OTHER TITLES BY CHAD ZUNKER

The Tracker

SHADOW SHEPHERD

CHAD ZUNKER

Text copyright © 2017 by Chad Zunker
All rights reserved.

Published by Thomas & Mercer, Seattle

www.apub.com

Amazon, the Amazon logo, and Thomas & Mercer are trademarks of Amazon.com, Inc., or its affiliates.

ISBN-13: 9781542045544
ISBN-10: 1542045541

Cover design by Jae Song

Printed in the United States of America

To Lane, my father,
who lived a life of relentlessly pursuing his God-given
dreams,
and by doing so taught his youngest son how to do the
same.
To Doug, my father-in-law,
who has always supported the crazy dreamer
who married his eldest daughter.

AUTHOR'S NOTE

Dear Readers,

You may recognize I made a transition to third-person omniscient storytelling with *Shadow Shepherd*. This means you get to read the story through multiple character viewpoints and sometimes know things that even Sam Callahan doesn't know. This is different from *The Tracker*, where I wrote strictly in first-person narrative and told all story threads, past and present, through Sam's unique but limited view. I felt writing *The Tracker* in first-person narrative was an intimate and powerful way to introduce Sam to readers, so you could truly connect with Sam's voice and heart, his struggles and pain, and how he views his life in relationship with others—all while on the run! In many ways, *The Tracker* was both autobiography and thriller, all packed into one book.

However, as I began to explore this next Sam Callahan adventure, I yearned to expand the scope of the story and further develop other important characters—especially Natalie Foster, who will continue to play such a pivotal role in Sam's journey. Telling this sequel and future Sam Callahan stories in third-person narrative will allow me the flexibility to write even more exciting story lines, as well as help readers connect on a much deeper level with supporting characters. I'm very excited about what it allowed me to do with *Shadow Shepherd*. I hope you will enjoy it, too.

 Sincerely,
 Chad Zunker

Everything that we see is a shadow cast by that which we do not see.

—*Martin Luther King Jr.*

If a man owns a hundred sheep, and one of them wanders away, will he not leave the ninety-nine on the hills and go to look for the one who wandered off?

—*Matthew 18:12*

ONE

Sam Callahan hung from the hotel balcony ledge, four stories up, and couldn't believe he was once again on the run from a man with a gun.

His adrenaline was pumping, his breath short, his mind racing.

It was all too familiar, like a recurring bad dream. The assassin had already shot and killed another man inside the hotel suite: Sam's new client, a guy he'd met only twenty minutes ago, before all hell broke loose. Sam hung from a brick ledge, looking down the sixty or so feet to the hotel grounds below. He shook his head, closed his eyes. He still had nightmares about last fall. The election. Redrock assassins. The FBI manhunt. His cancer-stricken mom kidnapped. The gray-bearded man. His face plastered all over national TV news. He was still hearing the thunderous echo of private military helicopters chasing him from overhead and seeing visions of bullets rain down from the sky. He was still waking up in cold sweats with the face of his nemesis, Square Jaw, fresh in his mind, like a mental tattoo he could never erase.

Now this. He thought of Natalie, the only woman he'd ever loved, and cursed.

He had to get out of this alive.

His fingers dug into the slippery brick, wet from the thick Mexico City humidity. The July afternoon heat was stifling. When he'd flung himself over the balcony railing a few seconds earlier, his left shoe had flown off and landed somewhere below in the central courtyard of the Four Seasons. He'd also torn a gash in the seat of his dark-blue suit pants, not that this was his biggest concern at the moment—that would be the killer still inside the executive suite. Sam's suit jacket was also inside, folded neatly over an expensive chair in the living room. His blue tie felt like it was choking him as it flapped in the hot breeze. He hated ties and hadn't grown accustomed to wearing them since starting at the Benoltz law firm three weeks ago.

Samuel W. Callahan, attorney at law.

He was still getting used to the new title and didn't like being an attorney at this very moment. His fingers trembled under the pressure of his dangling weight. They were already slipping. He wouldn't last too long.

With his recent graduation from Georgetown Law, Sam had thought he was finally moving on from the disaster of last November, getting a fresh start and putting the past behind him, finding a new normalcy in his job at the law firm. Until ten minutes ago, when his client had received a text. Sam had seen his face turn ashen, like his doctor had just sent over fatal test results. Moments later, a man had burst through the hotel-room door and then chased his client toward one of the bedrooms, where he'd put a silent bullet into his client's back. His client was dead. Sam was sure of that. He wasn't going to be next. He'd seized that moment to run. On instinct he'd moved to the only exit available near him, the balcony, and taken a flying leap.

Before getting gunned down, Sam's client had started spilling his guts, as if he knew these were going to be the final moments of his life, his last chance to hand over critical information from his case. So he did—sort of. Sam was still confused about his client's empty briefcase. None of it was information that he wanted. Not if it meant a man now chasing him with a gun. Not if it meant seeing more blood spilled. His boss, David Benoltz, may have recruited him—an attorney with a good grasp of the law who was even better at handling people in the field—to be his so-called fixer, but Sam didn't think this was what David had in mind when he'd sent him on a plane to Mexico City that morning to meet the firm's newest client.

If he did, Sam was resigning immediately. Provided he got out of this alive.

He needed to get off this balcony ledge first. They hadn't taught how to get out of a predicament quite like this in his three years of law school. There was no Running from an Assassin 101 class at Georgetown. Tragically, he'd learned to run as a kid, trying to escape the angry fists of drunken foster dads. He'd then mastered the art of running while living on the streets as a homeless teenager and stealing cars. And he'd gotten his PhD in running last November as a political tracker.

He was tired of running.

But life continued to give him no choice.

Sam again thought about his meeting with the client.

His client had shared *a lot* of information in a very small amount of time. He was neck-deep in something serious; that was for sure. A conspiracy involving very powerful and dangerous people. Any doubts about just how dangerous had all but been eliminated in the past few minutes. However, it was the very last thing his client had said to him, in his panic, right before the assassin had burst through the hotel-room door and started shooting that had left Sam reeling the most. They were words that were personal and shocking.

"You've got to find Rich."

"Who the hell is Rich?" Sam had asked, confused.

"My partner, Rich Hebbard. He instructed me to contact your firm and specifically ask for *you*."

"Me? Why would he say to ask for me?"

"Because he's your father."

Sam had shaken his head, stunned. He'd never met his father and knew almost nothing about him.

He couldn't hang on to the ledge much longer. Not only were his fingers slipping but the assassin inside saw him move toward the balcony. He had only seconds. He studied the area below him, the outdoor hotel courtyard, and let his mind begin to map out his surroundings. A huge water fountain, trees, flower beds that surrounded a tic-tac-toe board of landscaped sidewalks, and several outdoor seating areas, including a dozen tables directly beneath him. The tables all had huge canvas umbrellas that blocked out the blazing afternoon sun. His eyes settled on the multicolored umbrellas. It was his only chance without breaking both legs or, worse, his neck. He heard footsteps on the balcony. It was time to go. He chose the yellow umbrella, swung his legs once to get some needed momentum, said a prayer, and then he let go.

As he fell, he spotted the man with the gun peer down at him over the railing. They connected eyes for just a second. The man was probably in his early forties, black hair slicked back, sort of reminded Sam of Antonio Banderas in *Desperado*. He wore a sleek black suit like a normal businessman. A businessman didn't usually carry a gun and silencer—although Sam knew they sometimes did business differently in Mexico, so he guessed anything was possible.

It was surreal to drop from the sky.

He again thought of Natalie. *Always* Natalie.

TWO

Sam landed square on top of the yellow umbrella—a perfect fall tucked in a tight ball, like he was doing a cannonball off the high dive at the neighborhood pool. The heavy fabric instantly collapsed all around him. Then the glass table shattered beneath him, the gravity of his fall causing dishes to fly, chairs to bounce every which way, one loud and violent heap of destruction. He hit the concrete with a heavy thud, his breath completely knocked out, felt pain shoot up and down his left arm. But when he got his bearings, he thought he was okay. He could turn his neck both ways. It wasn't broken. He slowly tested his arms and legs. They all seemed to be working properly. He was sucking major air into his lungs and in devastating pain all over his body, but he was still alive. He could move around okay.

Sam was immediately swarmed by bystanders, who all stared and gawked. He was sure it was quite the spectacle to see a man fall from his hotel-room balcony. Two male staff members in uniform rushed over to him to make sure he was okay, speaking in rapid Spanish, and started to help clear all the debris away.

Sam peeled himself up off the sidewalk, spit glass shards out of his mouth.

One of the hotel staffers pointed at his forehead with concern. Sam touched it with his fingers, examined them, saw the blood dripping. There was *a lot* of blood. He felt dizzy but stable. The other staffer was trying to get him to sit down, to take it easy, but Sam rebuffed him when he spotted the second man out of the corner of his eye, one hundred feet out. This was just how his mind worked, even eight months after the Redrock episode. He found himself always watching his back, always studying others within his close vicinity, perpetually paranoid that someone was still out there trying to get him. Like a permanent scar, Pastor Isaiah, his mentor and the man who rescued him from juvie, had said, that feeling might never go away—he just had to learn to channel it the right way.

Certainly not now, not with this happening again.

The second man had a thick goatee, looked to be in his thirties, and wore a pair of sunglasses and a dark suit very similar to the assassin upstairs. He moved briskly across the courtyard around the large fountain, coming directly toward Sam and the growing crowd. Sam recognized his purposeful gait. He'd seen it all too often a few months back. This man was not coming forward as a concerned citizen—he was coming to finish the job.

Sam stepped forward, felt his left knee buckle in pain, and nearly knocked over one of the hotel staffers as he pushed his way through the small crowd. They were dismayed. He had just fallen from his fourth-story balcony, and now he was up and running?

Sam paused briefly, scanned the courtyard.

His mind pulled up a quick map, like a mental GPS, and he could suddenly envision a dozen different possible escape paths. He'd discovered this heightened ability to see detailed maps in his mind as a street kid, which made him the best thief in his crew. He'd always had a freakish way to see around hidden corners and get himself out of tight spots. The mind-mapping didn't help him much in law school, but he certainly needed it right now. The courtyard was fully enclosed within the hotel property. He had to get to the outside. He had to get to the busy streets of Mexico City. He had to get to the crowds if he had any hope of losing them.

He chose a path and sprinted up the courtyard sidewalk toward the main lobby—away from the man chasing him—bound up the steps, and burst through the large glass doors. The spacious lobby was busy, with several guests at the front desk, dozens more sitting around in luxury, sipping their margaritas and cocktails from a hotel bar nearby. Everyone stopped and stared at the crazy man who'd just made the brazen entrance from the central courtyard. The maniac wearing only one black shoe with blood rolling down his face.

Sam pointed behind him, yelled, "He's got a gun. *Pistola! Pistola!*"

His words instantly raised the level of concern in the room. Panic ensued. Guests began to jump out of their seats, spill drinks, topple over each other, scrambling and darting for the nearest exits. Sam saw a uniformed security guard appear from around the corner. He didn't look like much: skinny and unprepared, even with a gun strapped to his waist. Sam doubted this guy could stop an assassin, and he certainly wasn't going to put his life in the guard's pathetic hands. Instead, Sam ran for the front doors of the hotel, pushed through them, spilled out onto a busy sidewalk near the hotel's entrance. There were a dozen cars parked while guests were dropping off luggage and checking in at the front desk.

Sam whipped his head left, right. He could hear a police siren nearby. He'd be happy to talk to the police, to start figuring out what the hell had just happened to him upstairs, and to find some asylum. He cursed again. It didn't look like he was going to get that option just yet. He spotted two more men, fifty feet to his right, standing beside a black Mercedes sedan. Dark suits, sunglasses, the same getup as the other two guys inside the hotel. There was a whole crew of them. One of them held a finger to his ear, as if listening to instructions in an earpiece, and then pointed in Sam's direction. When the man reached inside his suit jacket, Sam knew what was coming next.

Who were they? What had Sam's client done?

The white Range Rover was parked to his left, ten feet away, engine still running, an elderly man of probably eighty helping a valet unload bags from the back. Sam jumped into the driver's seat, put the SUV in gear, and punched the gas pedal down to the floorboard. The engine roared, and the thick tires spun powerfully. He yanked the steering wheel left, did a quick U-turn in the hotel entrance. In his mirror, Sam noticed the elderly car owner yelling, shaking a frail fist, his luggage toppling out the back—a suitcase rolled and spilled open, clothes littering the pavement. But Sam never slowed. He watched his mirrors. The two men in dark suits scrambled to their Mercedes and worked quickly to follow him away from the hotel.

The street in front of the Four Seasons was thick with traffic. As he'd learned on the cab ride from the airport earlier, everywhere in Mexico City was crowded—there were twenty million people! Sam barely slowed, however, as he zipped into oncoming traffic, causing cars to swerve and jam on their brakes. He punched his foot to the floor again. He was flying by other cars, left and right, swerving in and out of congested traffic. Blood started dripping into his eyes from the cut on his forehead. He could even taste it in his mouth. He quickly wiped it away. The Mercedes was already gaining ground on him. There was clearly a trained driver behind the steering wheel, and the sedan was sportier than his vehicle.

They came up on a roundabout in the middle of the street. Sam jerked the steering wheel left without hesitating, cut into oncoming traffic inside the roundabout, causing more cars to swerve out of his way. A gray truck veered right and slammed into another car. Glass shattered and metal crunched. Sam clutched the steering wheel in tight fists. The tires of the Range Rover were squealing under intense pressure as Sam circled the water fountain in the middle at nearly full speed, looking for a good exit outlet.

In his mirror, Sam noticed that the Mercedes driver was even bolder. He pulled the sedan straight into oncoming traffic, an effort to catch Sam on the other side of the roundabout. More cars swerved and crashed, a red van losing control and smashing directly into the water fountain in the middle. Water spewed everywhere. The Mercedes was headed straight for Sam, clearly aimed at stopping him at all costs.

Although on a collision course, Sam had no time to reverse direction. He punched the gas pedal down even farther, swerved at the last second to avoid a direct hit. But the SUV was not brisk enough. The Mercedes clipped the back end of Sam's vehicle at high speed, jolting him, sending the Range Rover into a spin cycle in the middle of the street.

Sam came to a screeching halt with his front end now facing the Mercedes.

They were thirty feet from each other. He could see the driver. A quick staredown.

Sam quickly took in his surroundings, his heart hammering away. Smoke filled the air from the other crashed-up vehicles around the roundabout. Some drivers were already getting out of cars, dizzy, angry. The water fountain was now shooting an erratic stream of water more than a hundred feet straight up into the late-afternoon sky. There was a growing crowd of shoppers watching wide-eyed on the nearby sidewalks.

Sam's eyes again settled on the Mercedes.

The driver's door of the black sedan opened.

A man leaned out, aimed a gun at him.

THREE

Sam heard screams come from the crowd of onlookers on the sidewalk.

He punched the gas to the floor, yanked the steering wheel right, and ducked as low as possible in the driver's seat. His back window suddenly shattered, and then he heard three more consecutive gunshot punches hit the back end of the SUV. He kept the gas pedal to the floorboard, the expensive vehicle rocketing forward. He had to swerve repeatedly in and out of traffic, so as not to crash and burn. He'd never driven a car quite like this, not even during his stealing spree as a teenager, and it was only his heightened mental abilities that now somehow kept him on the road. Up ahead and across the median, he saw a series of flashing lights coming toward him in the opposite lane. As he flew past them, he counted three white cars with swirling red-and-blue lights and the word *Policia* on the side. All three police cars swerved to cross the median to come after him, right behind the speedy Mercedes still on his tail. He was happy to talk with the police but not with the men in black suits nearby.

A red light up ahead momentarily delayed traffic in front of him. Sam knew he couldn't stop in this crowd, not with the Mercedes still so close, so he yanked the SUV up onto the sidewalk, where he darted around the stalled traffic. He cut through the grass to avoid several sidewalk vendors and their carts, and then he nearly took out two men riding bikes. He made it through the red light and yanked the Range Rover back safely into the street on the other side, where he narrowly evaded a large white moving truck. The moving truck swerved and skidded to an abrupt stop. He watched his rearview mirror. The Mercedes driver was attempting to take the same sidewalk route, but it got stuck at the red light as the white moving truck stalled and completely blocked traffic in all directions. The police cars also got stuck in the sudden traffic jam. A chorus of honking horns ensued.

Sam figured it was time to make his move. To ditch the SUV and get lost.

Up ahead, he spotted a sign: LAGO DE CHAPULTEPEC. He could tell it was a huge lake inside a popular city park. He looked over into the passenger seat, noticed a metal cane—the old man's walking stick. He quickly played out a scenario in his mind, then he reached over and snagged the cane. He thought about it for only a second before he swerved the Range Rover up onto the sidewalk again, punched the gas, ducked his head, and rammed the SUV straight through a wrought iron fence that separated the park from the main road. He was accelerating through a grassy area now, the car jarring him with bumps, the lake just a hundred yards ahead of him. He carefully placed one end of the old man's metal cane onto the gas pedal, and then he used the seat dial on the side to secure the cane in place against the front seat.

The Range Rover was gaining rapid speed, like a jet about to take off.

Sam aimed the SUV toward a small hill to his left, away from the crowds of people inside the park, as well as the numerous paddleboats and recreational watercraft he spotted out on the lake. He wasn't trying to take out anyone else. He grimaced in anticipation—this was going to hurt like hell. He opened the driver's door, dove out, hit the grass hard but kept his arms and legs tucked tight to his body. He flipped and rolled a dozen times, his head getting whipped back and forth, before finally sliding to a stop on his stomach.

He turned, watched, as the Range Rover catapulted off the hill and sailed through the air, like one of those slow-motion scenes with a whale jumping in the ocean. The SUV hit the water with an enormous splash and began to sink almost immediately. People from all over the park started running up to the shoreline to watch. A few people were already jumping into the water from nearby rowboats and swimming toward the vehicle, probably thinking someone was still trapped inside. Sam noticed a couple of others looking over his way. He quickly got to his feet. His left knee almost gave out. He might have also broken a bone in his shoulder. It felt like someone had stuck a knife in it. He hobbled over into a wooded area to his left, away from the park crowds, and then hid behind a small dock house. He watched the scene unfold from a distance. He didn't spot the men from the Mercedes. Surely they were smart enough to avoid the chaos and crowds.

He'd survived. Just barely.

Within seconds, a swarm of police cars were on the scene. The crowd was growing bigger. Sam slid down to the concrete, sat on the ground, his back resting up against the dock house. He exhaled for what felt like the first time in fifteen minutes. His head hurt. His knee hurt. His shoulder hurt. Hell, *everything* hurt.

He wiped his face with both hands, a mix of sweat and blood.

He tried to get his bearings. He needed to call his boss, David, tell him that their client was now dead and David's newest law associate was a very close second. But his cell phone was back at the Four Seasons. As a matter of fact, *everything* Sam had brought with him to Mexico City was either back at the Four Seasons or still inside his hotel room at the Hyatt.

He had nothing else. Not even two shoes.

He took another deep breath, winced.

He would talk to the police, sort this out, see if they could tell him who these men were who were trying to kill him. Find out what kind of minefield he'd walked into this afternoon. Sam knew very little about his new client. Only that he'd immediately paid the expensive retainer, and for Sam's travel for this off-site meeting, so David had tossed Sam on a last-second flight from DC. He felt stunned by the sudden turn of events. Another man had been shot and killed right in front of him, just twenty feet away. He did quick math. It was the seventh time in the past year that Sam had seen someone killed up close and personal. After last November, he'd hoped he'd never have to go through another experience like that for the rest of his life. But no such luck.

Life was throwing him another vicious right hook. Why?

FOUR

Natalie Foster was on the move, as usual.

She quickly locked the front door to her third-floor DC townhome, trotted down the wooden stairwell to the first floor of her building, and found the back exit to the tiny parking lot reserved only for residents. Her silver Jeep Cherokee was parked in her normal spot, the faded Saint Louis Cardinals sticker permanently stuck on the rear bumper—her allegiance to both her dad and her youth. She'd already changed out of her suit and heels for the day when the text had arrived. She was curled up in her usual spot on the sofa in comfortable blue jeans, her favorite gray Missouri Tigers hoodie, bare feet beneath her, a warm mug of coffee in her hands, and a good book loading up on her Kindle. Then she grabbed her cell phone, read the text, and had her evening blitzed. This was not unusual for her.

As a reporter for *PowerPlay*, a popular DC political blog, she always had people reaching out to her about something. Her cell phone went off two dozen times every hour. Some were known sources, but many were unknown. She was okay with her phone number being out there for public consumption. It was all part of the gig. She needed the city; the city needed her. They'd had a great relationship the past four years. *Everyone* loved to be involved in a good political scandal. The most powerful and corrupt city in the world always provided her plenty of news fodder.

She'd understandably been even busier the past eight months. Ever since she and Sam Callahan had survived assassins and broken the story last November involving the sinister conspiracy between congressional candidate Lucas McCallister, of the powerful McCallister political family, and Victor Larsen, CEO of Redrock Security, her cell phone had nearly tripled in activity.

It was a story that had sent shock waves throughout the country.

A story that had changed her own life in many ways.

She thought of Sam, put the keys in the ignition.

The anonymous texts were always wild cards. Very rarely did they ever amount to much. There were *a lot* of nutcases out there in this city. She had to be careful. For every twenty text messages from mysterious sources, she usually found only one decent news lead. It was most often a lot of work for very little payoff. But she loved every minute of it. It was all part of the job and her life calling—even if it interrupted her evening plans with a good book.

This specific text exchange felt legit because of the detail involved. Which was why she'd thrown her brown hair into a ponytail, put on her running shoes, and grabbed her keys.

Text: You still working on the Hansel story?

Natalie: Who is this?

Text: Can't say. But I know something. Can we meet?

Natalie: What do you know?

Text: Proof he knew of payment to Barnstorm. That worth meeting?

Natalie: I can meet now. Where?

Text: City Center. Top floor of parking garage off 11th. Red Nissan Altima.

Natalie: I'll be there in 15.

She backed out, put the Cherokee in drive, sped out of the parking alley.

Natalie was working on a story involving Senator Todd Hansel of Mississippi amid rumors that he'd knowingly accepted money from a risky PAC called Barnstorm. A PAC started by a Mississippi businessman named Dennis Janey, who had recently been exposed as a twenty-year member of the Ku Klux Klan. Reelection was at stake. Everyone was in full-on denial mode.

Natalie swiftly navigated busy DC traffic. The streets were crowded as the city's buildings emptied for the end of the workday and sent everyone back to apartments, brownstones, and the suburbs. Paused at a stoplight, Natalie took a double glance in her rearview mirror at the driver directly behind her in the unmarked white van. He was bald with square glasses and a dark beard. Her eyes narrowed. She could've sworn she'd seen the driver earlier that day. But where? Her mind jumped through hoops, but she couldn't quite place him. She kept her eyes on her mirrors as she moved through downtown. The white van remained behind her for several blocks, always a vehicle or two back.

When Natalie reached the parking garage at City Center—a downtown development with condos, offices, and shopping—she slowed her Cherokee to the curb before entering, eyes locked on her rearview mirror. The white van slowly eased past, the driver staring straight ahead, and then the van turned at the corner in front of her and disappeared from view. She exhaled, relaxed. Maybe it was all in her head. She'd been on heightened alert for the past week. The reporter who'd broken the story about Dennis Janey's KKK involvement had had his car torched outside a restaurant six nights ago. The reporter was okay, but the incident had made everyone a little jumpy. Not that Natalie needed any extra help in the paranoid department. The past eight months had admittedly been difficult for her after her near-death experience with Redrock assassins last November.

She turned into the parking garage, got her ticket at the machine, and circled up the levels. The parked cars in the garage started to thin as she neared the top level, which was obviously her source's intention. This person didn't want anyone else around for their meeting. There were only a dozen or so cars still parked on level ten, with several spaces between each of them, and Natalie spotted the red Nissan Altima parked near a column in the very corner. A young guy in his early twenties was leaning up against the back of the car, waiting, hands in pockets. He wore khaki pants and a white button-down, looked like any number of political interns she met in her job throughout the week.

She parked in an empty spot five cars over, got out.

He seemed to register who she was and stiffened. She walked toward him. The guy had bushy brown hair and a blue tie that was loosened around his neck. He had a coffee spill on the front of his white dress shirt. She did not recognize him. He rocked on his heels, looked anxious. All good signs. If he didn't look nervous, she would never believe his story.

"Thanks for coming," he said.

"You work in Hansel's office?" Natalie asked, stopping five feet from him.

"I'd rather not say."

"Okay, where's the e-mail?"

He patted his front pants pocket. "What will you do with it?"

"Work quickly to verify authenticity."

"It's the real deal. I swear."

"Then verifying it should be easy."

"You'll keep me out of your story?"

"Unless you're brave enough to go on record."

He gave his first quick smile. "Not a chance."

She already knew that would be the case; otherwise, she wouldn't be parked on the tenth level of a random parking garage. They'd be meeting in a café in public somewhere.

"How did you get this e-mail?" she asked.

He shrugged. "Friend of a friend."

"Okay. Sure."

He sighed. "Look, I know you can track me down, if you really want, but I'll deny ever being here with you if you do. I'm not looking to commit career suicide."

"Then why're you doing this?"

He shrugged. "I have my reasons. Can we just get this over with? No offense, Ms. Foster, but I don't really want anyone seeing me with you."

"Sure, let me have it."

He pulled a folded white sheet of paper out of his pocket, held it out for her. She stepped forward, reached for it. When she did, the guy suddenly grabbed her by the wrist, yanked her forward, nearly off her feet. He twisted her right arm behind her back, causing pain to shoot up her shoulder, and he reached around with his other arm to cover her mouth with his other hand before she could scream.

Natalie felt a rush of adrenaline. She reacted on instinct. She bit down hard on his hand, felt the skin give, and then she slammed her head backward into his nose as hard as she could. She heard something crack in his face. He yelled out in pain. The collision also made her dizzy for a moment. The guy didn't let go. He was much stronger than she'd imagined. She squirmed again, fighting violently to get an arm free, jabbed her right elbow into his gut, and heard him gasp for air.

His grip momentarily loosened. She wiggled free.

Before Natalie could run, she heard tires squeal around the corner. Then the same unmarked white van from the street appeared right in front of her, the bald driver with square glasses and beard slamming on the brakes, blocking her escape path. In her hesitation, the intern again grabbed her from behind, squeezed her tightly in both arms. The back doors to the van opened, and two more men jumped out. They wore all black, looked to be in their thirties. Nothing too distinguishable about them. While being held from behind, Natalie raised up her legs and kicked the first guy—a stocky man with a crew cut—directly in the face. He was not expecting it and dropped immediately. She couldn't get a good lick in on the second guy, who grabbed both of her legs and lifted her up.

Even though Natalie fought with everything she had and would not go down easy, she was greatly outnumbered. All three men now had her secure in their grips and lugged her into the back of the white van. The door closed behind them. She kept fighting them, but moments later, she had duct tape wrapped around her wrists, her ankles, and finally covering her mouth. She felt helpless.

And then she had a black hood pulled down over her head.

The sudden darkness was unnerving. Panic swelled up inside her.

The van started moving. She stopped fighting. There was no point. There was nothing she could do to escape. Instead, she did everything she could to not think about what was happening and the fear that was steadily building up within her. She tried to steady her emotions, to somehow still feel in control of her situation. She began putting together a mental file of everything she could remember about the four men. The bald driver. The young intern. The two guys from the back of the van. Physical traits. Dialect. Sounds, smells. She kept mentally repeating the van's license-plate number in her mind, something she had locked in on upon seeing it reappear in the parking garage. DC plates.

Who were they?

Were they connected to the Hansel story?

She thought of her fellow reporter's scorched car.

The Klan? Barnstorm? Had Senator Hansel hired these guys himself?

As the van exited the parking garage, she tried to listen to the sounds of the city streets, maybe gauge where they were going. It was nearly impossible. Her eyes grew wet, but she immediately fought off the tears. No way in hell would she give these guys the satisfaction of seeing her cry. She was pissed about getting captured. If there had been only two guys, she was sure she would've gotten away. As a kid, she would put on boxing gloves and duke it out with her older brothers in the barn, once breaking Gary's nose with a right hook. She'd taken self-defense classes when she first got to DC and could handle herself well. Maybe they knew that about her, which was why there were four of them. That was a lot of guys to send after one little reporter girl.

She heard a quick muffled conversation from the front of the van.

Maybe the driver's voice. Sounded like he was on the phone with someone.

She tried to block out all distraction, listen closely.

"We got her. We're twenty minutes out . . . yeah . . . time to send Callahan the message."

Callahan?

She felt her stomach drop, her mind immediately switching gears.

This wasn't about Janey and Barnstorm. This wasn't about Senator Hansel.

This was about Sam.

FIVE

Sam rode in silence in the back of a *Policia* car.

Two uniformed cops sat in the front. Only one spoke any English. Sam had given his statement to two different officers, but there was a lot of confusion, a lot of suspicious stares, a lot of off-line conversations with other Mexican police officials. They'd finally led him to a police car and ushered him into the backseat. He wasn't handcuffed, but he wasn't sure if he was being considered a witness or a suspect, as the cops seemed leery of him and his version of the story. He still wore only one dress shoe, his pants were gashed and grass stained, his white dress shirt soaked in sweat and blood. He'd tossed the tie. One of the cops was nice enough to give him a dirty rag to wipe the blood off his face. He could still feel gooey clumps of blood in his hair. No one offered him a medic, even though he was wincing in pain with each breath, and there were two ambulance crews on the scene.

That made him feel more like a suspect.

His whole body ached from head to toe, and his side now throbbed something fierce. Maybe a broken rib. He wasn't sure. Every time he tried to clear the phlegm from his throat, he felt like someone was jabbing him with a needle. He ran his tongue over his front teeth—one of them had a small chip in it. He shook his head as he took his own physical inventory. A train wreck, but he was alive. Considering the events of the past hour, and the fate of his firm's newest client, Sam felt fortunate. However, he did feel completely lost without his cell phone or his wallet. No American citizen ever wanted to be sitting in the back of a police car in the heart of Mexico City without his passport or *any* proper identification. That was a recipe for disaster, especially when that American had just jumped from a hotel-room balcony and driven a stolen SUV into a city lake, right after having caused at least a dozen car wrecks all along the way.

The cops weren't talking to him, so he just sat quietly, went for the ride.

Thirty minutes later, Sam found himself in a clean, though dimly lit, holding room on the sixth floor of a federal police building. He was still hobbling around on only one shoe and getting irritated. Could someone at least get him a matching pair of shoes? He'd explained to three different officers that he had a bag back at the Hyatt with extra clothes and shoes, but they were in no hurry to get him back over there. They either pretended to not speak English or, more likely, chose to ignore him altogether.

Although it was hot as hell outside, it was freezing inside the building. A female federal agent had noticed him shivering and had given him a black windbreaker to wear a few minutes ago, right before they'd stuck him in the holding room. After Sam sat there for a few minutes, a man probably in his early forties in a brown suit finally entered the room. He spoke with a heavy Mexican accent, but his English was very good. Sam was grateful for that. The man was neat and proper and articulate. He was clearly in charge, to Sam's relief. He wanted to talk to someone who could actually do something for him. The man shut the door behind him, stared at a manila folder in his hands.

"Sorry for the wait. My name is Agent Mendoza."

Sam was sitting in a metal chair opposite the table, hands in front of him. He already knew from the fact that he hadn't been hauled to a dumpy local police station and instead was in a shiny federal police building downtown that this thing had escalated to the next level. It was like the FBI taking over a local investigation back in the States. Now he was speaking to a high-ranking Mexican federal agent.

Again Sam wondered what exactly he'd walked into this afternoon.

"Can you tell me what's going on, Agent Mendoza?"

"I get to ask the first questions here, Mr. Callahan."

"Call me Sam."

"Okay. And you can call me Raul."

Great, they were buddies now. "I've already told them everything in detail."

That wasn't totally true. He'd left out *a lot* of what his client had shared with him in his sudden panicked state. Understandably, Sam didn't completely trust cops.

"*Sí.* I just need to follow up on a few things," Mendoza replied. "Get our facts straight."

"Sure." He tried not to huff.

"When did you say you arrived in Mexico City?"

"This afternoon. Three o'clock. Delta flight. I have the ticket stubs back at my hotel."

"You're staying at the Hyatt in Polanco?"

"Yes. One night. Then back to DC tomorrow. At least, that *was* the plan."

"You say you were here to meet with a client?"

"A man named Tom Hawkins. I'm a lawyer."

"Had you ever met or spoken with this man before?"

"No. This was my first time to meet him."

"Why here in Mexico City?"

"I don't know. I'd say ask Hawkins. But you can't—he's dead."

"When was your first contact with Mr. Hawkins?"

Sam shrugged. "He called our law firm yesterday, asked for the meeting, paid the retainer. That's about all I know. I met with Hawkins a little over an hour ago at his suite at the Four Seasons. We talked for maybe ten minutes. Next thing I know, a man in a black suit broke into our hotel room, shot and killed Hawkins, and then chased after me. I was fortunate to get away. It should all be in the report. I've told this same exact story to four people already, including two of your agents when I got here."

"There is no record of a Tom Hawkins booking a hotel suite at the Four Seasons for today. We checked with the registry."

Sam thought about that for a second. "I had nothing to do with the booking of the hotel suite. I just showed up for the meeting that he requested. Maybe he didn't want anyone to know he was there at the hotel. Used a different name. Makes sense to me now, considering what happened."

"Yes, maybe."

"Have you checked his body for ID?"

Agent Mendoza slowly sat across from him, put the folder down, and folded his hands. "You see, *amigo*, that's the biggest gap in your story. We've been unable to locate *any* body in the hotel suite, like you've suggested. And there have been no reports of a shooting or a disturbance from anyone else on the floor."

Sam was stunned and having serious déjà vu. No dead body? "That can't be right. I'm telling you, a man came into our hotel suite and began shooting. I saw him put a bullet into Hawkins. Did you check the hotel-room door? He shot through the damn door!"

"So you say. We checked all the floors, just to be sure." He glared at Sam from across the table. "You want to tell me what really happened?"

Sam stood suddenly, knocking his chair back. "Are you kidding me? Why the hell do you think I would jump from a four-story balcony and almost break my neck? Just for kicks? Look at me. I've been beat up to hell. You think I did this to myself? There was a guy with a gun inside the hotel room. He was going to kill me."

Mendoza raised a palm. "Sit down, Sam. Now. Before I have you handcuffed."

Sam reluctantly obliged. Mendoza stared at his folder again.

"You caused *a lot* of damage at the hotel," he continued. "And then a lot more destruction out on our streets driving around recklessly. You took our local police with you on quite the run. You're lucky no one was killed. Including yourself."

"I don't feel so lucky. Did you find the guys in the Mercedes? Or let me guess. There are also no reports of a Mercedes chasing me through the streets?"

"We're looking," Agent Mendoza replied, but he didn't seem convinced. He stood, turned toward the door. "You say you have proper paperwork back at the Hyatt?"

"Yes. Room 414. Unless someone made that disappear, too."

"You'd better hope not," Mendoza warned. "Sit tight. I'll be back."

He shut the door, left Sam alone again in the small holding room.

Sam stood, paced in a slow circle, thinking. This was not going well. He needed to get in touch with David. The last thing he needed was to be stuck in a federal police building with an agent who didn't believe his story, and with no way for him to personally verify any of it. A body had disappeared. Impossible. Although he knew after last November, when another dead body had disappeared on him, that *anything* was possible. Apparently, no one from the hotel was coming forward to corroborate his version of events. Why? There were people everywhere. Someone had to have seen the guys chasing after him. He felt his chest tighten up, cursed again. He had sudden visions of being dumped into a dirty Mexican prison cell for the next twenty years, never to be heard from again.

Standing there, Sam felt a vibration come from the left pocket of his police windbreaker. He reached in and pulled out a small black smartphone, something he'd noticed earlier when he'd first entered the holding room. It was not his phone, of course, so he'd assumed it belonged to the female agent who had loaned him the jacket. He had been pondering using it to call David when Agent Mendoza had entered the room. Sam glanced at the phone's screen and was shocked by what he saw. A text message clearly intended for him.

> Sam, do not say another word to the police. Get out of the building. ASAP. Keep this phone. Wait for further instructions.

He wasn't sure how this was possible.
He hesitantly typed a reply: Who is this?
A new text appeared a few seconds later.

> Do exactly what we say. If you don't, Natalie dies.

He squinted at the phone. *Natalie dies?* What were they talking about?

Seconds later, a third text arrived, along with a five-second video attachment. His eyes narrowed. He pushed Play, opened the video, and suddenly felt like someone had violently swung a baseball bat straight to his chest—a feeling that was much worse than falling from the balcony or diving out of the SUV roughly an hour ago. He slowly sat, his legs wobbly, his mouth dry.

The high-quality video showed Natalie sitting in a chair, alone in a dark room, her hands bound in front of her by the wrists and a strip of duct tape covering her mouth. Her eyes were puffy, and he could see the fear in them as she stared directly at the video camera. He immediately recognized she was wearing her favorite hoodie. She wore it almost every night. A hand reached in from out of view and tugged the duct tape loose from her mouth. Natalie yelled, "Sam!" and then the video abruptly ended.

Panic rippled through him. Someone had taken her.

Who did this?

What the hell was going on?

His fingers were trembling. He typed: Please don't hurt her.

The reply was swift: Get out of the building now. Don't say a word to anyone. We'll be in touch.

SIX

A wave of rage gripped Sam, his breathing growing rapid and heavy. Clearly this was somehow connected to his being in Mexico City and to the events that had transpired this afternoon. It had to be connected to Tom Hawkins's death, to the assassins who were chasing after him, to Sam now being stuck inside this federal-police holding room. How else could someone have planted the cell phone on him? He thought about the black-haired female agent who'd given him the windbreaker. She'd barely said a word. She'd just appeared from out of nowhere while he was standing in the hallway, offered him the windbreaker, and then disappeared. He really couldn't remember that much about her. Who was she? Was she really a federal agent? What was happening?

Sam hesitantly watched the video of Natalie again. When she screamed his name, he felt bile surge up the back of his throat. He had to take several deep breaths to keep from vomiting and try to regain control of his emotions. There was nothing distinguishable about where they held Natalie. He checked the time on the cell phone. Did she just get home from work? That would explain her blue jeans and the gray hoodie. Did they break down the door and drag her from her apartment?

He took another deep breath, exhaled, and tried to calm down.

He knew he couldn't focus on the details of her abduction right now. He had to move quickly, as instructed. He had to protect Natalie at all costs. They'd endured so much. After he'd cruelly broken her heart nearly two years ago, Natalie had somehow summoned the courage last November to give him another chance. It had been anything but easy between them—mainly because of his ongoing struggle with abandonment issues. However, if Sam dreamed of any possible future with her, he had to get out of the building immediately.

He moved to the door. Locked. He cursed. Bolted with a sophisticated electronic card-key system. He couldn't just walk out. And he unfortunately couldn't use the expert lock-picking street skills of his youth. By the time he was twelve, he could pick a standard lock within seconds. An older street kid had shown him the engineering of a lock system, and Sam had practiced for countless hours. Because of the way his mind worked, he was a natural. At one point, he used the skill to steal from the back storage room at the local grocery and keep food in his stomach. He did what he had to do to survive life on the streets. But that wouldn't help him now. There had to be another way. He looked around the near-barren room, more panic flowing through him. How the hell did they expect him to get out of the building when he was stuck inside a small room on the sixth floor with an electronic lock sealing the door? He had his answer a second later when a white card key suddenly slid under the tiny crack beneath the door and bumped up against his socked foot.

Sam cursed again, reached down, snagged it, and swiped it in front of the black box on the lock system. He heard the electronic lock release. He quickly cracked open the door, peeked out, searching for his unknown accomplice. The holding room was in a hallway lined with several other rooms. To his left, the hallway dead-ended into another cross hallway, one that he knew led to the main elevators. To his right, the hallway led to a large open space filled with dozens of cubicles where officers and agents were milling about. He thought he saw the back of a black-haired woman disappear into the office space to his right. Was it the same woman who had given him the windbreaker? Did she also slide the card key under the door? He wanted to go after her, but that path would take him straight into a swarm of federal agents.

Instead, he stepped out, shut the door behind him, and walked to his left. If Mendoza came upon him unexpectedly, he'd simply say he was looking for the restroom and plead ignorance about how he got out of the room. From there he'd have to figure out plan B. He tried to be casual, cool, but his heart was pounding. As he passed by others, he kept his eyes up, so as not to draw extra attention to himself. He certainly didn't want anyone looking down toward the floor and noticing that he was wearing only one black shoe. He entered the cross hallway, paused, looked both ways. More offices, more conference rooms. Sam desperately needed a wardrobe change. That was always the first rule of survival on the run. He needed something to blend. He glanced inside an open office door, found a man who looked up at him curiously from behind a desk. Sam nodded, smiled, kept moving, and looked for more options.

He peeked inside another open office door on his left. The light was on in the office, but no one was currently sitting behind the desk. Sam noticed an item that he wanted right away. He stepped inside, gently shut the door behind him, quickly peeled himself out of the police windbreaker—the last thing Agent Mendoza had seen him wearing. He grabbed the black sport coat that he'd spotted hanging on the back of the desk chair, pulled it on over his arms. The sport coat was maybe a size too big but nothing obvious.

He noticed a blue duffel bag in the corner. He took another glance back at the door, felt sweat on his brow. He was unsure what he'd do if someone returned to the office and caught him in the act. Take a swing and run for it? However, he knew he had to take risks. He had no choice. He unzipped the duffel bag, began rummaging through the contents. Inside, he found a pair of blue running shoes. He kicked off his one black shoe, slipped the running shoes onto his feet, felt relieved. The shoes were tight—his toes were jammed all the way up in the front—but they would definitely work. He also found a gray bath towel, running shorts, T-shirt, and a brown leather toiletry bag. He peeked inside the toiletry bag, took quick inventory, and then he packed everything up, slung the duffel bag over his shoulder, and headed for the office door. On his way out, Sam grabbed a random manila folder off the desk to use as cover and stepped back into the busy hallway.

Still no noticeable eyes on him. No one coming around the corner as if he'd been reported missing. No Agent Mendoza. Now that he'd done a wardrobe change, Sam knew his initial defense of looking for a restroom was no longer valid. He had to make his way out of the build-ing ASAP. As he started walking again, he opened the manila folder and pretended to be scanning paperwork, as if he was in the building on official police business. He didn't want to stand out. Fortunately, he wasn't the only white guy there. He could blend in if he kept moving. He knew half of pulling a successful con job was simply acting like you belonged, with brash confidence and bold movement. He was trying to find that confidence right now. It was difficult surrounded by hundreds of police officers.

While his eyes were mostly on the folder, Sam soaked in movement all around him in his peripheral vision, making sure Agent Mendoza did not sneak up on him. He headed straight toward the main elevator corridor. Although he would much rather take the stairs, he felt that might be overly suspicious should he encounter someone coming up. He sidled up to the elevators along with three uniformed officers. One of them glanced over at him. Sam gave a subtle nod, had it returned. The door to one of the elevators parted, and a small group exited. Sam entered with the officers, and three more men quickly followed. It was a crowded carriage. Sam felt a large bead of sweat drip down his back. He hoped the moisture wasn't noticeable on his brow. He tried to casually wipe it with the back of his hand.

As the elevator doors fully closed, Sam spotted Agent Mendoza running up to them from the hallway. Their eyes momentarily met, but the doors shut before Mendoza could utter a word of warning. Thankfully no one else seemed to notice the exchange. However, Sam was now panicked. If Mendoza knew he was inside the elevator, he recognized that Sam was on the run. All it would take was a quick call, and Mendoza could have the building go on complete lockdown, with men with guns at every corner.

Would Mendoza make that call?

Would he treat Sam like an escaped suspect?

Sam could take no chances. He knew he had to make alternate plans. The elevator was rapidly dropping. He slid between two officers and punched the button for the second floor. As he slipped back to his spot in the corner, he brushed up against a plainclothes gentleman of sixtysomething in front of him who was wearing a gray suit, said, *"Perdón."* In that same moment, Sam stole the black eyeglasses poking out from the man's left breast pocket, his hands every bit as quick as when he used to do the same thing as a thirteen-year-old kid at the grocery store. He could pass by an old guy reading the cereal boxes and snag a wallet without ever slowing a step. Sam hid the glasses in the palm of his hand.

The elevator stopped on the second floor. Sam held his breath, said a prayer, unsure if a squad of agents would be waiting on the other side to grab him. The doors opened, and he exhaled. All clear. He eased through the others, found his way into a hallway that was nearly identical to the one on the sixth floor. He knew the clock was now seriously ticking. He had to do something drastic to get outside. His guess was that Mendoza would do his own searching at first—only because it might be embarrassing to admit he'd lost a potential suspect inside the building. But eventually Mendoza would call in the full army.

Sam spotted a door in the hallway marked Custodio. He'd noticed a similar door up on the sixth floor. The janitor's closet. He walked over, put his hand on the knob. Locked. Standard lock with a key slot. The manila folder with the paperwork in his hands was held together by a metal paper clip. Sam slipped off the paper clip, twisted it straight. He took a quick peek left and right to make sure no one was paying attention to him. With his back to the door, he leaned up against it, like he was taking a moment to review something inside the folder, and without even looking, he stuck the paper clip into the lock slot. He wiggled and scraped, felt the sensation of the familiar metal gear of the tiny lock system. Like riding a bike. He was inside the janitor's room within seconds.

He shut the door behind him, locked it again, hit the lights. There were two metal shelves filled with all kinds of cleaning supplies against one wall, a rolling custodial cart for laundry in the middle, and three tall, gray lockers on another wall that sat next to a small sink with a mirror. He searched the lockers first, finding what he wanted inside the third locker: a standard gray janitor's jumpsuit. Wardrobe change number two. He quickly took off the black sport coat and pulled the janitor's outfit on over his clothes, zipped it up tight to his neckline. The janitor's jumpsuit fit well. Whoever owned it was about his size. The name tag sewn on the front of the gray pullover said CARLOS.

Could he pass for a Carlos? He was about to find out.

Sam pulled out the toiletry bag, unzipped it, and grabbed the items he wanted. A razor blade and a can of shaving cream. He moved in front of the sink and got his first good look at himself in the mirror. He shook his head. He looked like he'd been run over by a semitruck, which was about right. He studied the deep gash on his forehead. It was nearly two inches long. He badly needed stitches or it would certainly leave a permanent scar. There were scrapes all down the left side of his face. Sam noticed that the tiny chip in his front left tooth was legitimate. His eyes took in his wavy, brown hair. It was completely disheveled, like he'd just stepped out of bed. He tried not to think about what he had to do next. It sucked, but he had no time to stall or second-guess himself. Not with Natalie currently bound with duct tape.

He grabbed a pair of scissors from a sewing kit he'd found on the shelf and began trimming his messy hair down to the scalp. It took him several minutes. The scissors were dull, and his hair was thick. It was a real mess. Once he finished that, he quickly wet the remainder of his hair with cold water from the sink and began rubbing gobs of shaving cream all over his head. Next, he took the razor blade and started going to town. Quick strokes back and forth, some of them catching skin. He didn't have time to do a careful job. He just had to get it all off. Finished, he dried his newly bald scalp with the bath towel, dumped all the hair remnants from the sink into a trash bag, sealed it up tight, and stuffed it into a trash can in the corner.

Sam again examined himself in the mirror. It was the exact same way he'd looked at the very end of his tracker assignment last November. Within days, he'd gone from a full head of brown hair, to black hair, to blond hair, and finally to no hair at all. Staring at himself, he felt chills, finding it hard to fathom that he was in this position again: on the run from assassins *and* the police.

Why did this keep happening to him?

He put on the stolen black glasses. The final piece of his new look. They were a mild prescription and easy enough to navigate around. He took another peek in the mirror. He was hardly recognizable from a few minutes ago. It was time to make his bold exit.

He returned to the hallway, pulling the janitor's laundry cart along with him. Carlos the janitor. He hoped no one would ask him anything in Spanish or his cover might be blown. He knew *yes* and *no* and little else. When the elevator doors opened, he pushed the rolling cart inside. Two men joined him. No one made a fuss. Neither of them even acknowledged him, his newly bald head, or stared at his misplaced name tag. They all rode down to the first floor together in silence. The doors opened, and the two officers walked out, Sam last. He tucked himself in close behind the rolling cart.

Nearby he immediately spotted Agent Mendoza, who was huddled with two uniformed officers. Sam felt a jolt of nerves but kept steadily moving. Brash and bold. It looked like Mendoza and the two officers were all staring at what was probably a photograph of Sam clutched in Mendoza's right hand. With his left hand, Mendoza was pointing this way and that inside the lobby, giving instructions. The federal agent glanced up as Sam stepped clear from the elevator corridor. Sam could've sworn Mendoza looked straight at him, but there was not a hint of recognition. The agent quickly went back to his animated discussion with the officers.

Sam exhaled, eased right past them without incident.

Up ahead he could see the exit out the front glass lobby doors.

He kept a calm pace, even though everything inside of him wanted to make a dead sprint for it. Halfway there, he slid over to the side, pretended to fiddle with the rolling cart, and then when he made sure no one else was looking, he left the cart there unattended. One more quick peek behind him. Agent Mendoza was still hovering near the elevators. Sam walked toward the doors. On the other side of a roped-off area, a line of people was waiting to get through guards and security detectors. He did not have to pass through security on the way out, only walk by a hulking guard in uniform who was holding a big black assault rifle.

Ten steps. Five steps. Sam pushed through the door, felt a wave of humidity splash against his face. It felt good. Freedom felt good.

He thought of Natalie and clenched his fists.

He was not free. Not yet. Not even close.

SEVEN

He was called the Gray Wolf.

His real name was Alger Gerlach.

He was wanted in twelve countries.

He was given the nickname nine years ago by a German reporter because, like the animal, he could adapt and thrive in any environment—whether forest, desert, mountain, tundra, or grassland. He'd made kills in countries with every kind of terrain. He was five foot ten, 160 pounds, with a build that never stood out. He had an everyman face, which gave him the uncanny ability to disguise himself, play just about any role, blend into his surroundings, advance in the shadows, accomplish his task, and then disappear again into the crowd—although a group of college coeds in London had once mistaken him for the American actor Edward Norton. He'd played along because it was the easiest path back to their hotel room. Truth was, after so many surgeries to change his appearance, he wasn't sure what he really looked like anymore. It didn't matter. He would change it up again next year.

In eleven years, he had nineteen kills to his name. At least, those were the kills that the world considered significant. Politicians. Ambassadors. Top executives. Powerful people. There were dozens of other peripheral bodies that only family and close friends mourned. And twenty years ago, there were numerous legal kills as a sniper in the German army.

His résumé was established. If you knew the right people, had powerful enough connections, or you were loaded, you could hire the Gray Wolf. Two million dollars was his current rate.

Gerlach exited the cab four blocks from the Lincoln Memorial, a stone's throw from the White House. He wore a black jacket and a dark-blue wool cap. The goatee was fake. So were the spectacles. His vision was perfect. The sidewalks were busy. It was nearing dinnertime, and people were out and about.

Gerlach entered the coffee shop and stood in a short line. Behind the spectacles, he scanned the counter near the front window. A man wore a maroon windbreaker, jeans, and gray Nike running shoes. He sat on the very last stool. All as instructed.

After ordering black coffee, Gerlach strolled toward the front. There was a stool available next to the man in Nikes. The man in Nikes did not know him and did not know what he looked like. Gerlach slid onto the stool, took a glance at the laptop screen in front of the man. A web browser was open to the Washington Redskins home page.

"Super Bowl this next year?" Gerlach said in perfectly crafted Midwest English.

The man didn't look up, so as not to lock eyes with an assassin. He said, "Maybe. If our quarterback finally stays healthy."

It was the necessary exchange in this killing game.

The man in the Nikes quickly shut the laptop and gathered his things. Before leaving, he set a folded newspaper on the counter. Gerlach casually grabbed the newspaper, slid it over in front of him. He unfolded it, found the manila folder waiting for him inside. He took a finger and opened the folder. There were several eight-by-ten color photographs of a good-looking man in his midtwenties. Some shots were of the man jogging in runner's clothes. In others he was wearing a black suit and tie, holding a briefcase. Gerlach casually flipped through the photographs and then found a stapled report behind them.

A full profile on his target.

Age. Height. Weight. Background information.

Gerlach quickly scanned through the background, found it quite intriguing.

He was an orphan boy just like Gerlach.

The Gray Wolf read the name at the top.

Samuel Weldon Callahan.

EIGHT

Sam found a crowded, lively outdoor marketplace.

It was the perfect spot for him to get lost for a little while, to wipe the trail completely clean from Mendoza and the federal police, to secure a set of much-needed new clothes, maybe some cash, and certainly to borrow a new cell phone from an unsuspecting victim. He sighed, frustrated. Every time he thought he was finally done with his old life of street crime—the only life he knew while surviving on his own in Denver as a teenager—he felt like it was forced back on him by some divine hand. He'd worked so hard physically, emotionally, and spiritually to move forward with his life. So why did he always find himself back in this position? Was God really that cruel? Was he cursed? He was starting to believe it. Every time he thought he was finally finished boxing with God about his tragic past, someone out of nowhere took a new swing at him, and there he was, right back in the middle of the ring. Pastor Isaiah used to say that he shouldn't be afraid of boxing with God, that it could be a healthy exercise if done right. *God can take a punch,* Pastor Isaiah used to say to him with a wink and a grin. But Sam's mentor also warned that God just might punch back if that was the best thing for Sam.

Sam thought of his mom, felt a twist in his gut.

There was no time to think about any of that right now. He kept moving.

He entered the sea of late-afternoon shoppers, began searching for targets. He found his first one almost instantly. Like it or not, Sam had an eye for quickly finding the right victims. The man of fiftysomething looked like he was out shopping with his much younger girlfriend. The designer clothes and the gold watch on his wrist told Sam that he was a good match for what he needed. The couple stood in front of a shop that was selling knockoff designer clothes, and the poor guy already had two hands stuffed full of items as his giggling girlfriend loaded him up with even more. Sam moved in, gave him a quick bump, and the wallet from the man's back pocket was securely in his palm. The man never noticed, never flinched, never turned around, not that Sam expected him to do any such thing. The old boyfriend just kept smiling away at his pretty girl. Sam knew it would be anything but pretty when the poor guy couldn't pay for anything at the counter.

Ten minutes later Sam spotted a group of five teenage girls all huddled together, laughing and listening to music on each other's cell phones, all while making eyes at a group of boys who stood fifteen feet away and were basically doing the same thing. Sam watched very closely for a few minutes and found his opening as a girl in a pink dress on the fringe of the group dropped her cell phone into her large pink bag. Sam had noticed earlier, when she'd pulled out the phone, that this girl did not type in a password to use it—which meant she did not have her phone locked down. A big mistake but one that could greatly benefit Sam. He did not need any extra hurdles right now. When the girl set her pink bag down on the ground next to her, then leaned in to watch something on her friend's phone, Sam moved in quickly. He scooted in behind the group, making sure he was in a wave of other shoppers, knelt abruptly to tie his shoelace, and then had her cell phone in his left hand a few seconds later. He was in and out of the crowd within seconds, and then gone.

New items in tow, Sam stole away to an isolated corner, away from the crowds, where he quickly pulled the cash out of the wallet. Thankfully, he'd guessed right. The affluent old boyfriend carried quite a bit of cash. Maybe $200 in pesos, which he knew would take him a long way in Mexico City. He tossed the wallet into a nearby trash can, kept moving, eyes now on a few police officers he spotted who had moved into the marketplace.

Were the police out looking for him now?

Had Agent Mendoza put out an alert for his immediate capture and arrest?

He had to keep moving around like he was a wanted man. He hated that.

Farther up the marketplace, he used the cash to purchase a new pair of blue jeans, a gray T-shirt, some knockoff Nike running shoes that actually fit, a small black backpack, a bottle of aspirin, and some toiletry items like deodorant, toothbrush, and toothpaste. He wasn't sure at this point if he'd ever see his room or his luggage back at the Hyatt again.

He kept checking the planted cell phone with Natalie's video on it every thirty seconds. He'd already texted the number: I'm out of the building. What now? But no reply yet. He was going crazy. What was the delay? He resisted repeatedly watching the video. It would only torture and paralyze him. He'd searched the entire phone. There were no other contact numbers. No apps, no pictures, no videos. It was likely a burner phone, meant to be used temporarily and then tossed. He again thought about the female agent who'd given him the windbreaker inside the police building. Was she a real cop? Or someone else? She was probably midthirties, black hair, a dark-gray suit. He remembered that she'd had an official badge, but he didn't recall seeing a name. He'd replayed the scene in his mind a dozen times and didn't remember her interacting with anyone else.

Who was she? How did she find him?

He already had a hundred questions. And no answers.

First things first, he needed to get out of this hot janitor's uniform.

Sam entered a small Catholic church up the street. A group of thirty or so parishioners were sitting up front in the main sanctuary, a priest performing in front of them. Sam slipped into a tiny one-stall bathroom in the back lobby, behind the sanctuary, and locked the door. He took off the janitor's outfit and his other clothes, gave himself a quick body wash in the sink, trying to get all the sweat and blood off him, used the deodorant and toothpaste, and then put on his brand-new clothes. His third wardrobe change in the past thirty minutes. He was still aching all over his body, especially in his shoulder and ribs—although the handful of aspirin he'd downed was helping.

He left the janitor's outfit and old clothes in the trash can, exited the bathroom.

NINE

Sam quietly entered the back of the sanctuary and sat in the very last row alone, the small crowd mostly at the front. He stared at the giant hanging crucifix of Jesus on the wall behind the Mexican priest, said another quick prayer for Natalie. He shook his head at his own hypocrisy. One second he was cursing God; the next he was begging him for help.

Story of his life, he supposed.

He couldn't help but wonder where they'd grabbed Natalie or what they'd done to secure her. She was a fighter. She would not have gone with them easily. No way. So how did they get to her? Did they drug her? Was she hurt? Again, he tried not to think too much about that, but it was damn near impossible. He stared at the screen on the burner cell phone, begging for it to ring or for a new text message to arrive from her takers.

Still nothing. He felt helpless.

He didn't know enough Spanish to follow much of what was going on with Mass down front, which was fine. He really needed to think, anyway, to clear his head, to start putting things together, and begin to map out a new plan. His mind drifted back to the brief meeting he'd had earlier with Tom Hawkins—before his world spun out of control when that assassin shot his way into the hotel room. He needed to remember everything about that meeting, every small detail, every single word that had come out of Hawkins's mouth. Natalie was in trouble, and Sam was convinced it had everything to do with his meeting with Hawkins.

He knelt in the pew, hands together, facedown, and closed his eyes. A proper prayer posture. So no one would pay him attention.

Then he relived the entirety of the meeting in his mind.

Sam was standing there alone, but Hawkins was already looking beyond him, searching for someone or something else—as if he recognized Sam but wanted to see if anyone else had come along for the ride. His blood-shot eyes traveled all the way down the hallway toward the elevators. Hawkins looked nervous from the very first moment Sam put eyes on him. His fingers were jittery; the glass of brown liquid trembled in his left hand. Sam noticed that right away. Hawkins wore tan slacks and an untucked Hawaiian button-down shirt. He looked to be in his midfif-ties, balding with gray hair on the sides, and very tan, like he enjoyed the golf course several days a week. Sam could see the tan lines at the sleeves, the collar, and around his left hand, where he might often wear a golf glove.

They'd had a meeting on the calendar for 5:00 p.m. that day, one scheduled just the day before when Hawkins had called the law firm. Sam was exactly on time. He'd actually waited in the lobby of the Four Seasons for five full minutes so as not to be too early. This was his first client meeting without his boss at his side. He wanted to make a good impression. David thought there might be good money here for the firm. He said when a potential new client calls you, immediately pays the expensive retainer, and offers to fly you internationally overnight for a meeting, it usually meant he is quite desperate and money is no object.

Those were the very best kinds of meetings, David had said with a grin.

His boss knew Sam didn't care too much about the money—that's not at all why he'd pursued law school and become an attorney. Still, Sam wanted to serve his boss well. David had taken very good care of him after the FBI manhunt last November, working diligently for many weeks to help restore Sam's public image, personally handling the hundreds of TV interview requests after Natalie's big story broke and exploded. Most important of all, David had amicably worked out his situation with Director Luther Stone and the FBI. His boss had been a fierce advocate for him throughout the whole crazy deal, had allowed him to return to his semi-normal life as a third-year law student, and he'd even made good on his offer to make Sam his newest associate upon graduation from Georgetown last month.

Sam felt very loyal to him. If this meeting was important to David, it was important to Sam. Besides, David had insisted, if the meeting turned out to be a bust, Sam could still go enjoy the Mexico City nightlife, all on the firm's credit card. Consider the trip a quick retreat, David suggested. Get a massage. Sip on some daiquiris. Lay by the pool. Play some golf.

"Callahan?" Hawkins said, eyes narrow.

"Sam Callahan, Benoltz and Associates."

Hawkins nodded without another word, and then he opened the door fully and allowed Sam to enter the luxurious hotel suite. Sam noticed he took yet another quick peek up the hallway before leading Sam to a sitting area in the spacious living room. Hawkins never took a moment to introduce himself or to shake Sam's hand or any of those normal pleasantries. Things felt off from the beginning. Sam could actually see sweat beading up on the man's shiny forehead, even though the hotel suite was a very comfortable temperature.

"You want something to drink?" Hawkins offered. His voice told Sam he was probably a native Texan. There was a touch of a drawl there.

"No, thank you, Mr. Hawkins."

"It's Tom, all right? Just Tom."

"Yes, sir."

Hawkins said it with irritation, although Sam didn't get the sense the irritation was aimed at him. Hawkins went back over to the bar area and refilled his glass, quickly tossed it back. Sam studied him. The man was a walking bundle of nerves right now, like he might unravel at any moment. Sam wondered why. He figured he'd find out shortly, even though Hawkins didn't seem to be in any hurry to get started.

"Make yourself at home," Hawkins insisted. "We could be here awhile."

Sam set his briefcase down, took off his suit jacket, and folded it over one of the chairs. Then he sat, crossed his legs, tried to get comfortable, which was easy in his new high-dollar business suit. He owned four of them now: two black, one dark blue, one dark gray. David had brought his own personal tailor into the office on Sam's very first day with the firm to take his precise measurements. As David's new right-hand man, Sam should be dressed in something more appropriate than the cheap off-the-rack numbers he currently had hanging in his closet, David had said, taking Sam through a complete wardrobe overhaul.

Sam was wearing the dark-blue suit. It fit perfectly on his lean six-foot frame. The black leather shoes were also pricey, although Sam never saw the actual bill. He knew David spared no expense. His boss worked hard and enjoyed the benefits, and he wanted Sam to do the same—even though Sam still felt like an outsider in his new world. He wasn't sure he would ever truly adjust to his new life as a well-paid attorney. After all, for more than two years of his street life, his one solid meal a day—usually a PB&J, an apple, and a hard-boiled egg—came from the free-food truck that regularly showed up on the corner of Vallejo and West Barberry.

Sam took in the hotel suite. Full living room, kitchen, and two bedrooms on opposite sides. Hawkins had splurged on the hotel accommodations. Was he staying at the hotel? Or just there for the day? Sam didn't notice much that told him he'd been there for too long.

Everything was cloaked in mystery. Sam was making mental notes, ready to get to the bottom of this deal, find out who this guy was and what he was doing there.

Hawkins didn't immediately join him in the sitting area; instead, he walked to the sliding glass doors of the balcony, pulled open the doors, and looked outside. Sam could feel a hot breeze push into the room. He expected Hawkins to get started, but he just stood there silently for a long moment. Sam tried to break the ice, get things moving along.

"There seemed to be real urgency behind this meeting, Tom."

Hawkins answered without turning around. "There is, believe me."

He did not expound. It was almost like the weight of the moment had rested on him, and Hawkins knew once he opened this door, he could never go back. Sam had a very thin file on Hawkins. The man was an attorney for a small firm in New Orleans called Hebbard & Hawkins, LLP. He was a name partner. According to their website, the firm had been founded only three years ago and specialized in oil-and-gas exploration and litigation. There was not much to Hawkins's online profile. Undergrad, Sam Houston State. Texas Tech law school many years ago. There were no details about Hawkins's specific problem or how they could help him—Hawkins had insisted they talk about his situation only in person today.

"I hear your firm is good at working out deals with the government."

"Which government?" Sam asked.

"United States," he clarified. "Hell, maybe Mexico, too. Who the hell knows what all I'll need to get out of this mess?"

"I suppose that depends on your situation. David has a very good working relationship with our government. I can personally vouch for that."

"Has he ever put someone into protective custody?"

"Like witness protection?"

Hawkins nodded.

"Yes. Many times. Do you need witness protection?"

"If we share what we know, we'll need to disappear quickly. They'll stop at nothing to eliminate us, believe me. How fast can you make that happen?"

Sam stared at Hawkins. *Eliminate?* "I'm not sure I can answer that until I know more about your situation."

Hawkins nodded. He then moved to the bedroom on the left of the hotel suite and disappeared inside. Hawkins had mentioned *we* in his declaration—*we* share what *we* know, *we'll* need to disappear. To whom else he was referring? Hebbard? The other name in the law firm of Hebbard & Hawkins? Or maybe a wife? Someone else? Hawkins returned with a small silver briefcase that had heavy-duty security locks on it. He set it on the coffee table in between them, took a seat on the plush sofa.

"There is *a lot* to go over," Hawkins began, finally getting serious. "This thing reaches beyond anything you can possibly imagine."

"Mind if I take notes?" Sam asked, reaching for his own briefcase.

"Sure, no problem."

The man's small briefcase seemed to have digital fingerprint readers. Hawkins set his right thumb on one scanner, and the lock clicked open. Then he set his left thumb on the second scanner, and it also clicked. Before fully opening the briefcase, Hawkins's cell phone beeped loudly in his shirt pocket. He paused, pulled his phone out, stared at the screen with bloodshot eyes. The change in Hawkins's face was quite noticeable. He suddenly went very pale, like someone had pulled the plug and the tan was instantly draining out. Sam actually thought the man might pass out right in front of him. A guy who had looked only nervous when he got there now appeared completely terrified. Whatever was in that text message was clearly alarming.

"They're coming," Hawkins announced. "We've got to get out of here. Now."

"Who's coming?" Sam replied. "What's going on, Tom?"

"Zapata's crew! That's who!"

That didn't register. "Who is Zapata?"

Hawkins cursed again, shook his head, his eyes bouncing all around the room, as if he wasn't sure what to do first. "It's all in the briefcase. We've got to get out of here right now, before it's too late. Do you hear me?"

"Who the hell is Zapata?"

Sam was getting pissed. The man was freaking out and needed to start answering his questions. A sudden pounding on the hotel-room door interrupted their heated exchange. Sam felt a spike of adrenaline push through him. Something told him the pounding wasn't from a room-service waiter. Zapata? Hawkins's eyes shot to the door, then he looked back at Sam and noticeably swallowed.

Sam didn't like the hollow look in the man's eyes. It was the look of defeat.

Hawkins reached around with a shaky right hand to his lower back, pushed up his Hawaiian shirt, and then pulled out a small black revolver. Sam felt a second jolt of adrenaline. The balding attorney was carrying a gun, seemed intent on using it.

Who the hell was outside that hotel-room door?

Sam tried to defuse the situation. "Whoa! Tom, wait. Let me talk to whoever is out there. I'm your attorney. Surely I can negotiate your way out of this. There has to be a better way."

Hawkins actually chuckled, although it was more a maniacal laugh. The man was losing it right in front of Sam. "There's no negotiating with these people. They're killers. They've already proven that. It's too late."

"What people?"

Hawkins was no longer listening to him. His mind was elsewhere. But then, as if he found a moment of clarity, he looked Sam square in the eyes. "You've got to find Rich."

Hawkins then tried to explain how Rich was somehow Sam's long-lost father, leaving Sam staring at the man, dumbfounded.

"He's already on the run." Hawkins held up his cell phone, as if that info had been included in the text message he'd just received. "Rich has what they want, too. He's the only other person who can bring them down. If you get away, find him."

Sam had no time to stand there and argue with Hawkins. His head jerked around when he heard three consecutive silent thumps at the door, and he could see that the wood around the door handle was splitting and being blown apart. Sam cursed. Someone in the hallway was shooting his way into the hotel suite with a gun *and* silencer, which was a very bad flashback for Sam. He immediately thought of Square Jaw, the ruthless assassin who relentlessly had hunted Sam last November. Only professional killers used guns with silencers.

As the door to the hotel suite burst wide open, Hawkins took off running for the bedroom on the right. Sam saw the man in the black suit holding the gun. Thankfully, the assassin's eyes were not yet on Sam but instead were locked in on Sam's fleeing client. On instinct, Sam dove to the carpet behind the sofa, to avoid being targeted and shot on the spot. Beneath the sofa, he saw the assassin's black dress shoes chase after Hawkins, who didn't get very far away. Sam heard another thump and then saw Hawkins drop heavily to the carpet in the entrance to the bedroom. Hawkins lay perfectly still. He was gone. Sam was sure of it. The assassin then knelt down and started digging inside Hawkins's pockets.

Sam had to get out of there. Hawkins was right. There was no negotiating with someone like that. His mind quickly splintered in different directions, showing him a couple of ways to get out of the suite. His options were limited. He chose one, scrambled to his feet, but then spotted Hawkins's silver briefcase still sitting on the coffee table. When he grabbed the handle, it fell fully open. Sam paused in shock.

There was *nothing* inside.

TEN

Spencer Lloyd surveyed the scene. He wore a standard dark-blue wind-breaker, zipped to the neck. Peering into the darkness down the side-walk, Lloyd gave a waving motion with two fingers. Three of his FBI agents appeared, deftly racing across the front yard to the opposite corner of the house. The neighborhood was just east of the Anacostia River, outside Washington, DC. The tiny brick house sagged, as if ready to sink into the earth. A trash can had toppled over near the front sidewalk, its contents littering the small yard. It was more like dirt. No grass. A rusted brown van sat in the driveway. Weeds were growing up around the flat tires. The van hadn't been moved in months. The house sat in the shadows, no lights on outside, one of a dozen identical dumps lining the block. One front window was boarded up; the other, though cracked and caked in dust, showed signs of life inside. The flicker of a TV set. They were looking for a man who was supposedly connected to an underground domestic-terrorist group responsible for killing a prominent American Muslim couple with a car bomb in Baltimore three months ago.

Lloyd turned to the two agents with him, whispered, "Let's go."

They pulled weapons out of holsters, scooted quietly up to the edge of the house.

Lloyd had already sent a group around the back. They had the place covered.

Inching toward the front door, Lloyd grimaced as a dog began to yelp across the street. He stared over and focused in on his nemesis. A white poodle, of all things, stuck behind a chain-link fence. He hated poodles. His ex-mother-in-law used to always carry around a little white yapper in her giant purse. This one seemed to be staring right at him. Mocking him.

He picked up the pace, met two agents at the front door.

Lloyd listened for any movement inside. Nothing. He turned to the agent directly across from him, gave a quick nod. The agent stood straight, stepped away from the door, and kicked powerfully. The front door splintered open, and Lloyd and the rest of the team rushed inside. Lloyd immediately heard the rear door collapse and the flutter of familiar footsteps. They had the house.

"FBI!" Lloyd shouted. "Nobody move!"

The agents covered the house, moving in practiced form, weapons drawn and ready to fire. Lloyd crossed to the center of a filthy living room. He found a small TV tuned to some random cop movie. Robert De Niro filled the screen. A worn leather recliner bandaged together with duct tape sat empty in front of it. The carpet was covered with beer cans. He noticed cigarette smoke rising from a cluttered ashtray. The perp was here. Somewhere. He turned to an agent behind him, mouthed silently, "Bathroom." The agent bolted down the hallway.

Stepping toward the recliner, Lloyd paused. His eyebrows dipped. He tilted his head. He could hear something. A nervous breathing pattern. From the opposite side of the recliner.

He alertly raised his weapon. "Freeze! Stay put! Don't move!"

But his demand was ignored. A skinny man with a black goatee and dressed only in white boxers dashed out from behind the recliner. Lloyd could easily take him out, but they needed him alive, and Lloyd didn't have a Taser on him.

"Stop! FBI!"

Lloyd saw the man's eyes. They were glazed over, drug induced, and he wasn't listening or stopping. Without breaking stride, the near-naked man raced straight toward the only available window in the room and dove headfirst through the glass, shattering it all around him before toppling over into the front yard. Cursing, Lloyd hustled to the window, peered out. The man gathered himself from the dirt, cut and bleeding all over, stumbled forward, and moved toward the street.

Lloyd yelled, "We've got a runner!"

Two agents were already in pursuit out the front door.

Lloyd hit the sidewalk, watched a group of his men chase down the street. The skinny man in boxers was surprisingly fast.

Lloyd's eyes dissected a path through the neighborhood, his old mind at work, predicting his runner's likely route. He'd driven the neighborhood beforehand, knowing something like this could happen. The legs surrounding him were twenty years younger, but he knew the criminal mind. He knew desperation. Instead of chasing along with the others, Lloyd hurried across the street and cut through a neighbor's yard. He shot a glare at the poodle, fought the temptation to put a bullet in the mutt. He hopped a chain-link fence and pushed through a wooden gate.

He circled another run-down house and paused at the next street. He leaned against a black truck, panting, his heart pounding in his ears. He rarely did the chase anymore. Maybe a jog on the treadmill every two weeks. As assistant director in charge of the Washington, DC, field office, he spent most of his time telling *others* how to run down criminals and terrorists. But every once in a while, it was good to shake the rust off, get dirty, show your team that you're just one of them. He was regretting that decision at the moment.

Catching his breath, Lloyd heard the sound of trash cans bouncing to the concrete a few houses away. He'd guessed right. He crouched behind the truck and peered around the bumper. He stared into semidarkness. Two seconds ticked passed. Nothing. And then he appeared. The skinny man looked frantic, fleeing wildly but swiftly, the other men unable to catch him on foot. The man stopped for nothing, not even trash cans, his bare feet slapping down on the sidewalk directly toward Lloyd. His agents were still thirty feet behind and losing ground. Lloyd pressed his eyes closed, grunted to himself. He knew what he had to do and could already feel his old body ache.

Hidden, Lloyd began to count down the seconds.

Three . . . two . . . one.

He leaped from behind the truck, tackled the near-naked man with his still-strong shoulder. They collided violently, a linebacker crushing an unwitting quarterback. The man let out a horrible gasp and landed square on his back, Lloyd on top of him. Within seconds, Lloyd had him flipped over and his arms pinned behind his back, nearly ripping them out of the sockets. The man continued to moan in agony.

Lloyd stood and let the younger agents take over. He rubbed his shoulder. His whole arm felt numb. He was way too old for this crap.

"You okay, sir?" asked a blond agent named Carter.

"Just splendid."

His cell phone vibrated in his pocket. Lloyd hobbled down the sidewalk, pressed it to his ear. His lead agent and good friend, Michael Epps, was checking in from the office.

"You get the guy?" Epps asked.

"You could say that." Lloyd grimaced. "What's up?"

"Just had something interesting come across my desk. Thought you should know."

"Okay, don't make me beg."

"You heard of Alger Gerlach?"

Lloyd ran that name through his brain. "Gerlach? You mean the assassin?"

"Yeah. They used to call him the Gray Wolf. Or I guess they still do."

"Sure, I've seen the BBC story." A BBC reporter had put together a profile piece on Gerlach several years ago. It was a fascinating tale of murder and mayhem. The Gray Wolf was part legend and part myth. "Why are you asking?"

"We think we just got a local hit on him."

"You're kidding? Where?"

"Reagan International. Just a few hours ago."

"Wait, I thought this guy was dead or something."

"I'm not sure, to be honest. There have been lots of rumors. Also heard he retired a few years ago. Hard to know what's really true. He's been known to move around the world under a hundred different aliases."

"And you're telling me that one of them popped up on our radar in our backyard?"

"Yes, sir. American Airlines flight from Paris."

"You send anyone over to Reagan?"

"I got TJ and Bartlett already headed over there to look around."

"Any chance this is a bug in the system?"

"Sure, there's always that chance. But Krieger thinks it's legit."

Agent Krieger was the genius tech lead on his team.

Lloyd sighed, rubbed his shoulder. "Okay, I'm headed back your way. Dig up what you can for me." He glanced at the near-naked man, who was now in handcuffs. "I should've never come out here in the first place."

"I tried to tell you, Chief. It's not necessary."

"I know, I know."

"You need a medic or something?"

"No, just a drink." Before hanging up, Lloyd again thought about Gerlach. "Hey, Mike, has the Gray Wolf ever worked on American soil?"

"Not to our knowledge. This would be a first."

ELEVEN

Sam left the small church, walked the busy streets of Mexico City. Although the sun was now setting, the heat was still palpable, the sticky humidity on his skin. Sam was not comfortable staying in one place for very long. He kept running the details of his meeting with Tom Hawkins through his head. Who was Zapata? Why was Zapata's crew trying to kill Hawkins? What did his partner, Rich Hebbard, have that they all wanted? Why the hell was Hawkins's briefcase empty when he insisted that all the sordid details of this conspiracy were inside? Was the guy crazy? Or just drunk? Or both? None of it made any sense.

Sam couldn't even wrap his mind around the very last thing Hawkins had said to him.

Rich Hebbard said he was his *father*? Impossible.

According to Sam's mother, his father was a small-time drug dealer who was living on the rough side of Denver when they'd met. She was a homeless teenager, only fourteen years old, and he was already abusing her when she became pregnant. He'd threatened to kill her if she didn't terminate the pregnancy. She ran away just to give Sam a chance. Sam had never questioned her story. It just made sense. And now, twenty-five years later, Sam was supposed to somehow believe that his real father might actually be a successful lawyer named Rich Hebbard who had his own law firm in New Orleans? Sam couldn't even entertain the idea as a real possibility. After all that he and his mom had been through, especially of late, he couldn't even fathom that she would've kept that truth from him.

So why had Hebbard told Hawkins that blatant lie?

After twenty minutes of walking around, hiding in the shadows, with still no reply from the burner cell phone, Sam huddled in a quiet alley, near a pile of cardboard boxes, away from the sidewalks. He took out the cell phone he'd stolen from the teenage girl in the marketplace earlier and dialed a number from memory. It was time to call in the cavalry.

David Benoltz answered on the third ring.

"Tom Hawkins is dead," Sam said.

A pause. "What . . . what happened?"

"Someone came into our hotel suite during our meeting, intent to kill. Shot up the door. A professional, David. And he pumped Hawkins full of bullets."

David was quiet for a moment. "Are you okay?"

"They tried to kill me, too. I got away."

David cursed. "Who were they?"

"He mentioned someone named Zapata. That ring a bell?"

"No, I don't recognize that name."

"Me neither. But I'm on the run."

Another pause. "Wait . . . are you messing with me, Sam? Is this a joke?"

"I wish! I've got the cuts and bruises to prove otherwise."

Not to mention a chipped tooth and no hair, Sam thought.

David cursed again. "Have you gone to the police? Why are you running?"

"The police can't help me. I tried."

"What do you mean, they can't help? Why the hell not? Let me start making some calls, get this sorted out. Where are you right now?"

Sam ignored his question. "When Tom Hawkins called the firm yesterday, did he specifically request for me to take this meeting?"

David thought about it for a second. "Actually, yes, he did."

"You didn't think that was worth mentioning to me?"

"Your name is on the website, you're listed as my associate, and if you'll recall, you made some really big headlines last year. So people have been calling. Why're you asking?"

"Just something Tom said, that's all."

Sam wasn't ready to mention anything about Hebbard possibly being his father. It still seemed absurd.

"Where are you?" David repeated. "Are you hurt?"

"No, I'm fine. I've survived worse."

"I've got to get you out of there."

"I don't have my passport or any ID. And I can't go back to get it."

"Why not?"

"Long story. Just trust me." He knew he could not mention Natalie. Based on the texts with the video, he was hesitant even to call David in the first place.

David sighed again. "Okay, listen, I know a guy there. We go way back. He's former military Special Forces. Did a lot of secret ops. He moved across the border when he got into some trouble here with the government. He's been living in Mexico City for the past ten years. He's not a bad guy, just kind of odd. I helped him out, so he owes me one. He knows his way around, knows who to trust."

"How do I find him?"

"Let me reach out to him right now."

Sam noticed two uniformed cops suddenly pass in front of the alley, look in his direction. He cursed. "I'll call you back in thirty minutes."

He hung up the phone, turned, hurried down the alley.

TWELVE

Thankfully, they'd pulled the black hood off.

Natalie took great pride in being more mentally tough than most, but even she wasn't sure she could've handled sitting in a solitary room for hours on end in complete darkness. That was a scary thought on the drive over. Although the hood was now gone, the duct tape was still securely in place, covering her mouth, wrapped tightly around both wrists, and firmly bundled around both of her ankles. She sat uncomfortably in a wobbly wooden chair in the middle of some dark warehouse, the only light from a yellowed bulb just above a door to maybe a front-office room directly in front of her, as well as from an outside security light shining in through two large windows at the top of one of the tall metal walls of the building.

Natalie felt they were still near DC somewhere. She tried to keep a running clock in her mind, guessing that the unmarked van had driven around for maybe forty-five minutes, but she couldn't be certain. The black hood made her feel disoriented. When the van doors opened, it was eerily quiet outside. They were in a remote location with no other car sounds to be heard. Strong hands carried her out of the van. Recognizing it was not a good use of her energy, she resisted the urge to fight them. She needed to preserve her strength for the right moment.

They moved her inside the building and guided her through a few doors. The clicking of the door shutting behind her echoed in the cold space. Finally, when they arrived at her current destination, they sat her in the chair.

Within minutes of arriving, the men had pulled off the hood.

The video camera was already in place on a metal stand right in front of her. A light stand was next to it, a bright bulb shining a spotlight in her face. It was blinding. The bald and bearded driver from the van calmly told her to talk to the camera. He pulled the duct tape from her mouth, and she screamed the first thing that came to her mind: *"Sam!"* Seconds later, the bearded man covered her mouth again with the duct tape. The bright light next to the camera went off. With spots still in her eyes, she was able to watch two men—the young intern from the parking garage and the bearded driver—pack up the camera and lighting equipment, and then they both walked out of the warehouse room together through the office door.

Natalie sat there alone for an hour. Maybe it was shorter or longer. She couldn't be sure. Although she tried, she had no way to properly gauge time. They'd taken her cell phone away in the van. She didn't hear a sound the whole time she sat there, other than the wind pushing against the metal walls of the warehouse. It was maddening. They were not in the city. She was sure of that. She couldn't hear any cars driving by, even in the far distance. Did they go north, south, east, or west? She couldn't be certain. The warehouse felt cold and damp. She spotted a rat scampering across the floor thirty feet from her. She prayed it would not come near. There was an oversize garage door to her left. Apparently, the garage was designed to fit school buses, as an old yellow bus actually was parked just behind her. From the looks of it, she guessed it had been sitting there for more than a decade. It was dusty, and all the tires were deflated. There were no longer any official school markings on the side of the bus. They'd been completely covered up with graffiti. She thought that might mean there were teenagers somewhere nearby, within walking distance. So if she somehow got out of here, maybe she wouldn't have to run too far for help?

After sitting there for a while without seeing or hearing anyone, Natalie finally got her nerve up. She refused to just wait around to be rescued. She inched herself to the edge of her wooden chair, then rocked twice and used her momentum to get up onto her feet. With both her hands and feet bound together by duct tape, it was difficult to maneuver. She couldn't just walk out of there. But she could hop slowly. Maybe she could find a tool of some sort to cut off the duct tape and run for the hills. As quietly as possible, she began to inch toward the large garage door, where the most light came in from the outside window, one small jump at a time.

One hop. Pause, listen. Another hop. Pause, listen. And so forth.

She got halfway to the garage door when the office door suddenly opened, and bright light poured into the warehouse. Natalie cursed. The stocky crew-cut guy from the parking garage entered the room. There was nothing Natalie could do. She had no freedom to flee, nor any way to defend herself. She just stood there and grimaced as the guy got closer, wondering if he would somehow punish her for getting out of the chair. She could see that his left eye was black and swollen, and Natalie thought it was probably from the swift kick of her foot in the parking garage. She'd struck quite the blow and left some damage.

When the guy reached her, he didn't say anything. He didn't punch her. He just lifted her up over his thick shoulder, carried her right back to the wooden chair. He set her back down, and then he calmly took out more duct tape and proceeded to secure her to the chair this time. He methodically wrapped the duct tape all the way around her upper body and the back of the chair. Then he fastened her legs to the front chair legs. She had just lost her small sense of freedom.

Sitting there, analyzing her situation, Natalie made two quick mental notes. First, they were obviously watching her somehow from the other room. She carefully scanned the warehouse. Were there video cameras? She wondered how many people were inside the front office. Just the stocky crew-cut one? Or were there others? How many men would she have to evade to get out of this place? Second, she was surprised, considering what she'd done to the crew-cut guy's face earlier, that he didn't take the opportunity to return the favor. She was grateful, of course, but it didn't fit the profile she was developing in her mind. She was fully prepared to feel the wrath of his fist. Or worse. But nothing ever came.

Finally, the crew-cut guy turned, found the black hood on the floor. Natalie cursed under her breath. The guy carefully pulled the hood back over her head without a word. She was in darkness again. She tensed up, wondering if he would now take his chance to clobber her when she was most vulnerable. No physical contact came. A moment later, she heard the office door open and close. She was alone again in the warehouse. However, she was not as frightened as she was the last time while wearing the hood. At least she had a feel for her whereabouts. For whatever reason, they were not violent with her. Was there no truth to beat out of her? Could she simply be a pawn in someone's game?

Sam. They needed her to get to Sam.

Why? Who were these guys?

In the darkness under the hood, she kept running these questions in her mind.

Anything to not think about that rat being in the same room with her.

THIRTEEN

Sam sat at a small table along a metal railing in a quaint second-story café, overlooking the Zócalo, Mexico City's famous main square, surrounded on all sides by massive old building structures. The Zócalo was the city's center for national celebration *and* national protest—where the Mexican people regularly gathered for festivals, religious events, royal proclamations, and military parades. A boisterous festival of some sort was currently in progress, as the square was already crowded with thousands of people. His eyes shifted back and forth from the square below to the front doors of the café, making sure no unexpected guests suddenly arrived in search of him. In twenty minutes, he was set to meet a man David called Uncle Jerry next to the giant flagpole, towering more than 150 feet high, that stood directly in the center of the Zócalo. An enormous red, white, and green Mexican flag swayed in the warm wind.

Sam's instructions from David were to stand on the north side of the flag, twenty feet away, and Uncle Jerry would find him. David couldn't really give him a current description of Uncle Jerry; he had not seen him in more than ten years. David wasn't sure if Jerry, now in his fifties, had altered his appearance. All he could tell Sam was Uncle Jerry once sported a braided black ponytail and a mustache. He'd been skinny with a perpetual cigarette. A tattoo of a creepy black scorpion was etched into the skin on the back of his left hand. All that could've changed. Sam felt uneasy with the vagueness. David insisted he could trust the guy.

Sam trusted no one. But he needed serious help.

Uncle Jerry would have to do for now.

The café was busy with patrons. It was nearing dinnertime—or drinking time—as most of his fellow guests seemed to be enjoying cold *cervezas* and cocktails. Sam ordered black coffee but barely sipped it. He wasn't hungry or thirsty. His stomach was tied up in thick knots. Although he tried to stop himself, he kept watching that damn video on the cell phone of Natalie being held hostage, kept hearing her scream his name. He'd already sent three more desperate text messages to the original number, each one escalating his anger. He still hadn't heard anything back. He was losing his mind. Watching the video was not helping matters, of course. He felt so lost, just sitting around, waiting.

He wanted to be in DC, searching for her. Rescuing her.

Especially with how things currently stood between them. This brought another rush of unwanted emotions, his mind flooded with scenes from the past few difficult months.

It had not been easy between them since last November.

March 4
Four months ago

The national fallout from Natalie's investigative story on the McCallister-Redrock scandal on the eve of Election Day last fall had created a political tsunami that rolled through DC and caused serious havoc. Politicians who had once backed Redrock as a viable global private-security alternative were now running for the hills. Natalie had material for months, with story after story to be written. With the best investigative reporters from all over the country pounding the same pavement in search of even more dynamic angles to cover—and there were many—Natalie refused to leave the center of the storm. Although she had agreed to give Sam another opportunity to make things right with her, the reentry into their dating relationship was difficult because of her demanding work schedule. Even though Sam was incredibly patient, he often told her he felt like he was working the corner of a prizefighter who had already thrown a knockout punch in round one but who was still insisting on going the full fifteen.

Natalie was a machine and rarely left her *PowerPlay* office. Many nights she even slept on the cheap sofa in the break room so she wouldn't miss a single second. She called it her World Series moment, her time to really shine under the bright lights on the biggest stage, and she begged Sam to try to understand—which, of course, he did. All in all, he was just grateful to get another chance with a woman he'd thought he'd lost forever. He'd screwed up their relationship so badly two years ago that it felt like a miracle that Natalie had even let her guard down just a little. Not to mention, he certainly had his own bumpy road ahead of him if he was going to put his life back together and somehow finish law school. So they agreed to play it slow, seeing each other mostly for lunch in her office a couple of times a week, a few quick dates here and there. Sam often wondered if Natalie was using her work as an excuse to keep some distance between them, subconsciously afraid that he'd run away again. If that was the case, he couldn't blame her.

The heartbreak of their first breakup had cut her very deep.

After four exhausting months, it finally took Natalie's boss finding her sleeping in her cubicle early one Sunday morning to force her to take some much-needed time off. He insisted she leave her laptop and phone, locked them in his desk drawer, then told her to get lost for *at least* a week.

Natalie chose the island of Saint Martin. She and Sam unplugged and jumped on a plane. She was grateful for his patience and excited to escape with him and let her hair down for a few days. Sam was in dreamland. Seven days on an island. No assassins. No helicopters. No FBI agents. Just Natalie in a bikini, unbelievable food, and an endless supply of daiquiris. It was a heck of a way to reignite their relationship. He knew they needed quality time together to heal old wounds and move forward in their relationship. Sam soaked up every moment with her, dreading the return home to the real world.

The voice mail that awaited him upon his arrival back in the States slammed him back to reality. Sam knew it wasn't good the moment he turned his cell phone back on. The voice mail was from Dr. Wilson, the head doctor at Angel Cancer Care, his mother's facility. He could not remember a time in the past year when Dr. Wilson had called to give him positive news. He called Sam only when it was bad.

He could tell by the tone in Dr. Wilson's voice that bad was an understatement.

His mom looked terrible. He'd been gone only a week, but she looked like she'd all but withered away during that time. Leukemia sucked. He hated cancer with so much passion. Dr. Wilson said it had come back in full force and was very aggressive. They were in desperate times. She needed a bone-marrow transplant. Fortunately Sam was a match. With no other family around, he was her only real hope. They would schedule the procedure ASAP. After having no relationship at all with his mother for the first twenty-four years of his life, and then finally tracking her down two years ago and wading through so much emotional pain to reestablish some semblance of a mother-son relationship, he refused to let her die on him now. Standing there in her doorway, looking in on her while she was sleeping, Sam could feel the anger bubbling up inside of him. He just didn't understand it. How could God let this happen? She was doing so well and responding to normal treatment. Then it all just spiraled in on them within a week, like a tidal wave crushing their whole lives. He grit his teeth. If God wasn't going to heal her, then he would do it himself. He'd give her his own flesh and blood. Whatever it took.

As he was standing there, still stewing, she opened her eyes and spotted him.

She looked frail, but the smile was as wide as ever. "Samuel! How was your trip? You got so much sun!"

He stepped into the room, moved close to her bed, gave her a quick hug and kiss on the forehead. She felt like skin and bones under the blanket.

"Where's Natalie?" she asked. Her eyes always sparkled when she asked about Natalie.

"She'll be here in a few minutes. She's grabbing food for us."

"Well, how was it? Beautiful? The online pictures looked spectacular."

Natalie had gotten his mom set up with her own Facebook account. So she'd been monitoring pictures that Natalie had posted while they were in Saint Martin.

"Mom . . . ?" Sam said, his voice heavy.

"I bet the water was as blue as your beautiful eyes."

"Mom . . . ?" he said again.

She ignored him. "And the sunsets, tell me about the sunsets there."

"Mom!"

Her brow furrowed. "Dammit, Samuel, don't walk in here and treat me like I'm already dead. Okay? I know what Dr. Wilson said. Just let me enjoy my only son and the beauty of his life. That's all I've got right now. You understand me? So stop your damn frowning and sulking. I won't have any of it. Not now. You don't need to feel sorry for me or angry at the world. Either way, God has got this, do you hear me? No more pity parties. Not for me."

He sighed. "You sound like Pastor Isaiah."

She smiled. "Well, there's a reason he's one of my favorite people on this planet. We can talk all about this damn cancer until we're blue in the face *later*; right now I want you to start telling me all about Saint Martin and the wonderful time you had with Natalie. Leave out no details."

Sam grinned. "You'd love it, Mom."

"Well, hell, get me out of this place, and let's go!" She laughed.

"That's my plan. I promise."

FOURTEEN

Agent Lloyd fiddled with a report in his fingers, rubbed his throbbing shoulder. He'd popped a handful of painkillers earlier, but they were barely taking the edge off. Special Agent Epps insisted that he see a real medic, but Lloyd continued to refuse. They were like an old married couple, always nagging each other. Epps was usually right. But Lloyd was the boss.

Lloyd stood in a room with a wall of digital screens on the sixth floor of DC's FBI Building, just a few blocks east of the White House. Several agents were pecking away at computer stations, different information popping up on the screens in front of him. Lloyd's cell phone vibrated in his front pocket. He reached for it, stared at the screen, frowned. *Pop.* He let out a deep sigh, shook his head. His father was calling. Pop called him at least three times a day, mostly at the worst possible moments. Pop was eighty-nine, half-senile, and lived with Lloyd in his cramped two-bedroom condo. He'd moved his father in with him two years ago when his father's health rapidly declined. His father had spent everything he had on medical care for Lloyd's mother, who'd lost a battle with dementia five years ago. Lloyd was also struggling financially because of a promising real-estate investment going bad. There was no extra money at the moment for a decent assisted-living facility for Pop. Now they were awkward roommates.

Lloyd felt guilty most of the time. He could go days without seeing his father, oftentimes getting home well after midnight if the job required it. It felt like having a dog at home but never taking it out for walks. Just cruel. His father was stuck in a dumpy recliner in front of the TV most days, watching old Westerns and war flicks, just waiting to die. The old man deserved better. He adored his pop, and it pained him to see a once-great man wither away into what he'd become. Edward Lloyd had been a faithful street cop for forty years, one of the best. He was the younger Lloyd's hero and the reason he'd gone into law enforcement in the first place. Now he did nothing but nap and eat candy bars all day.

Lloyd reluctantly pressed a button, lifting his cell phone to his ear.

Five years ago, when his beloved mother had passed, Lloyd had pressed Ignore to repeated calls from her paid caretaker. Lloyd was in the middle of an intense investigation and didn't have the time to be bothered. Which meant he didn't find out about his own mother's death until nearly eighteen hours later. That had haunted him for five years. Her body was ice-cold before he ever even knew about it. As painful as it was to sometimes answer these calls, Lloyd swore he would never let that happen again.

"Pop? What is it? You okay?"

He sighed again as his father began rambling off a grocery list. Mostly junk food and cheap beer. Lloyd got this same call at least twice a week. It was like having a teenager in the house. He tried not to sound too agitated.

"Sure, Pop. I'll go by the store soon. I've got to go now, okay?"

His father ignored Lloyd's urgency, as usual, continued to ramble on about a noisy neighbor. They lived in a sparse condo in a cheap building with thin walls.

"Okay, I hear you," Lloyd insisted, interrupting. "I'll talk to them. I've got to go."

He hung up with his father still spewing, which was normal. At least he was okay.

Agent Epps returned to the conference room with a folder in his hands. Epps was a tall black man of fifty who had starred as a shooting guard at Villanova back in the 1980s, before tearing up his right knee his senior year. He'd been a cop in Philadelphia, like his own dad and granddad, before joining the Bureau twenty years ago. He'd been on Lloyd's team for nearly fifteen years now. Lloyd trusted no one more than Epps. In fact, Epps was perhaps Lloyd's only real friend.

"Anything more on the Wolf?" Lloyd asked.

"Maybe," Epps began. "I'm not sure just yet."

Epps grabbed a remote, pointed it at the digital screens on the wall. An airport-security video appeared on the screen in the middle. It was a shot from behind an airline counter at Roissy Airport in Paris, pointing down over an airline agent's head at a nondescript-looking man of medium stature wearing glasses, a beard, a gray jacket, and a black bag over his shoulder. There was nothing that stood out about him. The profile of Alger Gerlach, the Gray Wolf, appeared on the screen to the left, along with a list of his most prominent kills across Europe. The Italian prime minister in '06. A member of the British Parliament in '09. The French minister of foreign affairs in '10. The Greek finance minister in '12. And the list went on from there. It was an impressive résumé for an already-legendary assassin. The picture on the profile looked nothing like the man in the video, which was not surprising. The Gray Wolf was known to blend in and regularly change his appearance. MI5 had once found a rogue plastic surgeon who claimed to have done a half dozen facial procedures in a five-year span on the great Alger Gerlach.

"That him?" Lloyd asked, pointing at the security video.

"In theory," Epps confirmed.

"I don't like theories, Mike. You know that."

"I'm not sure what we're dealing with here just yet." Epps walked over to the third screen on the right, where they both looked at a still shot of a computer screen. "This is what popped up on Krieger's radar, the alert I mentioned in our system, and why I called you in the first place. You see the name *Gildas Vaughn* with the red alert. BND tagged Vaughn to Gerlach just three days ago using facial-recognition software. However, as you'll see, only ten seconds later, the alert goes from red to green. And the guy is cleared to travel in the system."

BND was German foreign intelligence. Lloyd stepped closer. "What does that mean?"

"Krieger thinks it means someone was waiting online to make sure this guy got a free travel pass. Someone with the highest level of access. *Or* a brilliant hacker. Either way, someone manipulated the system and got Gerlach cleared into the United States."

"You talk to Germany?"

Epps nodded. "BND called it an orange-level tag based off security footage in Munich from last week, which is only a moderate alert requiring more investigation."

Lloyd stared at the man in the security video at the airport counter. He looked pretty relaxed. Was that because he already knew he'd have no trouble clearing the system? Or maybe an assassin like the Gray Wolf never sweats? Either way, he didn't like it.

"Why does Krieger think this is the same guy?" Lloyd asked.

Epps pressed another button, pulling up another security video next to the one from Paris on the oversize screens.

"This was taken seven years ago at a bus station in Cairo," Epps explained. "Egyptian intelligence tagged this to Gerlach, right before he assassinated a ranking member of the Shura Council."

Lloyd's eyes narrowed. Although the security videos had been taken years apart, the two men looked incredibly similar. Matching garb. Same eyeglasses. Beard. It was the same man, or they were twin brothers. He felt his heartbeat quicken.

"So this *is* legit," Lloyd stated.

"I think so, Chief. The Gray Wolf is here in DC."

Lloyd cursed. "Now the question is . . . *why* is he here?"

FIFTEEN

Sam stood twenty feet north of the Mexican flag inside the Zócalo.

The main square was still thick with people. Thousands of men and women, young and old, were out dancing and singing, marching and drinking, and the enormous crowd was steadily growing as the sun set over Mexico City. Sam wasn't sure what they were celebrating, but the Zócalo was apparently the place to be tonight—which was probably why Uncle Jerry wanted to meet there. It was easy to blend into the sea of people and the celebratory chaos. Sam checked the phone again, as he did every sixty seconds. It had now been more than two hours since he'd received the video with Natalie, and still no one had replied to his numerous text messages.

Had they hurt her?

Had something terrible already happened to her?

Was that why no one was replying?

The pit in his stomach kept growing deeper with each passing minute.

He stood with his hands in his pockets, his head on a swivel, his eyes alert, the massive waves of people shifting about all around him. He searched the faces. He watched for eyes that might engage his in a certain way. He was looking for a fifty-year-old white American with a potential ponytail and mustache. *Where are you, Uncle Jerry?* He felt exposed and vulnerable standing there in the middle of so many people, especially with Mexican policemen stationed all around the square. He'd counted twenty officers already, a pair of them standing at attention on every corner, monitoring the crowd. He again checked the time on the cell phone. Uncle Jerry was two minutes late. Sam decided if he was more than five minutes late, he would bolt. He would not take any extra risk for this guy, no matter what David thought of him.

Sam felt an unexpected tap on his shoulder, which startled him.

He spun around, stared at the guy. The man had somehow carved through the big crowd and managed to sneak up on him completely unnoticed. Sam didn't like that—it meant his survival instincts had dulled. David said the man was a former military specialist, so maybe Uncle Jerry was a trained and skilled professional. Either way, Sam felt uneasy about being approached in such a manner. The man was almost exactly as Sam had pictured in his mind. He still had the braided ponytail, a thin graying mustache, and aviator shades. He was skinny, with pale skin, and he wore a camo jacket, black jeans, and black army boots. Sort of a hippie-military look, like a product of the seventies.

Sam immediately got a weird feeling about the guy.

"You Callahan?" he said, leaning in close. Sam could smell marijuana on his breath.

Sam nodded. "Uncle Jerry?"

The man smiled, showing two tobacco-stained front teeth. "Right. A mutual friend said you could use my help."

"He said you know the city, know people around here."

"He's right. Let's go."

"Go where?"

"Away from this nonsense," Uncle Jerry explained, nodding right and left toward the crowd. "A secure place to chat. Figure out how to get you out of your mess."

"Then why'd we have to meet out here in the first place?"

"So I could make sure you were clean."

Sam studied him a moment. "Am I?"

Uncle Jerry nodded. Sam's eyes went to all the surrounding build-ings. He wondered from where the man had been watching him. It could have been anywhere. Uncle Jerry stepped forward, and Sam fol-lowed him. They began pushing through the people, working their way back to the edge of the square. The crowd suddenly parted ahead of them to let a marching band through. A parade of some sort was beginning. It was loud as hell and getting rowdier by the moment. Sam trailed Uncle Jerry closely as they circled around the marching band and the parade and headed across the square, making sure to avoid passing directly in front of any police officers. Across the street, Sam gazed up at the Metropolitan Cathedral—the massive old church structure that covered an entire block. He'd quizzed the café waitress earlier about the buildings surrounding the Zócalo, just to get a better lay of the land. The Metropolitan had dozens of ornate columns and several sky-reaching bell towers. The main doors of the church were open, and a lot of people were coming and going from the cathedral.

Sam followed Uncle Jerry across the street. They skipped the main entrance to the cathedral and instead trotted up some concrete steps farther down the sidewalk, where they entered through a more obscure side entrance. Uncle Jerry seemed to know exactly where he was going. He pushed open a heavy wooden door that looked hundreds of years old and quickly shut it behind them. Then he led Sam through a few dark rooms, opening and shutting more wooden doors, until Sam followed the ponytailed man up a very narrow stone stairwell that reminded him of being inside an old Renaissance castle—like something out of *The Hunchback of Notre Dame*. It was quiet and cold in the stairwell.

They circled up five flights of spiraling stone stairs, then finally stepped out into a dusty open-aired room that was filled with heavy ropes that crisscrossed in every direction. Sam recognized they were inside one of the tall bell towers as he spotted the giant bell hanging right in front of him. Sam stepped up to the ledge by the tower, peered out over a half wall down into the main square almost two hundred feet below. The party in the Zócalo looked even bigger from up high in the bell tower. The parade was growing longer, the marching band was getting louder, and the people were getting drunker.

Jerry lit a joint, took his shades off. "What kind of trouble you in?"

Sam turned. "Hard to say exactly. In the past few hours, I've been shot at by assassins, jumped from a hotel balcony and nearly broke my back, and went on a high-speed car chase through these crowded streets. If that wasn't enough, I had to break out of a federal police building."

"Sounds like fun," Jerry replied, grinning, puffing.

"Maybe for you. I don't need that kind of fun."

"David said you needed official papers."

Sam nodded. "Yeah, I lost everything. Passport. IDs. Credit cards."

"Gonna make it hard to get home."

"Can you help?"

He nodded. "Sure, I know a guy. You got any cash?"

Sam shrugged. "Maybe thirty bucks."

Uncle Jerry smirked. "I'll bill David. Let me make a call."

The man pulled out his phone, punched a button, and held it to his ear. Sam walked back over to the ledge by the large bell and studied the impressive celebration below. He guessed there were already ten thousand people down there partying it up and having the time of their lives. Considering his situation, he envied their carefree evening. What he wouldn't give to rewind the clock twenty-four hours and go in a different direction. He turned around again. For the first time, Sam looked at the back of Uncle Jerry's left hand. David had said there was a creepy tattoo of a black scorpion on it, but Sam noted that there was nothing there. Sam peeked down at the man's right hand, which was still holding his joint. No tattoos there, either. Sam thought that Uncle Jerry could have had the tattoo removed. Although considering the man's overall appearance, he highly doubted he would go to that kind of trouble for a scorpion tattoo.

Uncle Jerry looked up, locked eyes with Sam, who tried to play it cool. The man gave Sam a reassuring nod. Earlier Sam had noticed a black gun holster inside Uncle Jerry's camo jacket. Something didn't feel right. At that very moment, Sam heard the sound of the last wooden door they'd just passed through a few minutes ago, twenty feet down the spiral stone stairwell, open and then shut. Then he heard the patter of shoes quickly ascending up toward the bell tower. Full-on adrenaline pumped through his body. Someone was coming! His eyes again connected with Uncle Jerry; however, this time the military man must have noticed the sudden panic wash over Sam. Uncle Jerry stiffened, alert, reached inside his jacket for his gun.

Sam spun around, spotted the small opening beside the giant hanging bell, and then quickly jumped up on the ledge and dove through it. He heard Uncle Jerry yell something behind him. Sam got to his feet on the other side of the bell and was now standing right outside the tower, staring down over a short wrought iron railing two hundred feet or so down to the sidewalk below. He couldn't jump for it. The fall would definitely kill him.

Sam's eyes shifted left, where he noticed a terrace only two stories down. If he could get across the tiny ledge on this massive column without falling, he had a chance. It was a big *if*, but he had no choice. And he had no time to be cautious. He grabbed the railing, swung his legs over. His first huge risk was a ten-foot drop to another very narrow ledge below him that was maybe six inches wide. The only way to get there was to jump, land like a skilled gymnast on a balance beam, and then hope he could somehow grab an edge of the building with his fingers.

He heard movement inside the bell tower coming toward him.

He thought of Natalie, and then he jumped for it.

The toe of his right shoe caught the six-inch ledge at the same time that his left hand grabbed an ornate curl poking out of the column. He was literally hanging by a thread, half his body swinging wide out over the sidewalk below. He quickly pulled himself in, got his balance, and pressed himself up flat against the cathedral column. Then he began to scoot a few inches at a time around the corner of the tower. He took another peek up from where he'd jumped and spotted two faces staring down in search of him. One belonged to Uncle Jerry. The other was his new pal, Desperado, the assassin from inside the hotel suite. Had he been tricked? David?

He couldn't even fathom that possibility. He quickly slipped around the tower corner and ducked completely out of view. He was now twenty feet above the fourth-story terrace. He found more ledges on this column, so he was able to quickly scale his way down like a rock climber.

At eight feet, he jumped, hit the terrace, and rolled.

Getting to his feet, Sam raced to the nearest door and stepped inside an empty banquet hall. He crossed through the room, hurried down a quiet hallway, until he found himself staring down over a railing from more than thirty feet into the massive church sanctuary below him. A priest was at the front, standing near the ornate gold altar while several hundred people sat in dozens of wooden rows. When Sam spotted Uncle Jerry appear in the back of the sanctuary, searching the area, he tucked back behind a wall column. He waited a few seconds and carefully peered out again. Uncle Jerry was gone. But where was Desperado? Sam had to somehow get out of the building, create space between them, and get lost in the night.

He found a set of roped-off stairs, descended carefully. A large crowd filled the lobby. Most were tourists reading the various plaques, studying the artwork, and taking selfies with all of the ancient gold statues. He did not immediately spot his pursuers inside the lobby, but Sam knew he couldn't simply walk out. He needed extra help—something to throw the men off and buy himself some time to operate. He again needed a quick new look. He eased his way into the crowd, searching for options, and then he noticed two young men of maybe twenty hanging out by themselves against one wall and looking bored. One wore a blue ball cap with the words *Cruz Azul*. The other guy looked to be about Sam's size and wore a blue-jean jacket. Sam pulled out some cash from the small wad in his pocket, stepped up to them.

"*¿Habla Inglés?*" Sam asked them.

They both shook their heads. Sam pointed at the blue cap on the one guy's head and then the blue-jean jacket on the other guy and held up the cash. The young men gave each other a curious look, shrugged, nodded, took the cash, and handed over the requested items.

"*Gracias,*" Sam replied.

He immediately put on the cap and jacket, stepped closer to the stream of people moving in and out the main doors. He was within five feet when Desperado suddenly appeared right in front of him. Sam tried not to panic and blow his cover. Instead, he pulled the bill of the cap down even farther, blocked his eyes, held his breath, and kept a steady gait. Desperado brushed past him, their shoulders nearly touching, Sam's heart in his throat—the man had coldly pumped a bullet into his new client! When he cleared him, Sam took a swift but cautious glance back. The assassin kept moving farther down the lobby.

As calmly as possible, Sam stepped into the exit line and walked outside of the cathedral. He remained very close behind a large group of people who were with a tour guide, as if he belonged with them. He stayed with the group until they were at least fifty feet farther up the sidewalk. Then Sam veered off, took his first breath. He stared back up at the tall bell tower from where he'd just narrowly escaped, shook his head. None of it made any sense.

Why had Uncle Jerry betrayed him?

How was the man involved with Desperado? What was the link?

Sam knew he could no longer rely on David for help. Although he refused to believe that his boss had anything to do with this, there was clearly a breach somewhere in their communication. He'd have to go in a completely different direction. First, he had to get away from the Zócalo. He ditched the jacket and cap, hustled up the sidewalk. His brisk walk soon turned into a slight jog. The boisterous sounds of the party began to slowly fade behind him, but the intense emotions of the moment were growing even louder in his head.

The slight jog eventually shifted to a full-on sprint.

His running shoes now pounded the cracked sidewalks.

Sam ran deep into the dark streets of the foreign city.

SIXTEEN

Text: El Ángel, Paseo de la Reforma, 8:30

Sam stared at the burner phone, still breathing hard and sweating. The new text came only five minutes after he'd fled the Metropolitan Cathedral. He caught a cab at a street corner with the final remnant of cash he still had left in his pocket. He was flat broke again. He would need to put his street skills back to work if this continued much longer. He considered going back to his hotel room at the Hyatt but quickly dismissed that idea. Agent Mendoza would likely have a pair of federal agents waiting for him right outside his room door. He would have to continue to do this the hard way.

The cab driver spoke broken English but seemed to know exactly where to go when Sam passed along the info he'd received in the text message. Sam was unsure what he'd find when he got there, but he was certainly eager and hopeful that this was finally coming to a place of reckoning. He was already tired of the cryptic text messages. He was furious that there had been no follow-up to Natalie's situation.

He wanted answers, right now. He wanted to actually talk to someone.

He again thought of David, wondered how Uncle Jerry had turned on him.

It just didn't make sense. David would never do that. Or would he?

He watched the video of Natalie again. He needed to see her face, hear her voice, even if she was bound and frightened. He'd do whatever he needed to do to protect her.

Even give up his life.

He thought about his mom, felt a catch in his throat.

After all, Natalie was the closest thing to family he still had left.

March 7
Four months ago

They called it a harvest, where they were supposed to take about two pints of Sam's bone marrow and then immediately transplant it into his mom. Sam wondered what would've happened to his mother had he never gone to look for her in the first place. She might already be dead. She might never have gotten the type of care that she did by moving to DC to be near him. Without him, she might have died alone in a hospice room back in Houston waiting for doctors to find her a bone-marrow match. He had Natalie to thank for that. When they'd first started dating, she'd helped him push past the fear and the anger that had held him hostage for so long and encouraged him to finally make the effort to reconnect with his mom. He would never have done it without her. He would never have had the courage to face his demons head-on. Lying there in bed, recovering, he felt overwhelmingly grateful. He didn't deserve her.

He felt very emotional. Maybe it was the drugs.

At his bedside, Natalie leaned over to him.

"How're you feeling?" she asked.

"A little sore. But okay. How is she?"

"We don't know yet. They haven't finished on her end."

He sighed. "This has to work, Natalie."

"It will, Sam. Don't worry."

"She's a pain in the ass, but she's all I've got."

"She's not going anywhere. Have faith."

"I'm trying, believe me."

Natalie pushed Sam in a wheelchair to see his mom a few hours later. She was in a private hospital room with her name, Nancy Weber, on the door, and being monitored very closely. The doctor had come by earlier and told them they felt everything went well. Now it was up to her body to behave the way they wanted and expected. The next twenty-four hours were critical. His mom was awake and wanted to see him. Natalie pushed him up close to her bed. He didn't need the wheelchair and felt embarrassed by it, but the doctor made him promise to wait until at least the next day before he started walking around.

"Mom?" Sam said, touching her arm.

She looked skinny as hell, even worse than yesterday. Barely any color in her cheeks.

Her eyes slowly fluttered open.

"Samuel," she said, gave a weak smile.

"How're you doing?" he asked.

"I'm fine. Let's get the hell out of here and go to Vegas."

He chuckled. "Not yet. You need to rest."

"Can I at least get a cigarette?"

Sam frowned. "No, Mom. No more smoking!"

"Then just let me die."

"Not a chance."

She put her hand on top of his, squeezed. "I'm just teasing. But I sure could use a cheeseburger. Maybe some fries?"

Natalie said, "I'll go check with the nurse."

"Thank you, sweetie," his mom said.

Natalie stepped out of the room. His mom looked over at him.

"Have I told you to marry her, Samuel?"

"Almost every day for as long as I can remember."

She frowned at him. "Then what the hell are you waiting for?"

Sam grinned. "Let's just get through this first, okay?"

"Don't use me as your excuse," she chastised him.

"I'm not, I swear."

"Good. I never want you to let your dying mom hold you back. I already did enough of that in your life." She sighed, grimaced. "I feel bad even putting you through this ordeal."

"Don't. I'll be up and running around again by tomorrow."

"You'd better be, or I'll give Dr. Wilson hell."

"You'll be giving him hell no matter what."

"True."

"You will be up again soon, too. Everything went well."

She smiled, patted his hand. "I sure hope so. I don't want to miss your wedding."

He rolled his eyes, shook his head. "Come on, Mom. Stop already."

She squeezed his hand, her eyes growing wet. "Thank you, Samuel. I really mean it. I don't deserve this from you. I don't deserve much of anything."

"You don't deserve cancer, either. So stop talking that way."

"Well, that's debatable." She swallowed, pressed her dry lips together, her pale forehead wrinkling. "I need to tell you something."

"Okay."

She again pressed her lips together, as if this was something more serious, and she was contemplating just how to say it to him. "It's something I've wanted to tell you for a long time, from the first day you showed up in Houston, but I never felt quite right about it. Honestly, I was afraid you'd get angry at me all over again."

"You're in the hospital battling cancer and recovering from transplant surgery. How angry could I really get with you right now?"

He smiled, tried to be reassuring. She smiled, too, but he could still sense some hesitancy. About that time, the doctor appeared in the room, breaking the moment, ready to give them an update on her situation.

Sam leaned into his mom, said, "We can talk about this later, okay?"

"Okay."

Sam had no idea he'd never get the chance to finish the conversation.

SEVENTEEN

El Ángel was a huge monument in the middle of a major roundabout in the heart of Mexico City. A giant gold statue of a goddess stood at the top of a one-hundred-foot column. The whole monument glowed under bright lights in the dark night. When the cab driver finally dropped him off on the sidewalk across the street, Sam noticed there were several others meandering about around the base of the monument. He stepped out, suddenly felt very vulnerable once again. He had no money, no ID, and was likely wanted by both the federal police and assassins. Standing out in the wide open for very long was not at all comfortable.

Hands stuffed in his pockets, he trotted across the street. Slowly circling the monument, he wondered who would show up and from where. He walked past a young couple strolling hand in hand. A family with two little girls was taking pictures. An older man in a brown jacket stood off by himself, staring at one of the smaller statues around the base. Sam watched him for a moment, wondered. But the man never turned to look at Sam. He was not the guy.

Sam made a full circle around the base of the monument, checked the time on the cell phone. The digital numbers read exactly 8:30 p.m. He looked up and noticed the woman. She wore a gray trench coat and marched quickly across the street directly toward Sam. When she got closer, he put it together. She was the same woman from the federal building—the agent who had given him the police windbreaker with the burner phone in the pocket. Although he now doubted she really worked for the federal police. So who was she? He guessed she was in her midthirties, with straight black hair that fell just below her shoulders.

"Sam," she acknowledged, stepping within five feet.

"Who are you?" Sam asked, already feeling pissed off.

"If you want to see Natalie alive again, you must complete your assignment within the next twenty-four hours."

The mention of Natalie caused him to ball up his fist.

She noticed, smiled. "You should control your emotions, Sam," the woman suggested, a quick nod across the street from where she'd just appeared.

Sam peered behind her, noticed two imposing men standing at the corner looking his way. Both wore black leather jackets and had angry faces. The muscle. Her protection.

"Where is Natalie?" he asked through gritted teeth.

"She's safe. For now."

"What do you want?"

She reached inside her trench coat, pulled out a manila envelope, stepped forward, and handed it over to him. Inside, he found a single eight-by-ten-inch color photograph of a fiftysomething man with brown-gray hair, combed neatly to the side, wearing a black suit and tie. The photograph looked like it was taken while the man was standing on a city sidewalk. There was nothing else in the envelope. Just the photograph.

Sam looked up. "Who is he?"

"His name is Rich Hebbard. He's *very* important to my client."

Sam immediately connected the name back to Tom Hawkins. Hebbard was Hawkins's law partner, the man Hawkins instructed Sam to find because Hebbard also held critical information in whatever conspiracy was going on. Hebbard was the man Hawkins implied was already on the run from Zapata's crew. And last but certainly not least, Hebbard was the same man Hawkins had claimed was Sam's real father. Sam stared at the photograph, studied the eyes and the other facial features. Were they the same as his? He had to admit there were some vague similarities. He shook his head. Ridiculous.

"What did he do?" Sam asked, as if he didn't know anything.

She gave him a fleeting smile. "You know I'm not going to answer that."

"Fine," Sam huffed, irritated. "Why me? You seem quite capable. Go find him yourself."

"We have reasons to believe that Hebbard will not hide from you like he will from us."

"What reasons?"

Another fleeting smile. She ignored his question. "Twenty-four hours, Sam. Find him and turn him in to us, Natalie walks away clean. Simple as that. If you don't, well, I know my client. It won't be pretty, I can promise you that. So I wouldn't waste any more time."

He again clenched his fist. "Where do I start?"

She shook her head. "I don't know."

"Look, lady, I don't have a wallet or ID or any other resources."

"You've already proven to be very resourceful."

"Assuming I somehow find this guy, how will I then find you?"

"We'll find you. One more thing, Sam. If you contact the police or any other agency, Natalie dies. Like I said, my client is a bit unstable. So please don't waste your time trying to figure out who I am or the identity of my client. That won't save Natalie. Just do your thing, find Rich Hebbard for us, and then you can go back to your normal life. Don't complicate this by being reckless or stupid. Every second you're not searching for Hebbard is a second Natalie is closer to dying."

EIGHTEEN

Sam knew the first person he needed to contact: Tommy Kucher.

The brilliant twenty-one-year-old computer hacker had been invaluable in helping him survive the McCallister-Redrock ordeal last year. Without Tommy and his underground band of misfit hacker friends, Sam would've been toast. Tommy kept him one step ahead of assassins and two steps ahead of the FBI. The guy was a magician with a computer. Sam badly needed Tommy to pull a rabbit out of his top hat right now. Although they were good friends, Sam couldn't just pick up the phone and call Tommy out of the blue. No direct text messages or e-mails, either, if at all possible. Tommy operated completely off the grid inside his own dark world of conspiracies—a world where no government agency could ever be trusted. Sam knew Tommy had stopped trusting anyone as a teenager when his father, a longtime government employee, had died under suspicious circumstances. That had been the main catalyst for his future hacker crusade.

Big Brother was *always* watching. If Sam wanted to communicate with Tommy, even about insignificant matters, he was required to log in to the most secure of websites and pass through a maze of security clearances. The long list of passwords and ID confirmations that Sam had to use to reach Tommy felt ridiculous and seemed to multiply with each passing month. Sam knew the global hacking movement had brought on a new kind of crazy to an already paranoid world. Tommy constantly beat the same drum with him. No phone calls were ever safe. No e-mails were ever safe. No text messages were ever safe. No social media was ever safe.

No one was ever safe, according to Tommy.

As if Sam needed more things to be paranoid about.

He found a metro station a few blocks from El Ángel. It was busy in the main lobby. With twenty million people in the city, *a lot* of citizens traveled by train day and night. Almost everyone was glued to smartphones and tablets, just like the rest of the world. Zombies bumping around with their faces aglow. Sam searched for a new target. He needed a way to connect with Tommy. Within minutes, he found an older man with gray hair, a thick mustache, and a large belly sitting on a metal bench against the wall of the lobby. The man wore tan slacks and a short-sleeve white button-down. He looked like a college professor. A worn brown leather briefcase sat on the bench right beside him. More important, the old man held a computer tablet in his hands, resting on top of his robust belly, and he was intent on reading something—when he wasn't dozing off. Sam noted that the man was having a hard time keeping his tired eyes open. His head kept bobbing up and down every thirty seconds, before he'd attempt to reengage with the reading.

Sam casually sat beside the man on the bench, pretending to fiddle with the burner phone he held in his hands, as if he were texting back and forth with someone. He noticed the old man give him a quick once-over and then return to his reading—and his slumber. When his eyes fluttered shut again, his square head bobbed, and the tablet rested loosely on his broad chest, Sam took a swift glance around for wandering eyes. When he felt safe, he reached over and carefully plucked the computer tablet right out of the man's thick fingers. He watched the old man's eyes closely. No stirring. No recognition. For Sam, this exercise had always been like a game of Operation—work smoothly and quickly, and if you don't touch the sides, you won't get buzzed. Sam had steady hands. He'd been buzzed only once, when he was fifteen, and was fortunate to run *very* fast.

Sam eased off the bench, slipped into the crowd.

He found a door down an isolated hallway with a sign that displayed a male stick figure and the words *El Baño*. The door was locked. He waited impatiently for two minutes before a young guy in a soccer jersey finally exited. Sam stepped into the restroom, locked the door behind him. It was a one-toilet, one-sink room, and it smelled like vomit. He put the toilet-seat lid down and sat with no intention of going to the bathroom, then opened up the old man's tablet. He'd noticed each time the professor had woken from his brief nap, he had to reenter his security password, so Sam had taken a mental snapshot.

He typed in the numbers, gained access, and then found the icon for the Internet. As he'd expected, the metro station had Wi-Fi. From memory, Sam logged in to an obscure website called Leia's Lounge, where he always went to find Tommy. He then typed in a half dozen passwords, answered a few more identity questions, including providing a quick voice sample when prompted. Once inside, he pinged a user named Maverick for a secure video chat.

Come on, Tommy, be available. Now is not the time to be at the movies.

Seconds later, a video-chat box suddenly appeared on the tablet's screen—and there sat Tommy Kucher, sitting inside his dark and private computer lair, as usual wearing a plain white T-shirt and blue jeans, and looking as skinny as ever. The guy needed a protein shake. Sam had never been to Tommy's place. He wasn't sure *anyone* had—Tommy wasn't much for a social life. Through pieced-together conversations over the years, Sam knew it was on the second floor of a crumbling building in a seedy DC neighborhood and sat right above an arcade and a liquor store. Sam noted that since they'd last spoken, maybe a month ago, Tommy had shaved the sides of his head and now had a new purple streak running through the middle of the dark mop of hair he still had on top. Tommy had also added a new silver hoop ring through his right eyebrow. There were rings and tattoos everywhere. Sam could hear heavy-metal music pumping in the background. Tommy used to play in a metal band he called Tommy Cool.

"Dude, what's with the shaved head?" Tommy said.

Sam leaned in close to the tablet screen, spoke quietly but in a tone that let Tommy know this was serious. "I'm in real trouble, Tommy. I need help, like right now."

"Again?" Tommy asked, perking up.

"Yes. I don't have time to explain it all."

Tommy squinted, like he was looking beyond Sam. "Where are you, Duke?"

Duke was the nickname Tommy had given him long ago, named after the late Hollywood actor John Wayne, since Tommy loved classic Westerns. Usually the only time Sam saw Tommy out in the city was because an old movie house was showing one of his favorite flicks on the big screen. Sam got the invite every time and had joined Tommy on several occasions.

"Long story. I'm in a bathroom stall at a metro station in Mexico City."

"No way!"

"Like I said, long story. But I'm stuck here and need a new set of IDs to get out of the country. Do you have any contacts in Mexico City?"

"Hold on," Tommy said, began pecking away on his computer.

Even though it seemed out of reach, Sam knew better than to presume Tommy couldn't make something happen in this city. He would never underestimate him again. The guy was connected to a global underground network. Sam heard a knock on the restroom door. He cursed, ignored it. Could they hear his conversation outside? It didn't matter. He had to keep pressing forward. He did not have the luxury of taking extra precautions here. The clock was literally ticking.

"Okay, I got someone," Tommy announced. "I'll put it together and message you the details right now. Check your account."

"Thanks. As always, you're a lifesaver."

"What's going on? Why're you in Mexico?"

"Just bad luck, I think. Can you find out everything you can about a man named Rich Hebbard? He's a lawyer out of New Orleans."

"Sure, man. Shouldn't be too hard."

"I need *everything* you can find on this guy, both personally and professionally, as well as his clients."

"Anything else?"

"Yeah, this is a long shot, but see what you can also find on the name *Zapata* in connection with Hebbard."

"Zapata? That a first name or last?"

"I don't know. That's all I've got. But there's some kind of connection between this Zapata, Rich Hebbard, and a man named Tom Hawkins, who was Hebbard's law partner. Hawkins was the guy I came down here to meet today."

"*Was?*"

"He's dead now." Sam didn't explain further. Instead, he held up the burner phone so Tommy could see it inside the video-chat box. "One final thing. There's a video on here that I need to get off. Pretty sure it's a burner phone. Can you do that?"

Tommy smirked. "Give me the phone number."

Sam told him the number he'd found in the phone's settings. He waited. Tommy was pecking away and staring at another computer screen. He had the video downloaded within sixty seconds, as Sam could hear Natalie scream out his name on Tommy's end. Tommy turned back to Sam with wide eyes.

"Dude! What the hell?"

"I told you this was serious. Can you see if there is any way to track that video's location or maybe to analyze any of the markings you see around Natalie?"

"Did she go down there with you?"

"No. She could be anywhere."

"All right, I'll see what I can find. Who did this?"

"I don't know yet. But I need all of this ASAP," Sam reiterated. "I don't have a single second to spare. Her life depends on it. I gotta run now."

"I'm on it, man. Peace out."

Sam logged off the website. More impatient knocking on the door.

"Hold up!" Sam yelled.

He stood, turned around, dropped the burner phone into the toilet water, and then flushed it. He watched as the phone disappeared with the flow of dirty water, launched into the bowels of the sewer system of Mexico City. There was no way he'd allow them to use the phone to continue to track him. If he was doing this, he was going his own way.

He didn't care for any more surprises or cryptic text messages.

And he didn't want a shadow.

NINETEEN

Agent Lloyd had just walked through the front door of his tiny condo, eager to soak his throbbing shoulder in a hot shower for an hour and collapse into bed, when his cell phone rang. He pulled it out of his jacket and saw that it was the office. Never failed. He had a job where he was on the clock 24-7. Before answering it, he took a quick peek around the small living room. An old war movie was on the TV, but his pop was nowhere to be found. He thought he could hear snoring from a bedroom down the hallway. At least the old man had found his way back to his bed tonight. Lloyd usually discovered him asleep in the recliner with a can of beer spilled in his lap. Lloyd punched a button, stuck his phone to his ear.

"This better be good, Mike."

"Sorry, Chief. But I think you need to get back here."

"Seriously?"

"Krieger has something. He says he's been playing a serious battle of chess online—at least that's what Krieger called it. I've never understood the hacker thing. He's been going at it for a few hours, and he claims he finally has something significant for us on the Gray Wolf."

"No kidding. All right, give me fifteen minutes."

Lloyd hung up, stepped into the living room. He turned off the TV. In the silence, he could definitely now hear his pop snoring up a storm from his bedroom. He began to clean up the room. A worn plaid couch was against the wall, his father's beat-up brown recliner next to it, facing the small television. An open bag of Fritos sat on the cheap table beside the recliner. Lloyd walked over, grabbed the bag, and rolled it closed. He collected a stash of empty candy-bar wrappers that were stuffed into the cushions of the recliner. Mr. Goodbars were the old man's favorites. At first Lloyd had tried to ration them out—otherwise, his pop could eat an entire carton of candy bars in one day. But Lloyd gave up on that a while back. The old man didn't have much, so Lloyd decided the least he could do was let him have his candy.

Lloyd picked up his dad's dirty socks from the carpet, along with a few other clothing items, tossed them into a laundry basket in the corner of the kitchen. The kitchen was an equal wreck. Dirty dishes covered the sink and counters. An opened jug of milk sat on the kitchen table. His father would simply forget to put it back in the fridge. It smelled something awful. Lloyd poured it out in the sink. He grabbed a two-day-old pitcher of coffee, filled a mug, and then stuck it in the microwave. It would have to do for now. As he waited for it to warm, he surveyed his surroundings.

Home sweet home.

There was a time in life when Lloyd had actually lived decently. But it had been years. He'd married straight out of the police academy. Clara was a beautiful, sophisticated Harvard student from a high-society New England family. They were an odd pairing from the beginning. He was never certain of her draw to him. Members of his gritty middle-class family were more likely to change the oil in her family's fleet of BMWs or mow their estate's lawn. But when an attractive girl with class found you appealing, you didn't ask questions; you just enjoyed the ride. It was a disaster from nearly the beginning. They fought for a while to make it work. She was headed to law school. He was a third-generation cop. They were determined to be happy.

Their first place together was a tiny one-bedroom duplex four blocks from campus. It was small, but Clara turned it into an absolute work of art. They could have published pictures in a magazine. Life was good. But her parents never let up. They were constantly in her ear, telling her she could have done much better than Spencer Lloyd. That it was still not too late. There were no kids yet. Two years into the marriage, Lloyd got clipped in the stomach by a bad guy's stray bullet. Put him out a few months. Normal cop stuff. His family was used to it. It was their chosen way of life. Clara freaked. Her mom used it to manipulate. Finally, Clara broke. She said she couldn't handle it anymore. She couldn't be married to a cop. Lloyd knew she wasn't asking him to change careers—there was no chance of that. She was asking for a husband change. It got ugly. He loved her but hated her parents. He thought many times about taking a swing at her father, but he knew it could be a career killer. He finally relented.

She remarried within a year. An investment banker. She got everything her family wanted. Three kids. Two pretty dogs. A shiny sedan. Big house. Nice yard.

Lloyd sighed, looked around him.

No wife. No kids. No dogs. No yard.

Just dad. And the FBI.

He grabbed his coffee, took a sip, nearly spit it out.

He moved to the hallway, cracked the door to the first bedroom. His pop lay on top of the covers, snoring loudly, shaking the walls. Lloyd was used to it by now. It had given him nightmares as a kid. His mom could sleep through anything. She was an amazingly tolerant woman. A saint. He knelt next to the bed. His pop was still wrapped in the brown robe he wore every single day of his life. Lloyd grinned, shook his head, and grabbed the open container of Oreo cookies from his father's chest, set them on the nightstand. There were still black crumbs on his dad's dry and cracked lips.

Lloyd kissed the man on the forehead, whispered, "Sleep well, Pop."

His dad grunted, muttered, but stayed asleep.

The snoring grew even louder.

Lloyd headed for the door.

They met back at headquarters.

They were in the conference room. Agent Krieger was also in the room. He was in his late twenties, with blond hair and black square glasses, and he was a whiz with computers. The kid graduated near the top of his class from MIT and could have probably made millions already at a software start-up. Krieger was beyond brilliant. Lloyd respected that he'd chosen law enforcement instead of the corporate route. They definitely needed more agents like Krieger in this new age of cyberterrorism.

"How's the shoulder?" Epps asked.

"Fine," Lloyd grunted.

"Liar," Epps replied, shaking his head.

"Let's get started."

Epps turned to the young agent who was sitting behind a laptop at the conference table. "Show him what you showed me, Krieger."

"Yes, sir."

Krieger began pecking away, and screens popped up on the digital wall in front of them. Lloyd stepped around the table and moved closer to them. The digital screens showed several still images that had been

taken from Krieger's computer screen in the past few hours, document-
ing part of his online search.

"What am I looking at?" Lloyd asked Krieger.

"I basically followed the trail from this afternoon when we got the
first flag on the alias Gildas Vaughn—the one that quickly disappeared
on us, mind you. As I told Agent Epps, it's been a chess match for me
the past few hours. Whoever is behind this has been working overtime
to cover their tracks. To this point, I've been able to at least keep them
in sight. Until thirty minutes ago."

"What happened thirty minutes ago?" Lloyd asked.

"They pulled the rip cord and ejected."

Lloyd turned in frustration. "What the hell does that mean in
English, Krieger?"

"Sir, it means they shut it down so they couldn't be discovered."

"So we still don't know who *they* are?"

"No, sir. Not yet. But we think we know more about why Alger
Gerlach is here. Or, more important, *who* he is here for. We were able
to grab something in a file before they went dark."

"Pull it up," instructed Epps.

A photo appeared on the middle screen of a young man with wavy
brown hair wearing blue jeans and a Georgetown Law T-shirt.

"Who is he?" Lloyd asked.

Epps stepped in. "His name is Sam Callahan. Until recently, he was
a law student at Georgetown. He just graduated last month and joined
a law firm called Benoltz and Associates."

Lloyd studied the face on the screen. "Wait . . . isn't that the same
guy who was involved in the Redrock deal last year?"

"Yes, sir," Epps confirmed. "The same guy."

Lloyd turned to Epps, frowned. "You're trying to tell me that someone brought in the Gray Wolf, a million-dollar-a-job assassin, to take
out this rookie lawyer?"

"I'm not telling you *anything*," Epps countered, holding up a defensive hand. "All we know is that Krieger here found this directly attached to Alger Gerlach, in the same online thread where someone hacked security and allowed Gerlach safe passage into DC."

Lloyd studied the screens. It seemed far-fetched. "We know where to find Callahan?"

"I have his address. Just waiting on you."

"Well, hell, go get him. Let's talk to him."

TWENTY

Billarama Santa María was a dimly lit pool hall on the first floor of a two-story building in between a liquor store and a drugstore. Tommy's instructions were to meet someone he simply called Diablo. Sam didn't need to be bilingual to recognize the name meant *devil* in Spanish. As he entered the place, he could only imagine what kind of guy he would find owning that nickname in a smoky pool joint currently filled with dozens of tattooed and testosterone-laden men. A real badass, he figured. The place was busy. Men of all ages were crashing pool balls around with lots of drinking and yelling. Sam stepped carefully through the crowd, getting lots of glances. He obviously stood out. For one, he hadn't spotted another white face yet. Two, he had no apparent tattoos and wore nothing in black leather.

Sam found the bar off to the side. A bartender with beefy forearms and a thick black mustache made his way over to him.

"*¿Qué deseas?*" he said.

"Looking for Diablo," Sam said in his deepest voice, feeling weird about it.

The bartender nodded toward the pool table in the back corner. Sam thanked him and followed the dirty floor to the corner, where five of the biggest men he'd ever seen surrounded the pool table. The group looked like they could be the starting offensive line for the Broncos, all wearing matching black leather vests, dark goatees, and beards, and most of the men had tattoos crawling up and down both of their massive arms. One of the men's ink was nothing but huge flames—Sam's first guess at Diablo. He fit the mold. He was the biggest of the bunch and looked like he could lift a truck over his head. Sam sure as hell hoped Tommy knew what he was doing, sending him into this joint. He felt like a herring swimming into a shark den.

Sam waited for the man to finish a pool shot and then hesitantly stepped up.

The man looked at him, growled with his eyes.

"Diablo?" Sam asked. "Tommy sent me."

The man gave him a quick grin, which Sam found odd. The man then turned, gave a head nod toward someone sitting on a bar stool directly behind the pool table. A five-foot-nothing bleached-blonde girl in her early twenties. She wore tall-heeled boots that went all the way up above her knees, a short black leather miniskirt, and a formfitting pink T-shirt with a picture of a teddy bear on it. Was this guy messing with him? He stepped around the linemen and approached the young blonde.

She eyeballed him. "Sam?"

He nodded. "You're . . . Diablo?"

"Sí," she replied, as if it was no big deal.

She got off the stool, found her oversize black leather bag on the floor beside her. She knelt, reached inside, and pulled out a small pink Victoria's Secret shopping bag. She held it out for him. He took the bag from her and gave a quick peek inside. He spotted a new cell phone, a passport, and a bundle of new IDs, along with a thick roll of pesos. It was all there. He looked back up at the blonde, still finding this exchange bizarre.

"Gracias," he said.

"De nada. Buena suerte."

TWENTY-ONE

Twenty-two hours, thirty-eight minutes.

Sam kept his eyes on the clock, feeling the weight with each passing minute. He didn't understand the rules of this sinister new game. Twenty-four hours? Why had they given him a deadline to find this guy? Did they not think he would do exactly what they said, anyway, with Natalie in their possession? And did they also know that Rich Hebbard claimed to be his real father? Was that their true reason for pulling Sam into this mess? The meeting with the black-haired lady brought few answers and only initiated more frustrating questions.

Sam immediately took a taxi straight to the airport. He knew his first order of business was to get out of Mexico City. While riding in the back of the car, a text message from a random number appeared on his brand-new smartphone. Can you meet for pizza?

Sam immediately knew it was from Tommy, asking to video chat. *Can you meet for pizza?* was the string of code words that Tommy always used when wanting to get in touch with him, even just to invite Sam to the movies. The kid was cloak-and-dagger about *everything*. Sam logged in to Leia's Lounge on the cell phone and pinged his friend. Sam held the phone close to his face, although the driver seemed to be lost in his Spanish pop music, anyway.

Moments later Tommy was on his screen.

"I guess this means you got everything?" Tommy asked.

"Yes. Thanks."

"Don't use Sam Callahan for *anything* anymore. The federal police now have you tagged in their system, and they're on the hunt. An all-points bulletin has also gone out to local police. Everyone is looking for you right now, dude. You're officially a wanted man in Mexico."

Sam shook his head. "Okay, thanks. Please tell me you found something with Natalie's video."

Tommy sighed, shook his head. "Nothing, man. There is no way I can track it. The threads have been wiped clean. Whoever did this to Natalie knows what they're doing. And no matter how much I enhance the still images in the video, I can find *nothing* to distinguish her whereabouts."

"Damn."

"I know, dude. I'm sorry."

"You find anything on Hebbard?"

"Born in Shreveport. Second of three kids. Undergrad degree at Tulane. University of Mississippi School of Law. Worked as an associate for five years in Dallas for a big corporate firm. Then moved to Denver and spent two years at a different corporate firm. From there, moved to New Orleans and joined his third law firm, where he made partner. Spent over twenty years with that firm before starting his own firm three years ago with Tom Hawkins. I sent it all to your account."

Sam perked up. "When was he in Denver?"

"It was 1991 and '92."

Sam cursed. Twenty-six years ago.

"What?" Tommy asked, clueless.

"Nothing. He have a wife? Any kids?"

"He was married for ten years and then got divorced. Two kids. The boy is in law school in North Carolina. The girl is a nurse in Tallahassee."

Two kids? Or three kids? Sam couldn't believe where his mind was racing.

"What can you tell me about his clients?" Sam asked.

"Not much just yet. Looks like a standard client list. Mostly oil clients from Louisiana and Texas. Although I think I found a connection to Zapata."

"Who is he?"

"One of Hebbard's clients is Arnstead Petroleum out of New Orleans. I found a link between Arnstead's founder, a man named Lex Hester, at a banquet at a five-star resort in Cozumel with a man named Francisco Zapata. Zapata is a member of the Chamber of Deputies, Mexico's congress, elected from the city of Lázaro Cárdenas."

"A congressman?"

"Yes, correct."

"What else do you know about him?"

"Zapata's brother was the governor of the state of Michoacán when he got murdered two years ago. The police blamed the drug cartels. But Zapata publicly blamed another political party. Zapata had a brief military career where he was a member of Cuerpo de Fuerzas Especiales, which is Mexico's Special Forces. According to his political bio, twenty years ago, a group of thirty guerilla rebels known as EZLN took over a small town in Chiapas. Zapata led a Special Forces team to recapture the town, where they killed all thirty rebels and disposed of their bodies on a riverbank with their noses and ears sliced off."

"Lovely. Anything else?"

"There are rumors of corruption all over the place, as is the case with many of Mexico's politicians. Mostly involving drug cartels. Nothing that I can tell that's directly connected with the names you mentioned just yet."

"Keep digging, Tommy. And see what else you can find on Lex Hester."

"All right."

As the cab approached the airport, Sam watched the streets of Mexico City. Suddenly, the thought of a corrupt Mexican congressman sending a crew to kill him didn't sound so preposterous. Zapata certainly had the right military background and connections. But what kind of conspiracy did Rich Hebbard and Tom Hawkins know about that got Hawkins killed and forced Hebbard to go on the run? It appeared to Sam that Zapata wanted Hebbard dead. Was Natalie's abductor somehow connected to Zapata? If so, how?

"What's the last location you have for Hebbard?" Sam asked Tommy.

"He last used his personal cell phone a little over four hours ago at a hotel in New Orleans. He used his credit card three hours ago at Rubenstein's, a men's clothing store off Saint Charles Avenue. Nothing since then. All signs point to New Orleans."

TWENTY-TWO

His new alias identified him as Will Kane. Sam knew immediately where Tommy found the name. *High Noon.* The classic Western starring Gary Cooper. The movie was in Tommy's top-five favorites, although this list seemed to be ever-rotating. Tommy talked about "the list" all the time—which old movie had recently slid into the top five, which had recently been pushed out. Sam couldn't keep up with it all. He guessed *High Noon* was currently on the list. Under the new alias, Sam now had a new driver's license, a credit card likely attached to one of Tommy's hidden offshore numbered accounts, and a passport. It was his current DC driver's license photo on the fake license and passport. The passport was stamped with his trip into Mexico City that morning. Tommy knew these details all mattered.

Sam was now Will Kane.

The taxi dropped him on the curb outside Mexico City International Airport. Sam quickly ducked inside the building. He was not surprised to find the airport busy. Most of the traffic seemed to be coming from those arriving in the robust city. Sam was determined to get the hell out, as soon as possible. He found a digital board listing departures. There was a midnight option for Air Canada. If he could get a seat, it would put him in New Orleans at nine the next morning. That meant he would have just under twelve hours to find Rich Hebbard and some-how exchange him for Natalie. He quickly crossed through the airport concourse, looking for Air Canada, his eyes guarded and yet still taking in everyone around him—especially airport security, which had men stationed at every turn.

He found the counter for Air Canada. He had to wait only a few minutes for two people in front of him to move through. He stepped up to the counter and asked the female attendant if there was any room left on the midnight flight. She typed into her computer, said they still had seats available. Sam handed over his IDs and credit card and said a prayer. The attendant handed them back a few seconds later, along with a newly printed boarding pass. He was good to go. Sam exhaled. Tommy had again been his lifeline.

He stepped away from the counter, found an airport shop up the walk where he purchased small headphones, a bottle of water, and two prepackaged sandwiches. He was famished. He hadn't eaten since break-fast back in DC earlier that day, and he'd been running nonstop since midafternoon. If he was going to get through this, he knew he needed to keep his body fueled and hydrated for the next twenty-two hours. He quickly downed the sandwiches and then got into a long line for security to get to his terminal. He planned to find an isolated corner, far away from anyone, hide out for several hours, board the plane at the last minute, and then get some much-needed sleep in flight—if that was possible.

The security line plodded forward, each passenger showing his or her ID and boarding pass to the security guard behind the kiosk, taking bags through the conveyor belt, and finally getting the once-over from more security.

Sam was only ten people back from the security checkpoint when he noticed two men in uniform with security ID badges join the man behind the kiosk. One of the men held a piece of paper in his hands and set it before the guard. All three men studied it for a second, had a quick conversation, and then they looked up and began to scan the crowded line. Sam slipped in behind the tall traveler in front of him. He felt a sudden surge of uneasiness. Taking several slow, deep breaths, he tried to convince himself it was just nerves. He leaned around the tall guy, noticed the two security guards had taken a step back but were still monitoring the security line. The kiosk guard started to pass people through again.

Sam felt sweat on his neck. He inched forward. He was five people away now. One of the guards behind the kiosk guy placed steady eyes on him. He didn't move them away for a few seconds. Sam thought of Natalie. Twenty-two hours. He swallowed his growing fear and kept taking slow steps forward. He had to get to New Orleans.

Three people away.

March 7
Four months ago

A nurse frantically woke him up in the middle of the night.

There was an emergency with his mother. They needed to hurry. He was fuzzyheaded as he struggled from bed. *An emergency?* The nurse couldn't explain, said the doctor just ordered her to come and get him ASAP. He immediately felt fear grip him. An emergency on the heels of a bone-marrow transplant sounded ominous. Especially for a woman who was already in a desperate situation. He checked the clock on the wall: 2:15 a.m. Natalie had gone home around midnight. He wished more than anything he'd agreed to let her stay the night, like she'd wanted, rather than demanding that she go home and get some rest.

He was afraid. Natalie always made him feel stronger.

They took an elevator up the two flights to his mother's floor. A doctor met them in the hallway right outside his mom's door. There were several other medical personnel inside her room, but no one was scrambling about or acting like there was an emergency. He tried to peek into the private room through the window but was blocked by a medical cart. This was a different doctor from the one earlier in the day. His face was already dour.

"Sam, I'm Dr. Edgars," he began, a somber tone.

"What's going on with my mom?" Sam interrupted.

Dr. Edgars noticeably swallowed. "Your mom went into unanticipated cardiac arrest twenty minutes ago. We worked tirelessly to revive her, but her body was already incredibly fragile and weak. I'm sorry, Sam."

Sam felt sideswiped. "Wait . . . what are you saying, Doc? She had a heart attack?"

"Yes. There was nothing we could do."

"I don't understand. She's dead? My mom is dead?"

He nodded. "Yes, that's what I'm saying. I'm very sorry."

Sam felt the air knocked out of him, a numb panic traveling the length of his body, head to toe, like a powerful wave trying to carry him out to sea. "I don't get it. Did the bone-marrow transplant do this? Did my marrow do this to her?"

"*Nothing* did this, Sam," the doctor tried to reassure him. "Certainly not you. From all accounts, the transplant went really well today. Everyone was pleased. But her body was so weak, it just wasn't ready and able to handle an unexpected heart failure. We can monitor and be ready to respond, which we were, but sometimes the body just does what it wants to do, in spite of all of our advanced medicine and procedures. I'm afraid her heart just gave out and did not want to come back, no matter what we did. No matter how long we tried."

Sam couldn't believe it. The numbing wave was dragging him farther out. He could barely breathe. "Can I go see her, Doc?" he managed to ask.

"Of course."

Dr. Edgars opened the door, asked his team to clear the room for a moment. Sam was alone with his mom. The machines that were vibrant around her before were no longer beeping. It was quiet and surreal. His mother's eyes were closed. It looked like she was simply sleeping and *not* dead. He watched her chest for a moment. It never moved. He felt himself being completely dragged underwater, his chest feeling so tight, he thought he also might have a heart attack. He leaned over her bed. She looked peaceful, a small smile on her face, her hands placed at her sides. He noticed that in her left hand, the one closest to him that had the *Samuel* tattoo on her wrist, she was clutching her cross necklace in her frail fingers. The tears came fast and furious. He held nothing back.

His knees buckled; his face fell in her lap.

"I'm so sorry, Mom. I'm so sorry."

TWENTY-THREE

Sam's new phone vibrated in his pocket. Will Kane's phone. It startled him. He pulled it out, stared at the screen, felt panic swell in his chest. Tommy. A direct message, which was highly unusual coming from him.

Get out of the airport! Security has flagged Will Kane!

Sam peeked up, noticed the guard staring at him again with narrow eyes. Then the guard took a step forward, leaned over to the kiosk guy. Sam calmly stuck the phone back in his pocket, turned, and started to make his way back through the line. His heart was hammering away. He was halfway through the zigzag of ropes when he took another look over his shoulder. He noticed the same guard who had locked eyes on him now pushing his way aggressively through the security line. Sam cursed. He knew he couldn't just sprint through the airport—he'd stand out, be a sitting duck, likely be immediately tackled by a throng of security guards. He had to be careful and measured. He moved briskly, like a traveler simply late for a flight.

How the hell did security flag Will Kane? It was certainly possible someone could have matched his face with a picture of the real Sam

Callahan. However, the alias was brand-new, created only an hour ago by Tommy, and there was no way that Tommy or the blonde girl in the pool hall would've turned the information over to the federal police.

What the hell had just happened?

Sam rushed back to the main concourse, quickly ducked inside a tourist store with T-shirts, caps, coffee mugs, knickknacks. He watched from behind a rack of books. Seconds later, the same guard from the security line raced right past the store. Sam stepped around the rack, peered out. The man stopped fifty feet down the corridor, spun around, searching in all directions. Then he lifted a black walkie-talkie to his mouth and started barking instructions.

Sam cursed again. He knew he had to get out, right away, before an army descended upon the concourse. There was no time to spare. He frantically searched the store. He snagged a gray T-shirt with the Mexican flag printed brightly on the front. Then a pair of dark sunglasses. Finally, he grabbed something that, under any other circumstances, would definitely draw attention to himself. But he thought it might somehow deflect attention in this desperate moment. A big straw sombrero with red fringe. He quickly paid for the items in cash and stepped away from the counter. He pulled the T-shirt on over his current shirt, covered his eyes with the sunglasses, then put the sombrero on his bald head.

He looked like a cheesy American tourist.

At least that was the hope. He didn't want to be taken too seriously.

He took another deep breath, returned to the main corridor. He was two hundred feet from the nearest glass-door exit. He moved calmly down the corridor, his feet itching to run for it, his mind convincing them otherwise. A security guard suddenly ran right past him. Sam tried not to flinch, just got in a line of traffic moving toward the exit. A hundred feet. He saw three more security guards off to his left, hustling past him like they were on a mission. Activity was definitely picking up. He had to remind himself to keep breathing normally with each step.

At fifty feet, he turned toward the exit, noticed two beefy security guards stationed right in front of the glass doors. They were monitoring each person who passed by them on their way out to the sidewalk. They each held a piece of paper in their hands, which they continued to eyeball—clearly a photo of Will Kane. Sam knew he couldn't stop. There was no turning back. Every second he delayed from there would only invite more insurmountable odds. He had no choice but to move forward. Play the tourist card and chance it. He willed his body to behave normally. He knew his overall gait and demeanor would say everything.

Instead of trying to veer to the edge of traffic, as far away from the guards as possible, he decided to walk straight toward them. When he was within five feet, both guards put momentary eyes directly on him, his Mexico T-shirt, his dark sunglasses, his goofy hat. Sam never slowed. Instead, he smiled wide, as if half-drunk.

"Buenas noches, amigos!" he said straight to them.

The guards both acknowledged him but said nothing in return, their eyes instantly moving beyond the obnoxious tourist to the next set of travelers. Sam felt the humid night air hit his face a second later. He was on the sidewalk. He kept the sombrero in place as he moved more quickly now all the way up the sidewalk to a line of waiting taxis. He jumped into the back of the first available, instructed the driver to simply drive away. He really didn't know where he was going, only that he needed to get as far away from the airport as possible.

When the taxi cleared the airport property, Sam exhaled and removed the big sombrero, the sunglasses, and the T-shirt. He could feel sweat soaking his back. He wiped some of the beaded moisture from his face, took several more deep breaths, tried to regain his bearings. The driver spoke good English, so Sam asked him to take him to the nearest shopping center. Sam pulled out his new cell phone, hesitated. He wasn't sure whether he should still use it. Could they be tracking it just like his new ID? He pondered it for only a few seconds before deciding he had no choice. He needed to talk to Tommy and figure out what had just happened. He plugged the small headphones into the phone jack, quickly logged back in to Leia's Lounge, and summoned him. Tommy's face was on the screen a second later, as if he had been waiting for Sam to make contact again.

"What happened?" Sam asked, clearly frustrated.

"I don't know, man. Someone hacked into the airport's security system and directly flagged the new alias I just created for you."

"Who?"

"No clue. I'm searching. Did anyone else possibly see your new setup?"

"No one other than you and your contact."

Tommy shook his head. "Something else is going on here, man; it doesn't make sense. I covered all my tracks. There's no way someone cracked my code that fast, unless they were waiting on it. Unless they were waiting on me."

"You think someone is watching you?"

"Maybe. But you've got to ditch the new setup. Will Kane is already dead, as much as I hate to say it. I've got to get you something new."

"What about this phone?"

"Keep the phone. I can scramble it."

"Are you sure? How do we know it can't be tracked?"

"It'll work, trust me. Just give me some time."

Sam sighed. "I don't have time, Tommy. I've got to get to New Orleans by morning."

"I hear ya. I swear I'm working as fast as I can. It'll be much easier when you're back inside the States for me to get you new paperwork. Can you get to the border?"

Sam thought about it. There were *a lot* of hurdles. "What do you suggest I do if I get there, Tommy? Without proper papers, they're not going to just let me drive back through their security checkpoints into the States. They'll arrest me on the spot."

"Yeah, we have to find another way."

"Now is when I need you to be truly brilliant."

"Brilliance is forthcoming. Just get to the border."

TWENTY-FOUR

Sam had one new objective: steal the fastest car he could find in the next ten minutes. The quickest way for him to get to the border was by driving. Flying out of Mexico City was no longer an option. He didn't have the money to hire a driver, nor did he want someone else knowing he was trying to get there—that would only draw suspicion. He also couldn't rely on a dumpy bus that crawled along on crummy Mexican roads, even if that was a late-night option. So he was back to stealing cars—his first career and what landed him in juvie. He hoped this go-round would not land him in jail. Under normal driving conditions, the GPS map on his phone said it would take him eight hours. Sam planned to do it in much less than that. With Natalie bound to that chair in that dark room, and the clock continuing to click down, he had no choice but to chance an all-out high-speed pursuit.

The cab driver dropped him in a parking lot outside a commercial retail strip. He had a selection of about fifty cars. He needed something fast but not eye-catching. It would be foolish to steal a shiny red Corvette or a turbo-charged Porsche, even if they were options. He had to be more discreet than that. Something sneaky fast that didn't stand out. A car where he could stop and pump gas and no one would pay him much attention—yet a vehicle where he could still zip down the road at well over a hundred miles per hour. He walked through the rows of cars, searching. Hondas, Toyotas, Fords, Chevys. He didn't want a brand-new car, either. Technology had changed so much in the ten years since his glory days as a car thief. He needed a sure thing. He didn't want to waste any time on a new vehicle where his old tricks might not even work or some fancy new alarm system would blare at full volume.

He spotted it a few seconds later: a black '99 Saab 9-3 Viggen. Sam had stolen one of these before back in Denver. He'd been surprised at the velocity beneath the hood of the rather simple-looking five-door hatchback. He circled it, checked the tires, making sure they were all in good shape. He had one chance to get this done. He couldn't be having a flat tire at 120 miles per hour. Everything looked to be in working order. The vehicle was well worn but in good condition.

When stealing cars, a thief had several options to gain entry. One: check for unlocked doors. Two: search for a spare key. Three: pick the door lock. Four: break the window. If a thief was smart, he went about them in that order. Some car owners were either lazy with locking all their doors, or they felt they could hide a key where no one else but them could find it. Sam had stolen more than a dozen cars without ever having to pick a lock or hot-wire an engine.

Sam surveyed the parking lot. There was a young couple walking back to their car three rows over from him. Another man in a suit who was walking toward the commercial strip two rows in the opposite direction. There was no activity in Sam's current row of cars. He bumped the Saab forcefully with his hip to make sure it had not been armed with a new car alarm. Nothing happened. No beeping. No chirping. He bumped it again, just to be sure. Again, no alarm. Sam put his hand on the driver's door handle. Locked. He tried the rear door. Locked. He did the same thing on the other side, as well as the hatchback. All locked.

Sam began searching for a spare key. He reached under each of the wheel vents and felt around for a small magnetic box used for just this sort of thing. He found nothing. He then moved to the license plate in the back. No magnetic holder slipped under the plate. Finally, he dropped to the ground, used the flashlight on his new phone to search the full length of the undercarriage. Bingo. He found the small black case near the back bumper. He'd just saved himself valuable time and energy. He would not have to pick the lock, break a window, or pull apart wires under the dashboard. He could drop straight in and start her up. He took one last glance at the parking lot, felt like he was in the clear, and then stuck the key in the door. It unlocked without issue. He quickly sat in the driver's seat, shut the door behind him, and inserted the key in the ignition slot. The Saab started right up—a gentle rumble that Sam knew could get him down the road in a hurry.

He backed out, put the Saab in drive, and slipped out of the parking lot. One big hurdle down. He set his phone in the cup holder with the map showing on the screen. He had no idea what it would be like to drive more than five hundred miles through Mexico in the middle of the night.

He was about to find out.

He aggressively pressed the gas pedal down and drove north.

TWENTY-FIVE

Natalie heard a door open and shut in front of her.

Then the sound of shoes on the dirty floor. She was still in darkness, the black hood covering her head. The shoes approached. Sounded like only one pair of shoes. They stopped right in front of her. She couldn't say anything with duct tape covering her mouth. Seconds later, the black hood was pulled off. She squinted in the sudden brightness of the warehouse room. The young bushy-haired guy from the parking garage was standing in front of her—the one she'd mistaken for a political intern. He was still dressed in the same tan slacks and white button-down shirt. Same coffee stain on the front. His nose was swollen from her head-butt in the DC parking garage. He held a paper plate in one hand with what looked like a sandwich on top of it, a plastic water bottle in the other hand.

He knelt in front of her, eye to eye. "I have food and water for you. I'm going to take the tape off your mouth and hands. If you try anything, they'll be no more offerings of this sort. And the hood will go back on for the duration of your stay with us. Do you understand?"

She quickly nodded.

He seemed satisfied. He reached up and tugged the thick tape off her mouth. Then he unwrapped the tape that locked her arms down to the wooden chair. He kept the tape in place that bundled her wrists together. Natalie licked her dry lips and rolled her shoulders around with the new freedom. The bushy-haired guy then put the plate in her lap.

"Hope you like turkey and cheese," he said.

She wasn't hungry, but she wanted to somehow engage this guy. To probe. See if she could find an opening anywhere and gather any new information.

"I do, thank you."

She took the turkey sandwich in her hands, lifted it to her mouth, and took a small bite. The guy was just hovering and watching a few feet away.

"Can I have the water?" she asked him.

He unscrewed the cap, handed it to her. She took a big swig. She was really thirsty.

"Thanks." She handed it back to him. She took another small bite. "Why am I here?"

He gave her a fleeting grin. "Sharing that information is above my pay grade."

"Is there something you want? If I don't know, I can't give it to you."

"Just eat your sandwich, okay?"

Her eyes narrowed. She decided to take a different approach.

"What do you guys want with Sam Callahan?" she asked, studied him.

She saw the flash of recognition. Then he tried to play it off.

"I don't know that name."

He was lying. She could tell he was surprised she'd said the name.

"You work for Victor Larsen?" she continued.

Natalie was currently running with a theory that this was somehow connected with Victor Larsen, former head of Redrock Security, who was now in jail for his role in the conspiracy with Lucas McCallister last fall. Sam was central to his arrest. Maybe this was some type of revenge?

She knew that—even while in prison—Victor Larsen was still a powerful and wealthy man with the most sinister connections. It wouldn't take much for a loyal soldier to carry out lethal orders—which was why Sam had been so cautious the past eight months. The paranoia was draining, as if their other struggles weren't difficult enough.

"Stop with the questions, okay?" the guy said. "Just be a good girl and you'll be fine. This will all be over soon."

She nodded, ate her sandwich.

It seemed like these guys had done their homework. They'd smartly lured her with dangling a good lead on the Barnstorm story. They'd created a good setup to grab her off the streets. But she guessed they hadn't completed their homework, or else he'd have already known—she was *anything* but a good girl.

TWENTY-SIX

"Sam Callahan is missing, Chief," Epps said, entering the office.

Spencer Lloyd looked up from the papers on his desk.

"Missing?" Lloyd asked.

"We just got done meeting with his boss, David Benoltz. Apparently, Callahan went to Mexico City this morning on a business trip. I guess something went down, and his boss is unsure of his whereabouts at the moment."

"What the hell does that mean?"

"Benoltz was vague with details. But he seemed genuinely concerned." Epps dropped a report on his desk. "It gets more interesting. The federal police are searching for Callahan in Mexico City right now. He was added to Mexico's suspect list just this afternoon."

"Why are they searching for him?"

"The report mentions a potential connection to a murder in a hotel suite, a stolen car, a high-speed car chase, and Callahan's evading custody while under questioning this afternoon. Callahan was nearly apprehended an hour ago while trying to flee the country under an apparent alias at Mexico City International Airport. But he got away."

Lloyd picked up the report, leaned back in his chair. "How does this lawyer have an alias?"

Epps shrugged. "Not sure."

Lloyd scanned the report, sighed. "So we've got one of the greatest assassins in the world who was brought into the United States to eliminate this rookie lawyer. This guy gets paid millions. And this is the first time we know of that the Gray Wolf has accepted an assignment in the States. That can't be overlooked. Whoever hired him is a big deal. Not only do you have to have obscene money, you also have to operate in the most elite inner circle imaginable. Very few people would even be able to make contact with a guy like the Gray Wolf. And yet here we are. Gerlach flies into DC today, gets through security with help from what we believe is a hacker on the outside, with a twenty-six-year-old lawyer as his apparent target. Yet Sam Callahan is not currently in DC; he's in Mexico City. Not only is the kid across the border, Callahan is now on the run from Mexican police in connection with a potential murder. And now we think he's trying to get out of the country with an alias?"

"That about sums it up, Chief."

Lloyd shook his head, exhaled. "We're sure this has *nothing* to do with what happened last fall with Victor Larsen and Redrock Security?"

Epps shrugged. "We've turned over every stone there. We've found nothing that connects it. We've even spoken directly to Victor Larsen, who insists he's not involved. And we've found nothing in his network that would make us believe otherwise."

"So, what, Callahan is just a bad-luck kid? Last year, Victor Larsen's former military assassins are hunting him down and trying to kill him. And this year, Callahan draws the short straw yet again, with an international assassin trying to do the same thing?"

"I can't connect the dots yet, either."

"Do we know where Callahan was trying to go tonight with this new alias?"

"He purchased a ticket for a midnight flight to New Orleans."

"He have a connection in New Orleans?"

"Not that we can tell."

"We have any leads yet on Gerlach's whereabouts?"

"Nothing yet. We're keeping tabs on local hotels and motels."

"Alert the New Orleans office, just in case."

"Yes, sir."

"We need to find this guy, Mike. I don't like the idea of a skilled killer roaming our streets and creating collateral damage."

"Krieger thinks someone might have hacked into our system to keep tabs on our search for the Gray Wolf. His team found some suspicious activity."

Lloyd's eyes narrowed. "Same hacker that got Gerlach inside the country?"

"We don't know yet. His team is working on it."

"Our job was much easier before the damn Internet. We used to have real targets. Now they're all hidden behind invisible computer networks." Lloyd stared down at the report on Sam Callahan again. "I want to talk to this Agent Mendoza."

"Yes, sir. I'll set it up."

"Any other connections to Callahan that we can monitor? Family? Friends?"

"His mother died a few months ago. He has a girlfriend. A reporter. Natalie Foster. Both of them were knee-deep involved with the Redrock deal last year. But we've been unable to locate her. Sent two agents to her place an hour ago, and no one answered her door. Her car isn't there. She's not answering her cell phone, either."

"I don't like how any of this feels. Double down on your search for her. If Callahan is on the run, he's going to contact someone he trusts. It's just a matter of time."

"Yes, sir."

TWENTY-SEVEN

Sam drove the Saab north toward the Matamoros border crossing. There were roughly five hundred miles of open land to cover—basically the width of Texas—and he kept his foot nearly to the floorboard the entire way. With the potential conspiracy fresh in his mind, he kept running theories through his head. He tried to connect Rich Hebbard and Tom Hawkins with Francisco Zapata and whatever else might be going down, but he mostly thought about Natalie. With so much time on lonely dark roads, without seeing another set of headlights, it was difficult for him to think about much else. His thoughts kept drifting to dreadful places. He had visions of her getting tortured, or much worse.

He had to get to New Orleans at all costs.

Thankfully, Sam didn't have to fight traffic driving through the night. He was careful with his speed upon entering the dozens of small towns, but on wide-open stretches of road, Sam stomped on it hard— the Saab hitting well above triple digits on the speedometer. He prayed he wouldn't encounter a solitary police car out here in the middle of nowhere and see the sudden red-and-blue flashing lights behind him. He needed to catch a break if he planned to be at the border before daylight.

He was still unsure how he'd get across once he got there.

Using the cash roll Diablo had given him, Sam stopped to fill up with gas in San Luis Potosí around one in the morning. He figured he was more than halfway there. So far, so good. He quickly downed a can of Red Bull. Even at one hundred miles per hour, his eyelids were growing heavy. He couldn't chance a nod off and find himself upside-down in a dirt field in the middle of nowhere—if he survived the crash at all.

He hit the highway again, feeling the impact of the caffeine.

He was good to go. For a while.

Although he tried to resist it, he again began to ponder the crazy possibility that Rich Hebbard might be his real father. According to Tommy, Hebbard had been living in Denver when Sam was born. Was it possible? Did his mom have some kind of relationship with the guy? If so, why would she make up the story about the drug dealer? Why would she lie to him about it? What would be the point? He felt a sudden pang hit his gut, something he'd experienced quite often over the past three months, when the brutal reality that she was gone washed over him. He could no longer call her up and ask her about it. He couldn't ask her anything. He could no longer walk into her room and catch her sneaking a smoke. He could never again hear one of her crass jokes. He could no longer take the long walks with her through the neighborhood. He could never again see the love in the eyes of his own flesh and blood or hear the words she said to him almost every single time he was with her.

I love you, Samuel.

His mom was gone.

March 14
Four months ago

There was a small crowd at the funeral. Maybe twenty people.

This was not unexpected, of course. His mom had moved to DC only to get better care near him and had not established roots. Not that she had too many meaningful relationships back in Houston, either, where her life had been so wrapped up in doing drugs, and where she'd been in and out of rehab four times. Before that, she was a nomad who moved around constantly without keeping in touch with many. Sam, of course, had no other family members. So those who chose to attend were pulled from only a couple of places. Several of the workers from Angel Cancer Care attended, as well as her doctor, and a few of the other cancer-stricken residents. A group of the ladies came from the small church a few blocks up the road where his mom had started to attend a Bible study class. There was an old lady there who used to meet his mom at the park and feed the ducks.

That was about it. *A sad end to a sad life,* Sam thought.

The lone bright spot of an otherwise-sucky week was seeing Pastor Isaiah and his family. Pastor Isaiah had rescued him out of juvie as a teenager and given him a second chance at a normal life. He and his wife, Alisha, had invited him to live with them in their small home in Denver. They'd gotten him a job at the homeless shelter, helped him finish his GED, and even pushed him to enroll in college. The man and his family had rescued Sam from a surefire life of crime on the streets. Alisha looked as beautiful as ever and had whipped up a home-cooked meal their first night with him in the city. Their daughter, Grace, was already ten and much smarter than Sam. They held an impromptu spelling bee, and Grace beat him badly. It was hard to believe she was just a newborn when Sam had moved in with the family. The twin boys, Kevin and Myles, had just turned five and were full of energy. They nearly tackled Sam upon seeing him at the airport with cheers of "Uncle Sam! Uncle Sam!"

And, of course, in so many ways, Pastor Isaiah was his rock. An athletic-looking black man now nearing forty, Pastor Isaiah wrapped his arms around him, pulled him in close, and Sam nearly fell apart.

They held a simple graveside service. No bells and whistles.

Sam sat next to Natalie in front of the closed coffin. It was a cold and gray DC day. It felt even colder inside Sam's hollow heart. Although his mom had always told him that God could take her at any point, now that he'd restored her relationship with her son after all these years, Sam was *not* feeling that same sentiment at the moment. It just felt cruel. He was angry about it. Had he not faced enough already in his life? The abusive foster homes? His life on the streets? His time in juvie? Hell, what about the added trauma of just last fall when he had bullets flying at him? And, what, now God wanted to up the ante and snatch his mother away?

It didn't sit well. The more he thought about it, the angrier he got.

Natalie reached over and took his hand. He held it loosely.

Pastor Isaiah said some nice things, told a few funny stories about his mom, and read a few scriptures. Sam held together pretty well for most of it. It wasn't until Alisha stood up and belted out "Amazing Grace" a cappella that Sam completely lost it. The tears started to drip, slowly at first, but then he couldn't stop them. He just let them pour down his face.

Each person in attendance came by and tried to say something nice to Sam, a quick word of encouragement, a funny story about his mom, but he couldn't hear much of it. He tried to smile and acknowledge them, but he felt rather numb inside and out. Natalie kissed him on the cheek, walked with Pastor Isaiah and his family back to the cars, while Sam stayed behind for a few minutes.

He stood there, alone, stared at the coffin. He couldn't believe his mom was inside. He couldn't believe that, within the hour, a grounds-keeper would lower her into the ground. And that was that. It was over. His only family—gone.

It started to rain. Now it was really getting cold. But he didn't feel like running back to the cars to keep dry. He didn't care if he got wet.

Standing there, he glanced beyond the coffin, thought he noticed something in the distance of the cemetery. Not something, but *someone*. Maybe a hundred feet off, standing beside a tree, but definitely looking right at him.

Sam squinted through the falling raindrops. An older man in a black trench coat. Could it be? It sure as hell looked like the gray-bearded man. Marcus Pelini. The mastermind ex-CIA agent who had helped Lisa McCallister, the congressional candidate's wife, last fall during the Redrock scandal and toyed with Sam's life—first, by putting him in constant jeopardy against sinister assassins and even the FBI, then by repeatedly saving him. The same man who had taken Sam's mother from her cancer facility, with intent to harm, Sam initially thought, only to discover later it was to protect her.

A second later, the man was gone behind the tree. And Sam couldn't find him again. He rubbed his eyes. Was he seeing things? He'd been crying so much that his eyes were blurry. There had been a couple of other times the past few months he'd thought he'd spotted the gray-bearded man pop up in random places. When Sam was out running. Or walking across campus. But he could never be certain. The man was a spook. A spy. It always felt a bit like an apparition—and then the gray-bearded man was gone. Just like now.

Sam stared back down at the coffin. Then he kissed two fingers, pressed them against the wood. "Good-bye, Mom."

TWENTY-EIGHT

Sam was exhausted when he finally pulled the Saab within a few miles of the US–Mexico border crossing a few minutes after four in the morning. There were four empty cans of Red Bull and several PowerBar wrappers on the passenger seat. His head was spinning with a cocktail of fatigue, caffeine, and protein. His back ached something fierce from sitting six hours in one position in the stiff car seat, but he'd actually done it. He'd survived the long drive without any extra peril. He'd navigated more than five hundred miles of a foreign country and made it all the way to the border before sunrise.

But now what?

He pulled off into the empty dirt parking lot of an old schoolhouse in the border town of Matamoros. Then he used the cell phone to log in to Leia's Lounge. A few minutes later, Tommy was once again on the small screen in front of him.

"You still awake, Mav?" Sam asked.

"You know me, dude. Sleep is overrated. Where are you?"

"Matamoros. A few miles from the border."

"Perfect."

"How is that *perfect*?"

"Because I know how I'm going to get you across."

"I'm all ears."

"A drug tunnel," Tommy declared, letting the words dramatically hang out there.

Sam frowned at the screen. "A . . . what?"

"There's a secret tunnel dug deep belowground that one of the drug cartels uses to run drugs across the border and into the States. Right there in Matamoros. It's over a half mile long and begins inside a house on the Mexico side and comes out inside another house on the US side. This thing is an amazing piece of work."

"Are you kidding me, Tommy? How do you even know about this?"

Tommy frowned. "Come on, you think drug cartels don't have their own sophisticated online networks? You may see only the violence and the beheadings and whatnot on TV, but these cartels are billion-dollar business empires that hire guys just like me to run online intelligence for them. They're very dangerous people to mess with, but if you're bent toward making money, it can be quite lucrative."

Sam wondered if Tommy had been smoking weed—he couldn't be serious. "So, what, you're telling me one of these drug mercenaries is just going to let me walk into their house, buy a ticket like I'm at some kind of amusement park, and take their secret underground shuttle system into the States?"

"Look, you asked me to find you a way to get across the border, so I did. Actually pulling it off is entirely up to you."

"Fantastic," Sam muttered, having a hard time believing he was even considering the possibility. Were there any other options? This was crazy.

Tommy tried to give him a pep talk. "Dude, don't undersell your-self. You're the same guy who broke into Redrock Security headquarters last year—one of the most secure facilities on this planet—and walked away clean."

"Clean? I got shot at by military assassins and chased by friggin' helicopters!"

"*And* survived," Tommy clarified. "I'm just saying, don't underestimate yourself. That was a one-in-a-million task, and you actually did it."

Sam sighed, feeling resigned. "Where is this house?"

Tommy grinned. "I'm sending you the details now. There's an elevator inside."

"Are you serious?"

"I don't have the construction plans, so I can't tell you how to find it. I just know it's there inside the house, and it'll take you down belowground."

"Am I safe to cross through? Is this tunnel going to collapse in on me?"

"You're safe. They've been using it for about a year now. They've built some kind of ventilation system inside and even have lights. There's also a track system for carts to haul the drugs. It's a very impressive setup, if I do say so myself."

"If I somehow make it across, and that's a big *if*, what's next?"

"There's a five-thirty flight out of Brownsville to New Orleans."

"How am I going to board it?"

"I have something already waiting for you at the airport."

"Then I better get on with it."

Tommy smiled. "Attaboy!"

TWENTY-NINE

Sam parked the Saab a few blocks from the drug house.

He quietly got out of the car, walked the streets in the dark. No streetlights, no sidewalks, cracked and crumbling paved roads. Some of the houses already had graffiti-covered plywood nailed over windows and looked condemned. The drug house was a dingy white-brick number at the end of the road. Unkempt grass and weeds covered the yard, and an old green military-style Jeep was parked in the driveway. Sam examined the house from the street. No signs of activity. No lights on in the windows. It looked abandoned. He hoped perhaps no one was currently inside the house. Maybe he could just slip inside and get through this tunnel with no issues.

From driving slowly with headlights off through the neighborhood a few minutes ago, Sam noted that the backs of the houses on this street all bordered the river called the Rio Grande. On the other side of the Rio Grande was the United States. He could hardly fathom the idea that he might walk into this white-brick house in a few minutes, somehow find his way down a built-in elevator shaft, walk through a tunnel that had been secretly dug beneath an entire river, cross over an international border, and then reappear in a house on the other side. It never failed to amaze him the lengths criminals would go to for money and power.

Sam trusted Tommy. The guy wouldn't feed him bad information. The tunnel was there. Although this might be a crazy way to get back into the States, Tommy had at least given him a solid chance.

Sam took one last look up and down the street. No signs of life coming from anywhere. The sun wouldn't be up for a few more hours. Most lights were still off in the surrounding houses. He found a wooden gate around back. Half the boards were rotten. He pushed the gate open, held his breath so he could hear even the faintest sound. Scanning the yard, he found no menacing red eyes staring back at him, heard no sudden growls.

Sam stepped up onto a brick patio, cupped his hands around the dirty square glass in the back door. Complete darkness. He did not spot any tiny red lights on walls or notice any security wires coming from the door frame. He figured if the neighbors knew this was a drug-cartel house, which was likely, they sure as hell weren't messing with it. Not unless they wanted to be shot and dumped into the river fifty yards away.

Sam pulled out a pocketknife he'd purchased at the counter of the same convenience store where he'd grabbed Red Bull and PowerBars, thinking it could come in handy for a situation just like this one. He knelt by the back door, stuck the end of the small knife blade into the key slot. The blade fit perfectly. He wiggled and scraped for a few seconds and turned the door handle. He kept the knife blade open and squeezed the handle tightly in his right palm, just in case. He'd only stabbed one person in his life—a drunk foster dad who was abusing a young girl who lived with them—but he was ready to do whatever he had to do to get back to Natalie.

He stepped inside the dank house. The AC was either off, not working, or nonexistent. It was humid and sticky. He felt beads of sweat form on his skin. He used his cell-phone flashlight to look around. A small kitchen to his right. A living room to his left. A lone couch sat in the living room. No tables, no chairs, no TV. The brown carpet was in shambles and completely barren in spots. He walked into the kitchen, opened the yellow fridge. The light came on and blinded him. There was at least electricity in the house. He found two six-packs of Estrella Jalisco beer on the top shelf and nothing else. He shut the fridge, kept moving. He walked through the living room and found a hallway that led to two bedrooms. Inside the first door, he found a king-size mattress lying directly on the carpet. No blankets or pillows. No other furniture. He opened the closet. Completely empty. He checked the walls for any secret passageways. He didn't find anything. He stepped back into the hallway, poked his head into a tiny bathroom—it smelled something awful, like the plumbing didn't work.

He'd yet to encounter anyone inside the home—and been forced to use the pocketknife—but he still hadn't seen *anything* that told him an elevator existed. He moved to the end of the hallway, opened the door to the last bedroom. Although there was no furniture in the room, there were two dirty wheelbarrows. That was promising. He figured they were used to haul drugs around. He opened the closet door, and there it was. He shook his head in dismay. He stared directly at the front of a normal-looking metal elevator door, like he was staying at a Marriott, the Down button showing on the silver-metal casing. Incredible. A drug cartel had actually constructed a full elevator shaft inside a bedroom closet.

Sam was about to punch the Down button when he heard car doors slam outside. He raced back down the hallway, peeked out a front window. He cursed. A black truck with huge tires was now parked directly behind the broken-down Jeep. Four men were walking up to the front door, only ten feet away. Sam spun around, considered his options. He could either dart out the back door, hide, wait it out. Or he could go for the elevator right now, take his chances. Path one might keep him outside the house for several hours—or even all day. Not an option. He chose path number two. He had only a few seconds.

Sam hurried into the bedroom, jabbed the Down button on the elevator. Would it automatically work? Did the elevator have to be turned on somewhere? He felt panicked, sweating profusely. The elevator engaged, although the door did not immediately open. He could hear the elevator machinery pulling the carriage up from below. Inside the quiet house, it sounded to him like a loud construction site, the elevator's gears rumbling, creaking, and vibrating. He cursed again, knowing he'd just put a huge target on his back. He poked his head out into the hallway. The front door opened; someone turned on a light. The four guys were all casually chatting in Spanish as they entered; however, they immediately silenced upon hearing the unexpected sound of the elevator.

One of them said, *"¿El ascensor?"*

Sam jumped back in front of the elevator door as it opened. The carriage was completely empty, although caked with dirt on the floor and walls. He hurried inside, found the Down button inside the carriage, and started pumping it relentlessly with a finger. *Come on!* He knew the men would be inside the bedroom within seconds. There were four of them and only one of him. Somehow, Sam didn't think a small pocketknife would do the trick. If these guys caught him inside their drug house, he was as good as dead. It would not be pretty. They'd probably cut off both his hands and feet and prop his body up on a pole at the front of the neighborhood as a warning. The elevator door slowly shut.

Sam stepped to the very back, his chest feeling so tight, it might crack open. He stared at the closing gap of the elevator door, held his breath. When it was within an inch of fully closing, he heard what he thought was a string of Mexican curse words a few feet away. The elevator rumbled down. Sam took a quick breath. He had no idea what to expect when the elevator door opened back up. Either way, he knew he'd have to hit the ground moving at full velocity and swiftly find his way around. There was little doubt in his mind the four guys upstairs would come after him.

The carriage came to a jerking stop. The door opened.

Sam paused only briefly, staring out, praying no drug mercenary was waiting there to greet him. He was in the clear. The space in front of him was pitch-dark. He quickly looked around for *anything* inside the elevator carriage that might dismantle it. There was no Off button or any compartments inside where he might pull wires apart. Frustrated, he hurried out, the door closing behind him. The carriage began to rise again.

Sam frantically searched the cramped space using his cell-phone flashlight. There was another wheelbarrow sitting on the dirt floor off to his left. He looked for a light switch. He knew he wouldn't be able to go fast enough with just his flashlight. He needed to be able to book it. Tommy suggested the tunnel had working lights. He found a metal box screwed to a wooden stud against the wall to his right with a red switch on it. Sam flipped the switch, and a fluorescent light above him fluttered for a few seconds and illuminated the space, and then he saw more lights popping on like dominos down a cavelike tunnel directly in front of him. He could now see he was standing inside a ten-by-ten-foot room that had sheets of plywood for the walls and the ceiling. In front of him, a set of small railroad tracks disappeared down the tunnel. The tunnel was just big enough for him to duck his head and maneuver inside. At the foot of the tunnel, he found a metal cart twice the size of the wheelbarrows, made to fit the track system—clearly how they moved the drugs.

Sam heard the elevator engage again behind him. They were coming. Within seconds, he'd have four angry Mexican cartel members on his tail. The only question was if more cartel guys would be waiting for him at the other end of the tunnel. Only one way to find out. Sam sidestepped the metal cart, and then he rushed into the abyss of the tunnel, keeping his head tucked low. The tunnel veered slightly left and right in a few places but stayed relatively straight. There were individual light bulbs strung from the ceiling every hundred or so feet. Sam kept sprinting forward, trying not to think too much about how tight a space he was trapped inside and the fact that the dirt walls could collapse in on him at any point. He figured he was directly beneath the Rio Grande. The idea of river water possibly engulfing the tunnel gave him a scare. But not as much as cartel members cutting him into a hundred pieces.

Sam could hear yelling behind him inside the tunnel. He caught a toe on the railroad tracks, stumbled, jabbed his right knee into steel. He picked himself up, kept sprinting. He couldn't really tell how far he'd already gone. Five hundred yards? Maybe farther? It didn't matter. He would run until he hit the end. Sweat streamed down his face and stung his eyes. Seconds later, the tunnel veered left again, and he found himself spilling out into another room similar to the space below the other house. A matching elevator shaft stood in front of him. Sam pounded the Up button. The elevator doors immediately parted. He could hear the patter of shoes on the dirt floor inside the tunnel behind him. Maybe forty yards back. Before jumping into the elevator, he searched the plywood walls, found a metal box with a red switch. He flipped the switch down. The tunnel went dark. He heard more yelling and cursing.

Sam rushed inside the elevator, pressed the Up button. The door crawled to a close. He pulled the pocketknife back out, flipped open the blade, preparing for whatever he'd find waiting for him when the door reopened. He wiped the sweat from his face with his hand. He could feel his knee aching from his stumble. The carriage jerked to a stop. Sam held the pocketknife out in front of him. The door parted. His fist with the pocketknife was shaking.

He exhaled when no one was staring back at him.

Just like the other house, the elevator was hidden inside a back bedroom closet. He shoved a twin bed with no sheets or blankets against the closet doors, in hopes of blocking the men from getting into the house. He listened for only a second to see if he could hear anything.

There were no lights on in the hallway. A good sign, he felt. If someone was inside the house, he'd fully expect some lights to be on. He peered around into the dark hallway, stood still, tried to listen above the sound of his own heartbeat in his ears. Sam carefully moved down the hallway, using his cell-phone flashlight, taking quick peeks into two other bedrooms. Both were completely empty. He moved into a living room, found a square card table with metal folding chairs. A glass ashtray sat in the middle of the table and was littered with cigarette butts. The butts were dull. No signs of fresh cigarettes. Six empty bottles of Corona on the table.

Sam heard a vehicle skid to a stop right outside of the house. He cursed. Car doors opened and slammed shut. He turned, raced toward the back door. Before getting there, he spotted a shadow move by the window out back, the sound of a hand hit the doorknob. Someone had come around back. Sam moved toward the front door, stiffened again when he heard noise right outside. They were both in front and in back. He was surrounded. One of the guys from the other side must've called ahead, alerting them to his unwelcome presence. Sam had only a split second to get out or he was going to be filleted. His mind flashed and gave him a few escape options. He chose the first bedroom, rushed down the hallway, slipped inside, and shut the door behind him—just as he heard the men enter the house.

Sam twisted around, found the front bedroom window, one he'd spotted earlier upon quick inspection of the room. He knelt behind it, unlocked the metal tabs on the window. Hands at the bottom, he very quietly began to tug the window up. He paused. He could hear the men directly outside his bedroom in the hallway. They were speaking in rapid Spanish, clearly alarmed. When they moved past the bedroom, he pulled the window fully open, climbed outside, right into a prickly bush. The thorny branches of the bush jabbed into his hands. He bit down on his bottom lip, forced himself to be silent, pushed his way through the annoying bush, and crawled free into the front yard.

He surveyed the area, making sure one of the drug guys wasn't out front. He didn't see anyone. He heard voices again from inside the bedroom, where a light popped on and exposed his escape route. His first instinct was to simply sprint off down the street, get lost in the neighborhood on foot, but then he noticed that the engine was still rumbling inside the black Camaro the men had parked in the driveway. When he didn't spot any movement inside the car, he decided to be bold and ran straight toward the Camaro. He yanked open the driver's door, jumped into the front seat, shifted the car into reverse, and stomped on the gas. The Camaro roared backward. Sam hit the brakes, yanked the wheel to the right, turned in the street, just in time to notice two angry-looking men run out the front door with big guns in their hands.

Sam shoved the gear into drive, slammed his foot on the gas pedal. The sports car rocketed forward, the tires spinning and smoking on the pavement. In the rearview mirror, he could see the two men run into the street behind him. But neither man aimed his gun and started shooting. Probably because they didn't want to put bullet holes in their precious turbo-charged hot rod. Sam whipped the wheel left, right, zigzagged the streets, and he was out of their line of sight within seconds. He took quick breaths, tried to gather himself. He would not keep the vehicle for long.

He found the highway, felt his whole body exhale.

He was back in the States.

THIRTY

Sam parked the Camaro in a short-term paid lot directly in front of Brownsville's tiny airport. Only two airlines serviced Brownsville on three runways. It was enough to get Sam over to Houston and then to New Orleans by midmorning—*if* he could get a ticket and somehow get through security first. Tommy said he had something waiting for Sam to help make that happen. Walking away from the Camaro, Sam threw the car keys as far away as possible and fought the urge to punch holes in all the tires with the pocketknife. He couldn't waste a second.

He quickly searched the rows of other cars, looking for a Subaru Outback. He spotted a green one at the very end of the second row. The hatchback was unlocked. Sam popped the back open, searched inside, found a small black backpack. He quickly unzipped it, pulled out a white envelope. He tore open the envelope and dumped out the contents. A new set of IDs, a credit card, some cash. His face was on each ID along with the name Ethan Edwards, the name of John Wayne's character in the classic Western *The Searchers*. Another of Tommy's top-five favorites. He stuffed the IDs, credit card, and cash into his pocket, searched farther inside the backpack, where he found a black T-shirt, a pair of jeans in his size, a dark-blue Dallas Cowboys cap, and a small plastic bag of toiletries (deodorant, toothpaste, and toothbrush). Sam stuffed the items back inside the backpack, slung it over his shoulder, and then shut the hatchback. He checked the time on his phone. He had only twenty minutes. The flight left at 5:30 a.m. He needed to hurry.

He hustled across the drop-off/pick-up lane in front of the main airport building, where only a few cars were stopping and letting people out. Sam spotted one bored security guard way down the sidewalk to his left. He didn't expect to walk into the same kind of security barriers in Brownsville that he had in Mexico City. He quickly stepped through the glass doors and entered the building. Not much activity inside. With only two airlines servicing the airport, there was only one flight out at this hour. A small plane from United Express.

He hurried up to a ticket counter. A tired-looking but pleasant attendant greeted him.

"I need to get on the five-thirty flight to Houston. Is there room?"

She nodded. "Looks like it."

He dropped down his Ethan Edwards ID and credit card and held his breath. It was always nerve-racking to use a new ID for the first time. Had Tommy come through again? The attendant typed away, processed his boarding pass, and then handed everything back to him. Like always, Sam had no problem—*unless* someone tagged his new alias after purchase like they did the previous night. He'd find that out at security.

"Have a good flight, Mr. Edwards."

"Thank you."

Sam stepped down the corridor and into a short line for security. Only four people ahead of him. He made his way to the security kiosk quickly. His mouth felt dry. Hopefully, this time he would not have to turn around and hightail it out of the airport wearing a sombrero. The security guard gave him a quick glance, eyeballed his ID and boarding pass, then stamped it and let him through. No issues. Sam passed through the body scanner without a fuss, grabbed his backpack on the other side, and then quickly found a men's restroom. He grabbed an empty stall and changed into his fresh new clothes. He was glad to ditch his sweat-filled T-shirt and jeans. He stuffed the dirty clothes back inside the backpack, took a moment to wash his face at the sink, put on some deodorant, and brushed his teeth. Then he placed the Dallas Cowboys cap on his head and hurried out of the restroom.

He made it to the gate for his flight just before the attendant was set to close the doors. Seconds later, Sam was on the small plane. He moved down a narrow aisle that had two seats on his left, one on his right, toward the very back. He counted maybe forty other passengers, all looking tired and annoyed at having to be flying out this early. No one gave him a second look. He was grateful for that. He had no desire to fake small talk or personally engage any of them. He sat in the second-to-last seat on the right. All by himself.

First stop, Houston. Then on to New Orleans.

He eased down into the seat cushions, felt his body succumb to the exhaustion. The plane eased away from the terminal and minutes later was in the air. The pilot kept the cabin dark.

He closed his eyes, his mind drifting to Natalie.

How was she doing? Was she hanging tough?

Did she know this all had to do with him?

His thoughts were not only about his growing concern for her safety, but he couldn't help but relive everything that had happened this past year that had led them to this point.

May 9
Two months ago

Sam could feel himself pulling away from Natalie again, although he couldn't seem to figure out how to stop it. His mother's sudden death had hit him harder than he'd ever expected. Natalie was sympathetic and gave him a lot of space. She assured him that she was there for him, for love and support, but she also knew he had to work through the grieving at his own pace. She had once walked in his difficult shoes, losing her mother in a horrific car accident when she was only twelve. While her brothers had tried to push her along in the healing, it had only made her more frustrated—until her dad finally stepped in and told them to leave her alone. Their sister would heal in her own way and in her own time. Natalie said it had made all the difference. She would not push Sam through the healing.

Sam used this as an excuse to avoid Natalie. The truth was, losing his mother had reignited an even stronger fear that always bubbled just below the surface—he was terrified of losing Natalie. Every time he let people in too close, he seemed to lose them. Although he felt he could eventually survive losing his mother, Sam wasn't sure he could get over losing Natalie, who had somehow penetrated every part of his soul. He thought he'd finally dealt with these abandonment issues and put them to rest, but the death of his mother had unexpectedly yanked the chair out from under him and unraveled what good counseling had helped him slowly weave back together. Sam was once again a frightened little foster boy.

For weeks on end, he stopped returning her calls. Natalie would send simple texts. Love you. Praying for you. I'm here for you when you need me. Although a crummy way to behave, he couldn't even get himself to respond, as he spiraled into a dark place. He tried to get lost in his studies, but it didn't help too much. Although he would graduate from law school, he was limping across the finish line.

Several weeks of evading Natalie turned into a full month, until she was waiting for him one afternoon on campus when he stepped out of McDonough Hall. He paused, stared down the sidewalk at her, looking so beautiful in her black slacks and white blouse, her brown hair floating in the warm breeze. His heart was racing, but not in a good way. He did not want to hurt Natalie again. He hated himself for it.

"Hey," she said, with a warm smile. "Thought you might be hungry."

Natalie held up a bag from Ching Ching Cha, their favorite Chinese restaurant.

Swallowing, he couldn't even speak. She seemed to pick up on it.

"I miss you, Sam. I know this has been a hard month. But we really need to spend time together."

"I can't," he managed. "Not right now. I've got too much going on."

"There's going through the proper steps of healing, and then there's running away from them. I feel like you're running again. You don't need to do that."

"What if I can never stop?"

"I refuse to believe that. I know you now. The *real* you. I know what's inside."

"What's inside is broken."

"Okay, so we work on it together. You *and* me."

He swallowed again, his eyes beginning to well up. "I can't. I'm sorry."

He stepped around her, felt like he was going to vomit.

"Sam, please wait."

He didn't wait, just kept putting one foot after another.

THIRTY-ONE

Alger Gerlach was now Charles Lambert from Cleveland with a wife and three young kids. Gerlach even had generic pictures of kids in a worn leather wallet. Working for a small printing company, he traveled around the country selling notepads and special paper goods. He told his travel companion he grew up in a large family, the fourth of seven kids. Dad owned a construction company. Mom was a teacher until child number three, and then she stayed home. A good family man, he talked a lot about his brothers and sisters. The fortysomething blonde woman sitting in the airplane seat beside him on this crack-of-dawn flight from DC to New Orleans said she'd visited Cleveland ten years ago with her family and had taken the kids to an Indians game. He found it humorous that she had no idea she was actually sitting next to the great Gray Wolf. The most famous assassin in the world. What a story that would be for her kids. The truth was, Gerlach never knew his parents, who'd died in a bus bombing in Munich at the hands of Palestinian nationalists when he was only two. He'd moved in with an uncle who abused him in every way possible for more than a decade, until Gerlach finally ran away from home at age fifteen.

They carried on a conversation for the duration of the two-hour flight. Gerlach had no real interest in chatting with the woman, but he enjoyed the art and practice of deception. He wanted to know at any moment he could carry on a believable conversation with just about anyone in America—even law enforcement, if necessary.

His hair was gray now. He'd gotten rid of the black in a hotel bathroom in DC. He'd lost the goatee and replaced it with a salt-and-pepper gray beard. The green eyes were now brown with contact lenses. He wore a cheap gray suit that he'd purchased at a discount store. He looked forward to climbing back into his $5,000 Italian designer suits when this job was finally finished. He'd done some theater as a youth and had always enjoyed the makeup, the fake facial hair, the wigs, the constant costume changes. His teacher, Mr. Müller, always said he had a real eye for it and had a future in drama. If only Mr. Müller hadn't died before seeing just how far around the world Gerlach would take this cultivated gift.

Once on the ground, Gerlach took a cab from the New Orleans airport into downtown. He checked into the Omni in the heart of the French Quarter near the Mississippi River. The hotel clerk handed him an unmarked sealed shipping box slightly bigger than a notepad. He was supposed to have a suite reservation with a view of the river. The young hotel clerk with slick blond hair and a cocky grin typed into the computer and insisted that the reservation had only been for a regular room. *Sorry, Charlie.* Those were the clerk's exact words. Gerlach instructed the clerk to change the reservation to a suite with a view of the river and stop wasting his time. The clerk frowned at him, a look that said, "Who the hell do you think you are?" The kid told him they were booked solid. There was nothing he could do. Or wanted to do, Gerlach felt. It was really irritating him. The clerk asked in an annoyed tone if Gerlach wanted to speak with his manager. Gerlach said no. He did not want to draw unnecessary attention to himself.

He calmly took his key and left the counter. He noticed the clerk rolling his eyes and flipping the bird at him through a mirror on a column. The elevator escorted him up to the fifth floor. He put his black bag on the bed, pulled the curtains back. The sun was rising over the city. It was a view of buildings. Not the river. It wasn't too bad. But not what he wanted.

He sat on the bed, tore open the box. Inside, he pulled out a small computer tablet, powered it on, and waited. After loading, he opened the photo icon and began scanning a dozen color images that were clearly taken as part of security surveillance. The same face as the hardcopy photo he'd received upon his arrival yesterday, only now the young man in the image was completely bald. He also looked to have a gash on his forehead. In the series of photos, he wore a black T-shirt and jeans and was holding a cell phone. The last photo had a digital tag along the bottom. *Alias: Ethan Edwards.*

Gerlach set the tablet to the side, dialed from the hotel phone. A quick answer.

"Yes?"

"Where do I go to listen to jazz?"

"Jazz music?"

"Yes."

"The best place is Davenport Lounge."

The code words were out of the way.

"Do you have my package?" asked Gerlach.

"Yes. It's in the van, which is in the parking garage."

"Good. What happened with my hotel reservation?"

"What do you mean? We booked it to your specifics."

"It's not to my specifics."

"The hotel must have changed it. Sorry."

He hung up, pressed his lips together. The package mentioned was his trusted companion. He could not operate without it.

Forty minutes later, Gerlach was standing outside the hotel, in an alley near a service exit at the back of the building. He had watched several hotel employees come out the back door for a quick ten-minute smoke break. Cigarette butts littered the pavement. Gerlach was tucked behind a building column, watching, waiting. As expected, his cocky friend from behind the front desk eventually drifted out to the smoking area. Gerlach had smelled the smoke stink from the kid's breath, had seen the imprint of a cigarette box in his front left pants pocket.

The kid unbuttoned his hotel-clerk jacket, quickly lit up a cigarette.

Gerlach was behind him like a panther. The right arm went around the neck, the other arm around the top of the head. Gerlach ripped violently with both arms and heard the familiar snap of bones in the neck. The kid squirmed and then fell limp in his arms, the cigarette dropping to the pavement. Gerlach did a quick check of the pulse. He then dragged the hotel clerk over to the metal dumpster, where he tipped the body into the cluttered container filled with trash bags and cardboard boxes. He pulled a smelly black bag and several boxes on top of the kid, so he wouldn't be found immediately.

Satisfied, he stepped through the service door back into the hotel.

He was hungry. He'd read that Café du Monde was the place to go.

THIRTY-TWO

Spencer Lloyd barged into his apartment.

"Pop! Where the hell are you?"

The day nurse had called, said his father was acting more ornery than ever. He'd locked himself inside the bathroom, kept calling her a fat pig, among other much worse expletives, and demanded that she get the hell out and leave him alone. The nurse said she was never coming back to deal with his father again. She didn't need that kind of abuse. It was the third nurse to quit on him in the last nine months. Lloyd was fed up. He didn't need this crap right now. It was embarrassing even to have to tell one of his superiors that he had to leave a critical strategic meeting to go deal with his stubborn father and his overbearing ways.

Lloyd banged on the bathroom door. "Pop!"

"Go away!" his dad yelled back, his voice hoarse.

"It's me, Pop. Spencer. Open the damn door."

"Is that pig gone?"

Lloyd exhaled. "She's not a pig, Pop. You said you really liked her. And, yes, she's gone. She quit. You ran off another one."

"Good. That pig treated me like a little kid."

For good reason, Lloyd thought. "Are you going to open the door? Or do I have to break it open?"

"Break it open," he muttered. "What do I care?"

"Pop, open the door now. Or I'm serious, I'll drive you straight to the old folks' home. Let them deal with you. Do you understand me?"

There was silence on the other end. Lloyd took another deep breath. It was such a surreal thing to have the roles suddenly reversed in life, to have to treat his father like a child. Lloyd was about to go find a screwdriver to pry open the doorknob when he finally heard the lock click open on the other side. But his father did not open the door. He heard his dad sit back down on the toilet. Lloyd turned the door handle, parted the door, and looked inside. His father was sitting on the toilet, in a gray FBI T-shirt Lloyd had brought home, but with his checkered red-and-black pajama pants still pulled all the way up to his waist. And that's when Lloyd smelled it. An awful smell. The heinous odor of a kid who had crapped his pants. Except his kid was eighty-nine years old. Lloyd felt his heart sink. His father had obviously accidentally soiled himself and had locked himself in the bathroom out of humiliation. He wasn't going to let a young and attractive female nurse inside to deal with his mess, even though he needed help. It was one thing to have a nurse check blood pressure and get him to take his medicine. This was something altogether different. There was still some sense of pride in the old man.

His dad wouldn't even look at him. Lloyd put a hand on his shoulder.

"Come on, Pop. Let's get you some fresh clothes. Get you cleaned up. Maybe we'll grab some breakfast at the diner down the street together. You love that place."

"Fine," his father grunted.

Lloyd's cell phone buzzed. He stepped back into the hallway, pulled it out, saw that it was Agent Epps.

"Everything all right, Chief?" Epps asked.

"You don't even want to know. What do you have?"

"Krieger thinks he has a solid track on the Gray Wolf."

"Where?"

"New Orleans."

"You're kidding?"

"No, sir. Krieger is adamant."

"Wasn't Callahan trying to get to New Orleans?"

"Yes, sir. But we still haven't picked anything up on him since he was last spotted at Mexico City International last night."

"What about the girl? Natalie Foster?"

"She's still missing. She never came home. I had two guys at her place waiting all night. We checked in at her work this morning, but her boss said no one there had heard from her since yesterday afternoon, which he claimed was very unusual. He was very concerned."

"I don't like it."

"Me neither. We'll keep looking."

Lloyd glanced back inside the bathroom, where his father was slowly getting undressed. He shook his head, knew he needed to get in there and help the old man.

THIRTY-THREE

The same bushy-haired guy who brought her a turkey sandwich last night also delivered her breakfast. Sun rays poured in through the window at the top of the warehouse wall to her left. Natalie's body ached from head to toe. Sleeping secured to the hard wooden chair all night long, virtually stuck in one uncomfortable position, had been brutal—although she was grateful she'd been spared the black hood. Her eyes popped open at every creak, rustle, and gush of wind. Every time the fatigue took over and her eyes fluttered closed, images of a huge rat crawling up into her lap would creep into her mind, and her eyes would fly back open. Over and over again. But most of all, she feared the men coming in to check on her while she was asleep, desperate not to show any signs of vulnerability. She was determined to prove she was tougher than they were and could outlast them.

The bushy-haired guy still wore the same tan slacks and coffee-stained white button-down shirt as yesterday. Natalie guessed he hadn't gone home for the night and then returned. He'd been stuck in the front room. She'd made up nicknames for her four captors, just to keep her mind busy. She called this guy JB because he reminded her of the pop singer Justin Bieber, his face unusually boyish. The bald van driver with glasses was Abe because his thick beard reminded her of Abraham Lincoln. Named after his likeness to the movie character in *Forrest Gump*, she called the crew-cut guy Lieutenant Dan, only he had a new black eye—the result of a swift kick of her foot. Abductor number four was called Strahan because of his resemblance to the TV host and former football player Michael Strahan. Creating the goofy nicknames somehow made her feel more in control of the situation.

Walking over to her, JB set a paper plate with two croissants on the floor and tugged the tape off her mouth. She exhaled at the new freedom to breathe, twisted her dry lips all around to stretch them out. JB used a small pocketknife and cut the duct tape free that held her arms down to the chair. Although her wrists remained wrapped together, she was given just enough freedom to use her hands to feed herself. Natalie had been patiently waiting for this moment, anticipating an opportunity.

"You've got to let me go to the bathroom," Natalie exclaimed.

"I can't do that."

She frowned. "Are you serious? You really want me to pee myself? You can't possibly expect me to sit here all night long and be able to hold it any longer. I'm dying. Please."

He seemed to consider it, took a quick look back over his shoulder.

"Come on," she begged. "You can walk me to the bathroom and then bring me right back here. It won't take me but a few minutes, I swear."

"Fine. But you try to run, lady, it won't be good for you."

"You think I don't already know that? There are four of you and only one of me."

She watched him closely, but JB didn't tip his hat in any direction. The van had started up and left the property at some point during the middle of the night. An hour ago, the van had returned. She was sure it was the same van. Were they now working in shifts? Was JB alone at the moment? Or were Abe, Lieutenant Dan, and Strahan still on-site somewhere? Figuring that out was critical in discerning her next move.

JB knelt in front of her, cut the duct tape that held her ankles around the chair, and pulled Natalie up into a standing position. Although her wrists were still bound together, she was now free to walk like a normal person. She took a moment, thinking, and allowing the feeling to come back to her legs. Holding her firmly by the arm, he ushered her forward toward the front room. He opened the door, pulled her through, his grip tight on her arm. With a quick glance around the small front room, Natalie observed a round table covered with junk-food wrappers and soda cans. Four chairs surrounded it. A small TV with rabbit ears was sitting on a counter in a corner, currently showing a local morning talk show. The best news was that none of the others were in the room. No Abe. No Lieutenant Dan. No Strahan. So unless one of them was outside somewhere, which she highly doubted, she was one-on-one with JB.

He opened the door to a small single-toilet bathroom that was connected to the office and turned on the light. "Hurry up, and make this quick."

"What about these?" she asked, holding up her bound wrists.

His forehead bunched. "What about it?"

"I'm not a guy, okay?" she huffed. "I can't just stand up in there and take a leak. Not to be crude, but I need to be able sit down and use my hands, if you know what I mean. So I'd appreciate a little flexibility. Unless you want me to make a complete mess of this."

He sighed, took the knife back out, and slit her wrists free.

"Thanks," she said.

"Just get going already."

Natalie turned, stepped into the bathroom, shut the door behind her. She really did have to go to the bathroom, but she also had other intentions in mind. There was no fan switch in the bathroom, so she turned on the faucet water to full blast to drown out as much sound as possible—something any girl would do when using a public toilet with other people outside.

She quickly did her business but didn't flush. Her eyes were searching everywhere. There was no window in the bathroom—it was an internal room inside the building. She wasn't sure what to expect if she got this far. She checked the cabinet beneath the sink. Nothing inside that she could use for a weapon. Not unless she wanted to hit the guy with a small pack of toilet paper. Her eyes drifted up to the eight-foot ceiling. Standard white two-by-four acoustical-tile ceiling that she might find in any cheap office building.

Natalie quietly closed the lid to the toilet, quickly stepped on top of it. Then she carefully stepped onto the sink counter, where she accidentally bumped the wall loudly with her hip. She stood very still, listened. When she heard nothing from JB, she returned to the task at hand. From her heightened position on the sink, she could now easily push up ceiling tiles. She pushed the one ceiling tile directly above her all the way up, out of the bracket, and then moved it over to the side to be able to see into the space above the bathroom. A dark and wide-open space, just like the rest of the warehouse. She spotted a thick steel beam about four feet above the ceiling tiles; she couldn't quite reach it. Not without a little help. She searched the floor but saw nothing she could stack on top of the sink to give her an extra few feet of reach.

She felt the clock ticking. She didn't have forever.

Her eyes fell upon her gray hoodie, and she got an idea. She quickly pulled the hoodie up over her head, tugged her arms out, exposing the white tank top she wore underneath. She bent down and grabbed the clear plastic hand-soap dispenser. She tied the end of one arm of the hoodie around the plastic pump head on the dispenser, pulled the knot tight. She looked back up through the missing ceiling tile at the steel crossing beam. She probably only had one shot at this without drawing unwanted attention to herself. Holding the hoodie by one arm, she counted to three and then flung the second hoodie arm—the one tied to the plastic dispenser—up and over the beam above her. The dispenser landed right on top of the beam with a clang and then fell over the other side. She reached out and snagged the dispenser with her free hand and now had her hoodie completely wrapped around the beam.

"What's going on in there?" said JB at the door.

"Sorry, just dropped the soap bottle."

"Hurry up."

Natalie's heart was racing. It was now or never. Holding both arms of the hoodie together like a climbing rope, she reached up with her right hand and pulled herself off the sink counter. She was dangling now, her arm muscles straining. She reached her left hand above her right, began lifting her body up through the ceiling, like she was climbing the gym rope back in middle school. She had to ascend only a few feet before she was able to grab the beam with her right hand. Then she pulled herself up completely out of the bathroom ceiling and sat on the beam. Swiveling her shoes out of the way, she replaced the ceiling tile. She set the hoodie and the dispenser on the beam and left them there. It was already a hot morning. She set a mental countdown clock. She figured she had two minutes before JB would show more concern. Maybe three minutes before he angrily burst through the door when she didn't respond to him.

She studied the dark space. There were several big cracks in the warehouse walls, allowing just enough light through to help her maneuver around. Her eyes followed the beam over to the wall of the warehouse, where she noted it was attached to another steel beam—one that traveled the full width of the building. At the very end of the second beam, her eyes narrowed. Looked like a storage space with possibly a ladder. Like a gymnast on a balance beam, she quickly stood, held both arms out to her sides for balance, and then walked toward the wall. When she got there, she stepped over onto the second attached beam. She quickly put one foot after another, moved the full width of the building.

When she got to the end, she confirmed what she thought she'd seen from a distance. A makeshift plywood floor with stacks of boxes, and an opening with an attached metal ladder. She dropped to her knees, stuck her head down through the opening. It was an undeveloped front room with wooden crates stacked up against one wall. Natalie spotted the door to the outside. Her adrenaline kicked up a second notch. Behind her, she heard a muffled voice. She was sure it was JB, questioning her delay. Time was running out. She knew when she didn't respond, he would bust the bathroom door wide open.

Then all hell would break loose. She had only seconds.

Grabbing on to the metal ladder, she began swiftly scaling down into the dusty warehouse room. She heard another outburst from JB, even louder this time, and then the sound of him pounding a fist on the bathroom door.

Natalie dropped to the dirty floor, raced for the door to the outside.

Another crash from the other room. JB had broken into the bathroom.

Natalie turned the door handle, pulled the door open. She peered both ways. To her left, a dirt parking lot and the front of the building, where she spotted the white van. Straight in front of her was a long dirt road that was probably the only way in and out of the property. And to her direct right, at about one hundred feet, a thick set of woods. Although she needed to follow the dirt road, she couldn't go straight at it. JB would come outside and find her right away. She had to go the route of the woods.

More loud yelling behind her. Pushing away from the warehouse building, she sprinted toward the woods, saying a prayer that JB would not immediately step outside and spot her before she disappeared into the trees. If she could create some separation, she could make it out of there. The woods were a comfort zone—she camped every summer with her father and brothers. She knew she could find a track through the trees and make it back to the main road at some point. *If* she could get there.

Running at full speed, she was through tall grass now, the start of the tree line thirty feet ahead of her. Ten feet. Five feet. She hit the tree line like a sprinter crossing the finish line and kept moving deeper into them before she finally stopped, spun around, searched. She found a line of sight back toward the warehouse building; she could now see there were no other buildings on the property. The huge warehouse sat all alone, in the middle of nowhere, which was precisely why they'd chosen the place. Seconds later, JB exited the building and searched frantically in all directions. She ducked back behind a tree, slowly peeked out again. He was cursing and spinning every which way. Looking defeated, he finally pulled a cell phone out of his pocket, punched a button, and held it to his ear.

Natalie set a new mental timer. He was calling in the full gang. Turning, she stepped over fallen branches and ran even deeper into the woods—a safe distance from the dirt road but never fully losing sight of it. For the first time in twelve hours, she breathed a sigh of relief. She was free of the warehouse, free of her captors, free of that black hood, but now she had to somehow get back to DC.

And find Sam.

THIRTY-FOUR

Sam took his first nerve-racking steps off the plane in New Orleans. He hated being forced down a tunnel with no idea what awaited him—like a pig ushered toward the slaughterhouse. Was anyone waiting at the end for him? Federal agents? Mexican assassins? Drug-cartel mercenaries? It was a leap of faith to hope his new alias remained viable and no unwelcome greeters would be at the gate. He couldn't be sure if the police search for him in Mexico would transition into a search for him in the United States. Did the two agencies cooperate with each other? Would Mexico drop its pursuit of him if they found out he was back inside the States? Not that Sam wanted *anyone* to know he was back. He'd prefer Agent Mendoza and the Mexican police still believe he was stuck inside Mexico.

Sam stepped into the clearing of the gate, paused briefly, and took a slow panoramic view of the many faces inside Louis Armstrong New Orleans International Airport. No men in trench coats. No Mexican assassins. No cartel mercenaries. He moved into the flow of people traffic, found an empty gate up the corridor, and tucked himself away into a quiet corner. He quickly pulled out his cell phone, put in the headphones, logged in to Leia's Lounge. A few seconds later, Tommy was inside the video box on his phone screen. He noticed a collection of Red Bull cans scattered across Tommy's desktop. Sam wasn't the only one who'd gotten loaded with caffeine during the night.

"You made it?" Tommy asked.

"I made it. I'm here in New Orleans."

Tommy smiled wide, looking pleased. "So, no trouble with the tunnel?"

"Trouble? Let's just say there's a pissed-off cartel looking for me *and* their stolen car. But, yes, I made it through their tunnel. I'll give you the full story later, *if* I somehow survive this deal. You got anything for me?"

Tommy frowned. "Still no sign of Rich Hebbard. The man hasn't used a credit card anywhere since last night. No cash withdrawals, either. And there's been *zero* activity with his cell phone or e-mails. The guy just disappeared and hasn't resurfaced yet."

"He's here somewhere. I've got to find him."

"I did find out more about Lex Hester, Hebbard's client who owns Arnstead Petroleum. He's the man I initially connected to Francisco Zapata. Hester certainly is a guy capable of doing these heinous things. His hands drip with all sorts of corruption. There are rumors everywhere about bribes, extortion, backroom deals, and even murder."

"Tell me more about him."

"You ever read anything about the devastating hurricane that hit the Texas coast way back in the 1960s? Hurricane Carla?"

"Nope. Why?"

"That's where Hester's story starts."

Tommy took a few minutes to explain about how Hurricane Carla hit the coast of Texas as a Category Four back in 1961. Killed about forty people. Between a quarter and half a million people were evacuated. At the time, it was the largest peacetime evacuation in US history. In Port Lavaca, a small town of probably about eight thousand at the time, there was a local legend about an eighteen-year-old kid, an orphan boy who was known to be a real hell-raiser, who refused to leave town with everyone else. The kid got a fishing boat, packed it with a cooler of beer, pushed it onto the beach, and sat there as the fierce winds and waves began to torture the empty town. When morning hit and local authorities began searching the coast, they found the kid, still alive, and still inside his fishing boat. He'd tied himself to it with a thick rope. Only the boat was now more than two miles away from shore and planted on the roof of a three-story office building. They said when they climbed up, the kid just smiled at them and held up a beer.

"That was Lex Hester. After that, people around there began calling him Hurricane Lex. A shady local oil guy gave him a job to exploit the kid's famous story. That same local oil guy ended up stabbed to death behind a bar a few years later. Most felt it was at Lex's hands, although the police never made a case. By the time Lex is thirty, he's bribed and extorted his way into owning his own small oil company worth five million dollars. Today, the company is worth hundreds of millions. Through the years, Hester will spend time in jail for extortion and corruption; at one point, he's even tried and exonerated in court for the murder of a competing oilman. Hester got more involved in politics two decades ago, pouring tens of millions of dollars into secret PACs, playing both sides, and he began making a lot of new friends as well as enemies. Although he's constantly under suspicion of stealing, bribing, bullying, and everything else in between, he's gotten *very* rich in the process."

Tommy concluded by saying, "One of those friends appears to be Senator Liddell from Alabama. I've found a ton tying the two men together."

"Why does that matter?" asked Sam.

"Because Senator Liddell is also directly connected to Francisco Zapata. I actually have a photo of the three men together—Hester, Zapata, and Liddell, all looking quite chummy."

"What's the connection among the three?"

"I have a theory, but I can't substantiate anything yet."

"Let's hear it."

"There's a very lucrative deepwater government-oil auction scheduled for this coming September in Mexico. Ten blocks in the Gulf of Mexico worth an estimated *ten billion* dollars. It's a huge opportunity potentially worth over forty billion to Mexico in the long run. Apparently, Senator Liddell has played a significant role in negotiating opportunities for certain US oil companies, one of which is Hester's Arnstead Petroleum. For Mexico, Francisco Zapata seems to carry equal political clout when it comes to oil exploration. As I mentioned before, there are a lot of stories out there involving potential corruption with Zapata."

"So you think they were all working together on some secret deal?"

"I can't prove it yet. But I have travel records for Senator Liddell, who's been down to Mexico City six times in just the past year. Get this, Duke: all six times the senator has stayed in the exact same hotel as Francisco Zapata. While I can't confirm they were directly meeting, I don't think it's a coincidence."

Sam was starting to put it all together. "So Hebbard and Hawkins were representing Hester in this deal with Liddell, Hester, and Zapata. Then something happened, and both lawyers wanted out? But they couldn't just walk away? Hawkins mentioned to me that people had already been killed on this deal. So they were looking to turn to the government and seek witness protection. Zapata got to Hawkins yesterday, and now Zapata and Hester are on the hunt for the final key player: Rich Hebbard?"

"That's my working theory."

Sam sighed. "And somehow I managed to get caught in the middle of it."

"Just bad luck, man."

Sam knew there was much more to it. Unable to say the words out loud, he withheld the prospect of Rich Hebbard being his father from Tommy. He also thought back to Hawkins's empty briefcase—something that continued to baffle him. Why was it empty? Had someone already stolen what was inside? Had Hawkins lost his mind? There was still so much about this ordeal that didn't sit right with him.

"I've got to find Hebbard," declared Sam.

"I've got my antennas up."

THIRTY-FIVE

After finishing a four-mile run on the treadmill in the FBI gym, Lloyd met up with Epps inside Krieger's tech lab. Lloyd didn't even bother changing; he just came up in his running shorts and T-shirt, sweat still dripping. Epps said it was urgent. The tech lab had six computer stations that all faced a giant screen. Lloyd always marveled at the fact that all six agents in the room, including Krieger, had not even turned thirty yet. They were just kids. Hell, most were still in diapers when Lloyd first joined the Bureau. Yet these pimple-faced agents had quickly become the most valuable members of his growing team.

Epps and Krieger were already involved in an animated discussion.

"What do you got?" Lloyd asked, stepping into their huddle.

Epps turned to the giant screen. "We think we've got Callahan."

"How?"

"I'll let Krieger explain."

Krieger adjusted his glasses. "Sir, we took the airport-security video of Callahan from Mexico City last night and ran it through a full analysis with our facial-recognition program. Then we tapped into security video from over a hundred different points in Mexico City, as well as all along the southern part of the United States. Basically, anywhere we thought Callahan might show. Airports, train depots, bus stations, and *all* border crossings. We got a legitimate hit on him ten minutes ago."

"Where?" asked Lloyd, perking up.

"New Orleans," Epps replied, pointing at the screen.

Krieger punched a button on the computer directly in front of him, and airport-security video appeared in the center of the giant screen. A man was walking down the main corridor wearing a black T-shirt, blue jeans, and what looked like a Dallas Cowboys cap on his head. He held a black backpack over his shoulder. Krieger paused it, enhanced the video to show a clear and up-close image of the man's face. Lloyd had to admit it looked a hell of a lot like the same guy in the airport video from last night.

"How sure are you, Krieger?" Lloyd asked.

"Sheila says ninety-four percent."

"Sheila?" Lloyd questioned.

"Sorry, sir, that's what we call the facial-recognition program."

"Ninety-four percent is *really* solid," Epps mentioned.

Krieger nodded. "Sheila has never registered anything over ninety-six percent. It's about as sure as it gets in this situation."

Lloyd's head was spinning. "We still think the Gray Wolf is in New Orleans as well?"

"All signs point to it, Chief," Epps confirmed.

Lloyd sighed, cursed. "Okay, Mike, call Mitch and have them get the jet ready. We're going to New Orleans. And send all of this to the New Orleans office ASAP."

"Yes, sir," Epps said.

THIRTY-SIX

Natalie stayed off the dirt road, instead fleeing through ditches, woods, and farmland. She did all of it within eyesight of the road, knowing it had to eventually spill her out somewhere more prominent. Twice, she had to duck away behind trees—once when the white van sped up quickly behind her, JB behind the steering wheel, and then again, just now, when the white van raced back in her direction. Her heart had flooded with adrenaline when the white van skidded to a stop not fifty yards from her, dust circling up behind it. JB jumped out and began searching the woods in her direction. Natalie was on the ground, chest down, just barely peeking out from behind a tree. She could feel the rapid thumping of her heartbeat in her chest. JB's eyes slowly peered over her and then farther down into the woods. Frustrated, he climbed back into the white van and spun the wheels. The van moved down the dirt road, back toward the warehouse.

When the van was out of sight, Natalie was up and sprinting again. Fortunately, she was a conditioned runner, so long distances were nothing to her—although she didn't usually run at this fast a clip, and certainly not while jumping over tree branches and stepping through mud. Her familiarity with running allowed her to keep track of her overall distance traveled. She thought she was about two miles away from the warehouse already when the winding dirt road *finally* met up with a paved road. She stepped into the middle of the main road, panting heavily, not sure whether to head right or left. No cars could be seen in either direction. There were no road markers that gave her any indication of her current whereabouts, so she chose left. She stayed on the pavement this time, as the running was much easier, and she felt she had enough of a view in all directions to see if a car was approaching.

A mile down the paved road, Natalie spotted an old farm truck that was parked at the head of a long dirt drive. An old man in denim coveralls worked on a white wooden fence and hammered a new board into place. She was out of breath when she rushed up to him. He turned, startled by her sudden appearance. He looked to be in his seventies, trim of build, with a thick white mustache and a tan weathered face. He immediately reminded her of what her own father might well look like in ten years. Rugged but healthy.

"I need help," she exclaimed, trying to catch her breath.

"What's wrong, miss?" he said, looking genuinely concerned.

"I need to call the police. Do you have a phone?"

He shook his head. "I'm sorry, I don't carry a cell phone with me. Are you in some kind of trouble?"

"I will be if I don't get to the police right away."

The old man stood straight, wiped his hands on a towel. "Well, the police station is just up the road from here a few miles. I can certainly drive you there, if you want."

"Yes, please!" she begged. "Thank you."

She jumped into the front seat of the farm truck as the man climbed behind the wheel. He turned the key in the ignition, and the truck sputtered to a start. Natalie glanced in the rearview mirror at the street behind them. Still no sign of JB and the white van. She exhaled. The old man pulled out onto the paved road.

"By the way," Natalie said, finally recovering her breath, "where are we?"

He looked at her curiously. "Boonsboro."

Natalie nodded, felt relieved to finally put a pin in the map.

Boonsboro, Maryland.

They were sixty miles outside DC.

THIRTY-SEVEN

Boonsboro was a picturesque town of a few thousand, which meant they did not have a traditional police station. The station was actually an old two-story white colonial house with a front porch that sat in the middle of an acre of land. The only way to know it was a police station was the big wooden sign out front with the flags and the police cruiser in the driveway. Natalie thanked the old farmer profusely. She then hurried inside the house through the front door. There were only two people inside: a female administrator who sat behind a desk and looked to be in her fifties, with her red hair pulled back into a tight bun, and a balding uniformed cop of maybe forty who was standing nearby and chatting it up with her. They both looked genuinely surprised to have an unexpected visitor. Natalie figured there was probably not a whole lot of crime happening around this small town. Boonsboro was about to be introduced to a full-on abduction-and-hostage situation.

With urgency, Natalie began to explain the direness of her situation to the bald officer, who seemed genuinely shocked at the mention of an abduction. He quickly ushered her into a back conference room and began taking down copious notes. The red-haired woman, who introduced herself as Gloria, brought her a cold bottle of water. When Natalie told Officer Charlie Riddell everything she had stored in her mind, he said he needed to make a call to his chief. He left her alone in the room.

Gloria returned with a package of cheese crackers and a banana. She thought Natalie might be hungry. Natalie asked for the bathroom. Gloria walked her through the back door of the conference room and down a hallway that led to a single-toilet bathroom in the back of the house. Inside, Natalie cleaned the dirt and mud off her hands, washed her face in the sink, and tried her best to sort out her messy hair in the mirror. It wasn't much help. She badly needed a shower. She stared at herself in the mirror, took another deep breath, and exhaled. On the one hand, she was relieved to be away from her captors and the warehouse. On the other hand, like a good journalist, she was eager to start putting together the pieces of this complex puzzle. She wanted to talk to Sam.

She returned to the hallway and reentered the conference room. Gloria again checked on her, asked if she needed anything else, showing deep concern for Natalie's overall well-being. Natalie appreciated it but insisted she was fine. Gloria then said something that surprised Natalie.

"There are two federal agents out here who want to speak with you. They said they've been actively looking for you. Officer Charlie is giving them details of your situation right now."

Natalie felt a check in her gut. "How do you know they're federal agents?"

Gloria shrugged. "They have proper identification." She tilted her head at Natalie, her forehead bunched. "Everything okay, dear?"

"Yes, thanks."

When Gloria shut the door to the conference room, Natalie bolted out of her seat and went to the small window in the front of the room. She peeked through the blinds to the front room, cursed. Standing in a huddle with Officer Charlie were two of her new pals, JB and Abe—only now they were both wearing the dark windbreakers you might see on federal agents. She was shocked. Was there any way these guys worked for the government? She'd been grabbed, hooded, forcefully tossed into the back of an unmarked van. She couldn't fathom it was the work of the feds. No way. Natalie felt panic ripple through her. How did they find her? Who were these guys? What would they do with her next? She knew one thing for sure—she sure as hell wasn't going to wait around to find out.

She rushed to the back door of the conference room, quietly returned to the hallway. She'd noticed it a few minutes ago on the way to the restroom: a black purse hung on a hook by the back door, along with several sets of keys. Natalie grabbed the purse, then considered the two cars parked out back. A Jeep sitting up on huge tires. Probably Officer Charlie's personal car. The other was a black Honda Civic. She looked for a set of Honda keys on the hooks, found them. Natalie heard Officer Charlie in the conference room call her name. She opened the back door, jumped down a few steps, and ran over to the Civic. She unlocked the door with the key fob, jumped inside, threw the black purse into the passenger seat. She quickly started up the car, shifted it into reverse.

When she was shifting back into drive, she saw the men step out the back of the house, look over at her. Officer Charlie seemed confused. JB and Abe locked eyes on her and wasted little time in scrambling back around the side of the house, obviously intent on following her. Natalie slammed her foot down on the gas pedal. The Civic raced forward. She took the side road beside the police station, returned to the main road. Peering over to her left, she spotted Abe and JB jumping into a gray Chevy sedan.

Natalie hit the gas again, spun the tires. Zipping down Main Street, she saw a sign for US 40 Alt East—back toward DC. The tires spun again, and she raced around two puttering old trucks. She kept her foot down, and the Civic quickly sped up past seventy miles per hour and headed toward eighty. When the Civic hit ninety, she could feel the little car start to vibrate under duress. She was also under serious duress and had to remind herself to keep breathing. She hadn't driven this fast since she was fleeing from Redrock military helicopters last fall. If nothing else, that experience had given her a bit of confidence that she could handle this type of escape. She zigged in and out of slower-moving traffic on the highway. Squinting in her rearview mirror, she cursed again. They were back there and already gaining. Natalie knew she couldn't stay on the highway all the way back to DC. She'd surely wreck the car—or worse.

She needed a way to lose them, and quickly.

Thinking of a plan, she punched her foot down farther.

THIRTY-EIGHT

The Honda Civic inched its way past one hundred miles per hour.

At this point, Natalie wasn't sure she would even stop for a cop, should she spot the flashing lights behind her. Not with the gray Chevy sedan so close on her tail. If JB and Abe had fooled the Boonsboro cops with their fake credentials, she would fully expect them to convince a common patrol officer in Middletown or Braddock Heights. Even a highway cop would likely turn her right over, maybe help push her into the back of the Chevy sedan himself.

The thought was terrifying.

The Civic reached 110 miles per hour, the car seeming to barely hold together, pushing Natalie's heart up in her throat. She could still see the Chevy sedan gaining ground on her. Her hands felt sweaty on the steering wheel, which was not a good sensation with the small car flying so fast down the highway. Natalie saw a sign up ahead and veered onto Washington National Pike.

She was getting close now. Time to try a new evasion tactic.

She spotted the exit sign, slowed as to not crash the Civic, and pulled off the highway. The Francis Scott Key Mall sat right alongside the highway. She'd shopped there once before with some girlfriends when they were on their way back to the city after staying at a country bed-and-breakfast. Natalie ran a red light, causing a Lexus SUV to swerve and barely miss crashing into her. She stomped the gas again, entered the mall parking lot, and nearly took out an older couple walking too close to the middle of a row of cars. Natalie sped right up to the curb directly outside Macy's department store. She slammed on her brakes, shifted the car into park, and grabbed the black purse from the passenger seat.

Jumping out of the car, she hurried toward the glass doors. As she pushed through them, she took a glance back. The boys were right there behind her. The Chevy skidded to a stop on the curb directly behind the Civic. Natalie spun around, raced deeper into the mall. She dashed all the way through Macy's, hit the main shopping corridor. The mall was busy with shoppers, which is what she both hoped for and expected. She looked for a quick place to hide, darted inside a Victoria's Secret, and took a position behind a rack near the back but still with a clear view of the shoppers walking by in front of the store. She politely waved off a store clerk without taking her eyes off the corridor for a single moment.

Come on, boys. Where are you?

Thirty seconds later, she saw them. JB and Abe were still wearing the dark windbreakers. Ducking completely out of view, she peeked out again. The boys split up, headed in opposite directions. This made Natalie uneasy. Now she'd have to evade them from two different directions.

Easing back to the front of the store, she saw Abe heading away from her to the left. No sign of JB anywhere on her right. She couldn't hide out in a lingerie shop all day. The plan was to get in and out of the mall in a hurry, hope her tagalongs would waste a lot of time looking for her. Taking a deep breath, she stepped back into the main corridor and sidled up behind two girls. She then slipped inside an Aeropostale clothing store.

Pausing for a moment, she took inventory of the other shoppers, making sure JB hadn't stolen away for a look inside the store before her. Natalie went to work quickly, snagging a light-blue blouse off one rack, a new pair of white shorts off another rack, some deck shoes, and finally a dark-blue stylish baseball cap. Taking the items to the counter, she dug in Gloria's wallet and pulled out a Visa card. She said a quick prayer that Gloria had not yet reached her limit on the credit card or had not immediately reported it as stolen.

She handed the Visa card to the clerk, who swiped it through the machine. Natalie watched closely, her right leg bouncing up and down nervously. The clerk asked her to sign inside the digital box. Natalie exhaled, quickly scribbled an ineligible name. The clerk bagged up the items, and Natalie asked if she could use the dressing room to change into them. She got a curious look at that point; nevertheless, the clerk led her back to a dressing room.

Natalie peeled herself out of her white tank top and jeans and put on the new items. They weren't a perfect fit. She did not have the luxury of trying on different sizes. Tugging the bill of the new blue baseball cap low on her forehead, she stuffed as much of her brown hair up underneath the cap as possible. She stared at her appearance in the mirror, pleased with the dramatic change. Would it be enough?

After shoving all her old items into the shopping bag, she left the store and took a straight path back toward Macy's. She had to resist the urge to walk too fast and stand out. When she was within fifty feet of the department store, JB stepped out in front of her, causing Natalie to scream on the inside—although he was searching faces behind her. He'd been inside an H&M store on her left. It took everything within Natalie not to halt in place, like a deer in headlights, which she knew would instantly blow her cover. Instead, she kept walking. One shaky foot after another. He was ten feet to her left. Five feet. Natalie passed by him without incident, entered Macy's, again fought the urge to immediately spin around and put eyes on him. When she was well inside the store, she casually veered off behind a clothing rack, took her first look. She didn't spot JB anywhere, which made her nervous. She'd much rather know exactly where he was at the moment—especially being so close to her exit.

Natalie turned around, walked briskly toward the same doors she'd entered twenty minutes ago. Pausing by the doors, she peered out at the parking lot. Both cars were still parked illegally on the curb. She was glad to not find a tow truck hooking up the Civic. There were no eyes looking back at her from inside the Chevy sedan.

Natalie stepped outside, her breath short. As she neared, she couldn't help but run toward the Civic. She opened the driver's door, dropped inside, started the car. She shifted into drive, punched the gas pedal. As she exited the mall parking lot, she kept her eyes glued on her rearview mirror until she could no longer see the parked Chevy.

The boys were still inside the mall. *Search away, fellas.*

She exhaled. Now back to DC.

THIRTY-NINE

Sam took a cab from the airport to the heart of the French Quarter.

The address listed for Rich Hebbard's law firm put him on a busy sidewalk right outside a high-rise office building on Canal Street—the Mississippi River only a block away. Climbing out of the cab, Sam felt moisture quickly bead up on his skin; it was a muggy morning, the air thick and sticky. He entered the building, hopped on an elevator, and ascended to the sixth floor. Stepping out, he searched both ways, spotted a title company and a graphic-design studio off to his left. He walked down the opposite hallway, where he passed by a software firm and an insurance company before he finally stood directly outside a shiny wooden door at the end of the hallway labeled Hebbard & Hawkins, LLP.

Sam paused, feeling the weight of the moment.

Was there any chance Hebbard would be hiding inside?

Was he about to come face-to-face with his real father?

He took a deep breath, exhaled. Only one way to find out. He reached down, grabbed the door handle, only to discover it was locked. He tried to peer into the frosted window beside the door. It looked like the lights were all off inside the lobby, which seemed odd to him. After all, it was a normal business day and within normal business hours. Why would *everyone* at the firm currently be out of the office?

Sam examined the door handle. Just a regular key slot—nothing high-tech like a card key. He thought it would be unusual for the office to have an alarm system with security guards stationed in the lobby at all hours. He knocked, waited. No one came to the door. He tried a second time, just to be sure. Still no answer. He wanted to at least get inside the office and have a look around, see if he could find *anything* that might lead him to Hebbard. He glanced down the hallway when two men in suits exited the door of the insurance company. They gave a quick look in his direction and then walked away toward the elevators.

Sam waited until he heard an elevator door open and shut, then he quickly knelt in front of the door and unzipped his black backpack. He'd hit a hardware store on the way from the airport and had purchased a few items he thought he might need at some point along the journey: duct tape, a short bundle of black rope, several screwdrivers, and a four-piece pick-and-probe set, which is usually used in working with car engines. Sam had different plans for them. He grabbed two tools from the pick-and-probe set, carefully inserted them into the heavy-duty key slot. He put pressure down with one tool and used the other to scrub the lock pins until he heard the lock fully release.

He stepped inside the dark lobby of the law office.

"Hello?" Sam called out. "Anyone here?"

No reply. No sounds at all. He found a light switch on the lobby wall and flipped it up. The ceiling lights flickered on, leaving Sam completely confused. Although he was standing in what looked like a small lobby, it was completely empty. No receptionist desk, no chairs, no sofa, no rugs, no art on the walls. What the hell? He walked over to an inner hallway, where he found another light switch. The fluorescents in the hallway popped on. Again, he shook his head. There was a wide-open space in the middle of the office suite where he guessed cubicles would normally go, but this area was also barren. Just carpet and windows. He searched even further, hitting light switches in all six of the enclosed offices that hugged the right side of the suite, along with a large conference room. Every single space inside the office suite was empty. The *only* item he found in the whole place was a phone system that was plugged into the wall and sat on the carpet inside the corner office.

Sam pulled out his cell phone, dialed the main number he had listed for Hebbard & Hawkins, LLP. The phone on the floor in front of him rang four times, shocking him, and then a recording greeted him with words from a chipper female voice.

"You've reached the law offices of Hebbard and Hawkins. We're unable to take your call at the moment, but please leave us a detailed message, and we will return your call as soon as possible. Your business is very important to us. Have a great day."

When the voice mail beeped, Sam waited a few seconds without saying anything, then hung up. He watched as the voice mail light on the phone system went from dark to a blinking red. His call was the only voice mail? What was going on?

He stepped back into the wide-open middle space again, hands on hips. None of this made any sense. Why was the entire office suite empty? Had Hebbard and Hawkins already cleaned house and gotten rid of everyone and *everything*, as they prepared to turn on their own client? Was that part of their exit strategy? It seemed highly unlikely— shutting down an entire office of this magnitude was no easy and quick matter. It could take several weeks to coordinate. The dramatic ordeal with Hawkins and Hebbard felt like it had all blown up on them within the past couple of days.

There had to be another explanation.

Sam shut off all the lights, returned to the main hallway, and then stepped inside the office suite for the insurance company next door. A young female receptionist greeted him with a bright smile. He could hear the sounds of normal office activity coming from the hallway behind the reception area—phones ringing, printers churning, people talking—all the noises he expected to hear down the hallway.

"Can I help you?" the receptionist asked.

"I sure hope so. I'm looking for the attorneys who work in the office space next door. Rich Hebbard and Tom Hawkins. Do you know either of them?"

She shook her head. "No, sir. We haven't met anyone from the law firm yet. I actually don't think they've moved into the office. The sign on the door only went up a few days ago."

"Oh, okay. So you haven't seen *anyone* come and go from over there?"

"No, sir. Sorry."

"Thank you very much."

Sam returned to the hallway, looked back over toward the door for Hebbard & Hawkins, LLP, trying to make some kind of sense of the situation. Tommy had said the firm was started by the two men more than five years ago. There was no other office address listed. If the firm was somehow in the middle of an office move, Tommy would have discovered it and shared that with Sam. The firm listed a staff of ten people. Sam had names for members of the firm's administrative team, three paralegals, and even two associates. So where the hell was everyone? Why would a phone system be installed inside the office suite that was attached to the main number for the law firm? That perplexed him the most. He felt dizzy with this unexpected twist. However, he couldn't let it slow him down.

He still had to find Rich Hebbard.

FORTY

Hebbard's home address was within a few blocks' walking distance of his law firm's bizarrely empty office space. Sam moved up the sidewalk at a brisk pace, trying to stay in the shadows as much as possible, hesitating as he turned street corners, always watching his back. Although he felt slightly safer in New Orleans—and out of the direct dangers of Mexico City—he knew he could not become lax and take any unnecessary chances. The fact that someone out there might have the capability to infiltrate Tommy's secure network was cause for great alarm. There were certainly men out there still trying to assassinate Sam.

He turned a corner, came up on Governor Nicholls Street. According to the info Tommy had given him, Hebbard's residence was an exquisite three-level yellow town house with dark-green shutters and an upstairs balcony that sat on a row of other fancy town houses. It was upper-class living in the lower French Quarter, and Sam felt like it suited a wealthy attorney. He peered in the front window beside the brown wooden door. There didn't appear to be any activity going on inside. He saw no movement, spotted no lights that were on, and heard nothing coming from any of the rooms. Tommy mentioned that Hebbard had an ex-wife and two older kids who all lived in other parts of the country. There was no mention of a girlfriend or a roommate in Tommy's file on the man.

Sam knocked on the door. He figured he might as well go for the direct hit, see if the missing man might show up on his own doorstep. Not likely, but he could leave no stone unturned. No answer. He knocked again. Nothing. Just like at the law office, Sam was searching for any bread crumbs that might somehow lead him to finding the man.

Sam turned around, considered his options. There were *a lot* of people out and about on the sidewalks, many looking like tourists. Sam felt it was way too risky to try to pick the front door lock right there out in the open. Especially when he spotted a New Orleans PD patrol car parked only a block over. He stepped away from the front door, peered up at the balcony, tried to think of another way inside without drawing attention to himself. A potential answer came when he noticed a drive-through security gate at the very end of the row of town houses suddenly open and a shiny Mercedes SUV pull out into the street. Private parking—which meant there was a back way into the town houses.

Sam rushed down the sidewalk, a walk-run, trying to still look casual. He arrived just as the security gate was within a few feet of closing, took a quick glance around him again for any watching eyes, then slipped inside the gate at the last moment. Behind the gate, he found ten covered parking spaces that belonged to the five town houses on the row. Half of the parking spots were empty—including the two that had the address for Hebbard.

Sam walked past the parking spots and found a small courtyard with benches and a water fountain that led to the rear entrances of the town houses. Hebbard's place was the middle unit in the row. The homes all had second-story balconies in the back, too, and they overlooked the private courtyard. Sam didn't spot any residents currently sitting outside. He worked quickly with his tools to pick the lock of Hebbard's back door. When he opened it, he heard the familiar beeping of a security alarm waiting to be disarmed. He was ready for it—Tommy had hacked the code. Sam found the alarm pad on the wall, typed in the code, and the beeping went silent.

Exhaling, he hurried down the rear hallway until it spilled out into a large kitchen and dining space. Considering the situation, Sam had anticipated that he might find Hebbard's place completely ransacked, but everything looked normal. Had no one else come looking there? The town house was impeccably clean and well decorated, like it was the showcase for an interior-design studio.

Sam moved through the formal dining room, around an antique table with a huge crystal chandelier above it, and stepped into a small living room. A black grand piano filled one corner. A huge sofa was pressed up against the back wall along with two large chairs that sat in front of an ornate fireplace. Sam found it odd that there was nothing personalized about the space. No random mail sitting out on kitchen counters, no photos of kids hanging on the walls, no magazines with subscription labels, no personal mementos on bookshelves.

Sam quickly moved up the narrow stairs to the second floor, where he found two bedrooms and another small living space. The immaculate decorating continued on the second floor. All the beds were made, all pillows in place, all bathrooms perfect. He checked the medicine cabinet in the master bathroom and found common everyday toiletries: toothbrush, toothpaste, deodorant, shaving cream, cologne. No prescription medicine. The toiletries made him believe someone did live there, but he'd yet to find *anything* that told him it was actually Rich Hebbard.

He *finally* found personal items on the third floor—a large room that had been turned into a home office. An antique wooden desk sat in the middle, with a wall of floor-to-ceiling antique shelves behind it. There was a stack of business cards in a container on the desk: RICH HEBBARD, ATTORNEY AT LAW, HEBBARD & HAWKINS, LLP. He found a notepad with scribbled handwriting on it, probably notes on a case, but nothing that seemed pertinent to Sam's situation. There was no computer on the desk. Sam guessed that Hebbard used a laptop and currently had it with him. He hoped he would log in somewhere and Tommy could track him down. No word of that yet.

Sam checked the drawers of the desk, which were filled with common office supplies: notepads, pens, stapler, three-hole punch, and an assortment of random business cards. He searched through all the business cards but found nothing that seemed relevant. He moved in behind the plush leather office chair and scanned the antique shelves behind the desk. Mostly legal books. A few mementos like a football signed by Archie Manning and a basketball signed by Pete Maravich. There were also a few framed photos. Sam picked them up one at a time. The first framed photo showed a man maybe a few years younger than Sam at what looked like a ski resort. The man wore a blue ski jacket and goggles and was standing in the snow while holding his skis in one hand. The second framed photo was a woman of similar age on a sailboat. She was smiling wide, in white shorts and bikini top, sunglasses propped up on her head. There was a framed photo of the same guy and girl standing on both sides of an older man who matched the picture of Hebbard that the black-haired woman had given him in Mexico City. Hebbard was wearing a New Orleans Saints jersey. Hebbard had his arms around both, so Sam naturally assumed these were his two kids. A law student in North Carolina and a nurse in Tallahassee.

Sam set the photos back in place. Then he noticed a much smaller framed photo on the top shelf. He did a startled double take, couldn't believe his eyes for a moment. He reached up, snagged it off the shelf. It was an aged photo of a newborn baby wrapped in a blanket. It wasn't just any baby. The picture was the same exact photo that his mom had in her collection. Sam felt the air rush out of him and had to sit down in the office chair.

He couldn't believe it. He didn't want to believe it.

The baby in the picture was Sam.

He thought about his mom, wondered why she'd withheld this information. Was his whole life built on a lie? Then he thought about this man, Rich Hebbard, who perhaps was his real father. If Hebbard had known about Sam from the time he was a baby, why the hell had he never made an appearance in his life? Why leave him out there on his own to suffer so much? The man had resources. Why hadn't he helped? The biggest question of all kept pushing to the surface: Why was Hebbard making an appearance now?

Sam closed his eyes, feeling a new wave of confusion and anger.

Would the pain *ever* stop?

June 12
One month ago

Sam flew home to Denver.

After months of struggling, he decided he had to get out of town. He wasn't getting any better in DC—he was only getting worse. He needed to go somewhere else to clear his head and seek counsel. If he and Natalie had any future, he needed to find his way again. Pastor Isaiah and Alisha were surprised by his unannounced visit but nevertheless welcomed him like their own prodigal son. Sam knew he needed to do something vastly different. Natalie was being incredibly patient—more than he ever deserved. However, the hollow hole in his chest was not mending; it was only growing bigger with each passing day. He felt more lost every moment of every day since he'd put his mom in the ground. Natalie was scared. He could see it in her eyes and hear it in her voice. She had every right to feel that way since he felt a growing panic swelling up within him like a slow but emerging flood. She'd taken another chance on him. After going through so much pain during their first breakup, she'd opened her heart back up to him again and let him take full residence. Sam felt a growing sense of regret about it, as he was losing all faith in himself, even though Natalie tried to ease his anguish.

While sitting on the plane, he kept replaying her last words to him before he left for the airport: "I swear I'd do it all over again, Sam. I mean it. You're worth it to me."

Sam played with the kids in the living room while Alisha whipped up his favorite lasagna in the kitchen. He wrestled with the two boys, who couldn't get enough of it. They piled on top of him, grabbed him around the neck, wanting him to toss them both in the air. He happily obliged. Then he allowed Grace to show him her artwork. Pastor Isaiah returned from a meeting at Zion Baptist Church and asked Sam to accompany him over to the shelter, which was just up the street. Sam had volunteered at the shelter for a year when he first came to live with them. It was a transformative time and a big part of the reason he'd decided to pursue law school—he wanted to help people who struggled to help themselves. Pastor Isaiah allowed Sam to make small talk, catching him up on things around the church, how the kids were doing, but Sam knew a deeper conversation was stirring. Pastor Isaiah just had a way about him. Sam welcomed it. It was the real reason he was back in Denver. A desperate cry for help to the man who'd already saved his life once.

They made the rounds at the shelter, saying hello to many of the guests who were eating in the small cafeteria. Some of them Sam remembered from when he was there ten years ago. For a few minutes, they talked with the new shelter director, a huge black man of forty with the greatest smile. They worked up a good sweat unloading boxes of food from the back of a delivery truck. Pastor Isaiah grabbed two bottles of cold water and pulled out a chair at a metal table on the back patio of the shelter. He motioned for Sam to take the other chair.

"Tell me what's really going on," Pastor Isaiah said, his eyes already peering deep into Sam's soul. "I know you're not here on vacation."

"I just can't seem to pull it back together."

"It's painful to lose a loved one, Sam."

"Excruciating."

"But you're not here because of your mother. You're here because of Natalie."

Sam looked up, surprised by Pastor Isaiah's innate ability to discern the specific source of his pain and anguish, although he shouldn't be. Pastor Isaiah had always been able to read him like no one else he'd ever been around. It had been that way from the beginning, when Pastor Isaiah caught him sleeping in the pews of Zion Baptist Church when he was a sixteen-year-old homeless street kid. It continued after the man showed up unexpectedly at the Youth Detention Center, where Sam was serving a twelve-month sentence for juvenile car theft, offered him a second chance, and brokered a deal with the judge for Sam to come home with him. Pastor Isaiah had walked Sam through every difficult season of life ever since—including his first devastating breakup with Natalie two years ago.

Sam nodded but didn't say anything else. He took a swig of cold water. He'd longed for this moment with Pastor Isaiah for the past month, for the man to say the magic words that would make everything better, like he always seemed to do. However, the weight of this thing felt even bigger than Pastor Isaiah. What if there were no healing words? What if he got back on the plane to DC and *nothing* had changed? The gravity of the moment made his chest tighten. He felt another anxiety attack coming on. He'd been having them regularly the past few weeks, which was a big part of the reason why he'd finally gotten on a plane to Denver. He thought he was going to die if he didn't do something drastic.

"Sam," Pastor Isaiah said, authority in his voice. He grabbed Sam's knee in his strong hand and squeezed. "Look at me, son."

Sam hesitantly looked up, locked eyes with the man.

"It's okay. Do you hear me? You're going to be okay. You're not broken—at least not in a way that God can't heal. I promise you that."

Sam nodded unconvincingly.

"Do you believe that?" Pastor Isaiah asked him.

Sam nodded again but couldn't speak.

"I need to hear you say it, son," Pastor Isaiah instructed.

Sam somehow got the words out. "I believe it."

As soon as he said it, tears started falling. Pastor Isaiah pulled him in even closer, his arm wrapped around Sam's shoulders as he sobbed into the pastor's chest. Although he didn't fully realize it, Sam so desperately needed to hear Pastor Isaiah say those exact words. He was terrified that maybe this time the words wouldn't come from the man's mouth, that even Pastor Isaiah might finally recognize that Sam was a lost cause and beyond any divine hope. That maybe he really should be discarded, like a bag of trash, like so many of his foster dads had done over the years. Pastor Isaiah let him have a good cry for a few minutes before he pulled back and looked Sam directly in the eyes with that perfect smile.

"Okay, now that your head believes it, Sam, how about we spend the next few days trying to convince your heart?"

"Sounds good."

FORTY-ONE

The Pontalba buildings were redbrick four-story apartments built in the 1840s that sat alongside Jackson Square, the historic New Orleans landmark. The ground floors housed numerous shops and restaurants. The upper floors were apartments with outstanding views overlooking the pristine square, the statue of Andrew Jackson on horseback so prominent in the middle, as well as the dozens of artists, musicians, and street performers who currently occupied the street in front of the historic Saint Louis Cathedral.

The Gray Wolf stepped out onto the narrow balcony of a top-level apartment unit directly in the middle, took inventory of his surroundings. He glanced right and left. There was no one currently on the balconies next to him. That was good. Unwanted company could greatly complicate matters. For a few minutes, he watched a couple of the street performers in front of the cathedral. A unicyclist was pedaling while juggling bowling pins. Another performer was painted in solid gold, pretending to be a statue. Gerlach then peered over to the Mississippi River, a block to his left. He could see a classic American steamboat in the river waters, draped in red, white, and blue decorations, flags waving, and the word NATCHEZ painted in bold letters on the side of the boat.

His eyes went back to the square below him, where he scanned the sidewalks, the benches, and the people. Hundreds of tourists were out and about, as he had been just a few moments ago, enjoying coffee and beignets. The sun was drifting in and out of puffy clouds. He could hear jazz music coming from the sidewalks below. The southern city had a charm that suited him. If Gerlach wasn't there to kill, he felt he would like this place immensely.

Gerlach noticed the trees below him shift slightly back and forth. A subtle breeze was blowing in from the water. Not enough to impact his shot.

He stepped back inside the well-decorated apartment. A key to the unit had been left for him inside the minivan. When finished, he would dump the vehicle in a junkyard outside the city, where his accomplices were instructed to completely destroy it, leaving no trace of his use. Precise adherence to his process was critical for a successful mission.

He'd entered the Pontalba just a few minutes ago wearing a black-knit cap, glasses, and fake beard, and carrying his large black bag with him.

Gerlach checked his watch. Three minutes ahead of schedule.

Unzipping the black bag, he stared down at the impressive rifle. He worked only with a Dragunov SVD sniper rifle. The Russians knew how to equip to kill from a distance. It had been his trusted friend and comrade for more than two decades. As he had a thousand times before, he went through his meticulous routine of putting the rifle together and double-checking all the calibrations. Satisfied, he found a short antique cabinet against the wall and pushed it over into the balcony opening. He made sure it remained hidden inside the unit and behind the curtains. He set the gun's bipod on top of the cabinet and allowed the long rifle barrel to peek out from the curtains.

Gerlach removed the glasses and placed his sharp eye to the custom-built scope. He shifted and adjusted, scanned the buildings across the street, worked his way over to the artists and street performers, and then settled in on Andrew Jackson riding high on his horse in the middle of Jackson Square. This was one of the easiest kill shots of his career. His target would be within a block of his window. Gerlach had successfully eliminated at a distance of 1,520 meters. The prime minister of Serbia. A charming man with whom he'd actually had coffee once to discuss a different job. Four grandchildren, who'd called him *Deda*, played at the prime minister's feet as he spoke casually of eliminating an opponent. Gerlach had split the two bodyguards just a half second before the prime minister stepped inside the vehicle. There were strong winds that day, requiring extreme precision. Because of the distance and the conditions, he'd considered it the crown achievement of his career. That shot had turned him into a legend. It was the central focus of the BBC profile.

Gerlach smiled at the memory.

He repositioned himself, eye to scope, and took a few deep breaths.

He could feel the adrenaline begin to pump in his veins, like it always did when he was ready to engage a new target. While in most sports, adrenaline could enhance an athlete's ability to perform at the highest level, it was not an advantage in shooting at a distance. Gerlach closed his eyes, counted slowly to five in German. *Eins. Zwei. Drei. Vier. Fünf.* The nerves settled and gradually vanished. His breathing was normal again. Zen-like. Perfect calm spread through his entire being. Mind. Body. Soul. Spirit. He was in another place. A necessary place. A killing place.

The Gray Wolf waited.

FORTY-TWO

Sam was back on the sidewalk in front of Hebbard's yellow town house, his mind continuing to churn out questions after finding his own baby picture in the man's home office. How had Hebbard gotten it? Was it really true? Was everything he'd thought about his father a complete lie? Had his mom chosen to hide the truth from him for some reason?

Processing through dozens of different conversations he'd had with his mom over the past year, he searched for answers. One particular conversation stood out—a conversation they never got to finish, interrupted by the doctor just a few hours before her death. She'd told Sam that she needed to share something important with him. He could remember her exact words. *It's something I've wanted to tell you for a long time, from the first day you showed up in Houston, but I never felt quite right about it. Honestly, I was afraid you'd get angry at me all over again.*

Sam felt numb. Was this what she wanted to say?

While he was standing there, still dazed, a black kid of maybe ten, wearing jeans, Nike basketball shoes, and a Pelicans NBA jersey, came bouncing right up to him.

"Yo, mister, got something for you."

Sam looked down at the smiling kid. "Me?"

"Yes, sir."

The kid held out a folded piece of white paper.

Sam took it. "What's this?"

The kid shrugged. "Beats me. Some lady up the street gave me twenty bucks to bring it over and give it to you."

Sam unfolded the paper, read it. Short and sweet.

Jackson Square. Ten minutes.

"Who gave this to you?" he asked the kid.

"Some lady on the corner over there. I was minding my own business, and she said she'd pay me to walk this over to you."

Sam peered over toward the corner, didn't see any lady.

"What did she look like?" Sam asked.

The kid shrugged again. "I dunno. Black hair, gray jacket."

Sam felt a spike of adrenaline. Black hair, gray trench coat? It had to be the same woman from Mexico City. The same woman who'd given him the windbreaker while he was inside the federal police building and met him at El Ángel to give him his so-called assignment instructions. How had she found him? How could she possibly know he was in New Orleans?

Had he been followed? No possible way.

He suddenly felt very uneasy and exposed.

Sam briskly walked the five blocks to Jackson Square. His eyes were bouncing *everywhere*. Any sense of false security he'd felt after getting out of Mexico alive and making his way to New Orleans had disappeared. He stepped out onto Chartres Street next to Jackson Square and maneuvered slowly through the crowds of tourists gathered around the street artists, musicians, and performers. He glanced over toward Saint Louis Cathedral, as well as the Presbytère and Cabildo, the buildings on its right and left, but saw no one staring right back at him. A street band was pumping out jazz as a large group gathered around them. Sam crossed slowly through the crowd, searching for the mystery woman in the gray trench coat.

He stepped out into the landscaped grounds of Jackson Square. He paused behind a giant water fountain, scanned the circular sidewalks. His eyes moved slowly left to right, stopping at the statue of Andrew Jackson, and then continuing on from there. Then he spotted her. She was sitting alone on a bench under a tree, just waiting. Same woman. He was sure of it. She wore the same gray trench coat as last night in Mexico City. Only she was now wearing sunglasses. He surveyed the area all around her, looking for her two bodyguards. He didn't spot anyone at the moment, but surely, they were around somewhere.

His hands felt sweaty, his heart racing.

He walked down the sidewalk toward her, feeling hesitant with every step. His eyes continued to dart in all directions, looking for others. Nothing felt right about this. Yet he had no choice. These people still had Natalie. Like it or not, he was their pawn.

When he was within five feet, she stared up at him.

"Thanks for coming," she said, a grim smile.

"What do you want?" he demanded, not hiding his anger.

"My client desires an update on your progress."

"How the hell did you find me?"

"That's not important."

"It's important to me."

She patted the bench next to her. "Calm down and have a seat."

"I'd rather stand."

She sighed. "Please don't make this difficult, Sam. I'd rather not call help over."

That's when he spotted her two sidekicks standing beside a tree, fifty paces to his left. They looked as thick and menacing as ever. He reluctantly sat next to her on the bench.

FORTY-THREE

Tommy Kucher munched from a bag of Funyuns.

He sat in front of his bank of computer screens in a dark room inside the dumpy second-story apartment he'd rented for three years, since he'd first made the move to DC. Back in Chicago, his mom and younger sister still lived in the house where he grew up. Mom had been a special-education elementary teacher for twenty years. His sister was a senior in high school and had already been accepted into Harvard. He'd never admit to it, but she was even smarter than he was. His efficiency apartment housed a tiny bathroom and an even smaller kitchen. There was a futon stuffed in one corner of the room. A beanbag in the other. Posters of his favorite Western movies covered the walls. More than thirty of them. He'd been collecting them since he got the place. The L-shaped desk was directly in the middle of the room, five computer screens sitting on every corner. The cushioned swivel chair he'd bought at a consignment store was held together with duct tape.

Tommy had no real job. At least nothing traditional. He considered his work in his computer lair his calling. Someone had to hold the world's governments and powers accountable. So he and his team of hackers did their deal every day, their fingers pecking, their faces bouncing screen to screen. No concept of time. No need for much of a life outside the walls of his apartment. Very little need for real money.

Tommy's dad had introduced him to computers and networks when Tommy was only eight. That's when they built their first computer together in the garage. A computer engineer by trade, his dad was glad to finally find something that Tommy enjoyed that they could do together, since Tommy never showed much interest in sports, cars, or other typical boy hobbies. They spent hours every night in the garage. Tommy guessed they'd built more than a hundred computers together by the time his dad died unexpectedly when Tommy was only sixteen. Police called it a suicide. Two uniformed cops showed up at the door and told his mom they'd found his dad parked in his car in Burnham Park along the banks of Lake Michigan with a bullet hole in his head and a revolver in his lap.

Tommy was suspicious from the start. They'd had plans that very night to start a new project. His dad was excited about it, and so was Tommy. There was no way his dad would've pulled the trigger. There was no suicide note, no explanation, no hint to anyone that his father was on the verge or capable of such a thing. Tommy knew his dad worked for the government. Up to that point, he hadn't paid too much attention—he was a self-absorbed teenager, after all—so he wasn't even sure which department. But he'd noticed some digital files marked "Classified" on his dad's home computer. When two of his dad's so-called colleagues showed up at the house the next morning, flashing government badges in his mom's face—still teary—and demanded his dad's work computer, Tommy's suspicions grew.

Tommy did his first hack job on the government.

It wasn't an easy job. Someone on the inside had tried to wipe Daniel Kucher from existence, along with all his files. Tommy pieced it together. His father was working on a special project for the State

Department. Millions of dollars had suddenly gone missing. His father had traced it to a high-level department head, and the morning of his death, he'd turned his findings over to his boss. As it turned out, based on private and encrypted message exchanges Tommy discovered, his boss was also in on the crime.

Tommy anonymously turned his discovery over to a reporter for the *Chicago Sun-Times*, the story broke, and months later, a total of four men were indicted for crimes against the government and for the murder of his father. No one ever knew how the reporter got the information. But Tommy knew what he would do with the rest of his life.

He moved to DC two years later, right out of high school.

While Tommy was monitoring activity for Sam online, looking for any alerts on the reappearance of Rich Hebbard, he received a sudden and unexpected direct message on his computer screen. It startled him because *no one* on the outside should've been able to send him a direct message—nobody should have access to his system in such a profound way. Tommy prided himself on being a ghost. On being untraceable. He ran his operation completely off the grid. If someone ever tried to track him down, they'd first be bounced from Buenos Aires to Calcutta to Shanghai to Moscow. And the list went on from there.

They would never arrive at his apartment in DC.

Tommy nearly flipped his chair over, then straightened up.

Who had done this? How was this possible?

He moved close to the screen, read the message in the box.

Call Sam. NOW! Tell him to run. He's in Jackson Square. You have maybe sixty seconds before he's dead.

Tommy felt his throat tighten. Because someone had penetrated his *impenetrable* network to get him the message, he took it very seriously. He didn't know how they'd done it, and that caused him severe anxiety, but Tommy didn't feel like he could worry about that just yet. He really hated phones. Hated making direct calls. He hated exposing himself. But what choice did he have? If he hesitated any longer, Sam could be dead, and Tommy knew he could never live with himself. He felt trapped, panicked. He cursed, recognizing that he'd already allowed fifteen seconds to tick off. Sam could be dead in forty-five seconds.

Tommy picked up his secure phone, dialed the number directly.

FORTY-FOUR

"I want confirmation Natalie is okay," Sam demanded.

The black-haired woman stared at him for a moment, pressed her lips together.

"I'm serious," Sam insisted. "Or I walk away."

"I don't think you're in a position to make demands, Sam."

"I don't care what you think."

"Fine. I'll see what I can do."

Sam felt his cell phone unexpectedly buzz in his front pocket. There was no reason anyone should be contacting him right now. It buzzed again, letting him know that it wasn't a message but someone calling him directly. Who? He didn't want this woman even knowing he had a phone, but he needed to know who was calling him. He reached into his pocket, pulled out the phone, stared at the screen. He was shocked. Tommy. The name Maverick was on the screen with a DC phone number. Why the hell would Tommy be directly calling him?

"Sam . . . ," the woman said, trying to grab his attention.

"Give me a second."

Sam stood, stepped a few feet away, and answered it.

"Tommy? What the hell?" he whispered.

Tommy screamed at him. "Sam, are you in Jackson Square?"

"Yeah, man. How'd you know that?"

"Run! Right now! Don't ask any questions, just run. Someone is about to kill you."

"What? What are you talking about?"

Tommy screamed even louder. "Now, Sam! Run!"

Sam turned back around. The woman was watching him curiously. She had no gun. The goons were still by the tree. However, he trusted Tommy with his life, so he turned around again, took a step forward, and broke into a full sprint. Within his first step, something hit his backpack. It collided with so much force that it nearly knocked him over. He stumbled to the grass, peeked over his shoulder. There was a huge hole in his backpack. He flung it off, scrambled to his feet. He felt something buzz right past his face. Sam cursed. Someone was shooting at him. He ducked his head lower and sprinted as fast as he could back toward the huge water fountain. Right when he passed by the fountain, he heard something puncture the stone and ricochet. He kept running forward, straight toward the crowds of people. He hated to put others in danger, but he had no choice or he was a dead man. He moved in behind the jazz band and a large black man playing a tuba. When a bullet punctured the top of the tuba and knocked it completely out of the man's big hands, people in the crowd suddenly realized that all was not right. A man yelled, "Someone's shooting!" and panic quickly ensued.

Sam kept his head down as he scrambled away with the rest of the crowd. Then he saw someone—a man from his past. He was standing behind a column on the steps of Saint Louis Cathedral. The man was not panicking like everyone else. It was a blur—the chaos making everyone understandably crazy—but Sam was sure it was him. He knew that face well. He thought he'd seen it pop up in random places over the past six months, including at his mother's funeral. Sam was nearly knocked over by another man who collided with him while fleeing. When Sam regained his balance, he looked over and could no longer find the familiar face by the column.

The gray-bearded man.

The man behind the curtain last fall who'd played puppet master with Sam's life.

The face of Marcus Pelini.

FORTY-FIVE

The FBI jet landed in New Orleans at the old Lakefront Airport, and two agents from the local field office quickly grabbed Lloyd and Epps in a black Suburban with darkly tinted windows. Lloyd had arrived just in time to hear news of a sniper shooting in Jackson Square. He believed it had to be associated with the Gray Wolf—although there were no deaths reported yet. That gave him pause. Alger Gerlach rarely missed or made mistakes. It was why he was a legend and paid millions of dollars. So what happened?

The Suburban thundered through the streets of New Orleans before finally dropping them on the curb outside Jackson Square. There were more than a dozen police cars already on the scene. Several areas were blocked off with official yellow police tape. A large crowd of tourists encircled the blocked-off sections. A brown-haired man around fifty with a neatly trimmed beard met them on the sidewalk. Lloyd had interacted with him several times over the years: Jeff Caldwell, special agent in charge of the New Orleans field office. Caldwell wore a white shirt with the sleeves rolled up, a blue tie, and dark dress pants.

"Hey, Jeff," Lloyd said, eyes already taking inventory of the chaos.

"Spencer," Caldwell acknowledged.

"What do you know?"

Caldwell glanced behind him, over at Chartres Street near Saint Louis Cathedral. "Multiple shots from a distance. Two wounded. A musician got hit in the arm. A woman in the ankle. They've been taken to the hospital but nothing too serious. We've ID'd a shot that hit the water fountain and chipped the stone. And we found a black backpack in the grass with a bullet hole in it. There are some clothes inside, some toiletries, along with a bundle of rope, some duct tape, and other random tools, which is odd. No identification on the backpack."

"You having it checked out?" Lloyd asked.

Caldwell nodded. "Full diagnostics. We'll see if we find prints or fibers."

"Any witnesses?"

"No one that spotted a shooter."

"Anyone spot who they think was the target?"

Caldwell eyeballed him. "You're thinking Callahan?"

"Of course."

"Well, no one has mentioned anything that matches his description yet. But it was total chaos out here as soon as the first bullets started flying."

"What about location?"

"My guys are working it right now. We think the shooter was inside the Pontalba."

"Where's that?"

Caldwell turned, pointed at a four-story redbrick building that snugged up next to the square. "They're going room by room right now."

A thirtysomething agent with blond hair and the standard dark-blue windbreaker approached their huddle with a tablet in his hands.

"What do you got, Manny?" Caldwell asked.

"Security video from outside Café Pontalba."

Manny held the tablet out for all to see, punched a few buttons on the screen. Suddenly, they could see a wide shot that started with the artists and musicians on Chartres Street and captured all the way to those walking through the landscaped grounds of Jackson Square. One moment, everything was normal. The next, complete chaos broke out, with people ducking behind trees and scrambling to get away from the rest of the crowd.

"Run it again," Lloyd said, squinting.

They all watched it closely again.

"There!" Lloyd said, pointing. "Can you enhance that and run it back?"

"Yes, sir," Manny said, focusing in on the area where Lloyd had pointed and rewinding the security video.

The video showed two people in the distance sitting on a park bench. It was not a close-up shot but clear enough to see that it was a man and a woman. The man was wearing a backpack. He suddenly stood, looked to be talking on the phone, and took off running. That wouldn't have been odd in itself, as everyone was dashing for freedom—except that the man started running *before* any gunfire. Manny widened the screen enough to follow the path of the man, who sprinted through Jackson Square, behind the water fountain, and then got lost from the video in the crowd along Chartres Street.

"That has to be our boy," Epps said to Lloyd.

Lloyd nodded. "That's him. That's Callahan."

Another younger agent with a buzz cut approached the group with an update for Caldwell. "Sir, we think we found a location for the shooter."

"Show us," Caldwell ordered.

The group of them followed the agent over to the Pontalba, where they entered and climbed a stairwell up to the fourth level. They crossed down a hallway until Lloyd spotted a group of agents lingering outside an open door to one of the apartment units. They entered the apartment, where more agents were doing forensic work. Lloyd noticed that the balcony doors were open and the curtains were swaying slightly in the breeze.

"You found the balcony open?" Lloyd asked.

"Yes, sir," the agent replied. "And we found marks on the floor where it looks like a cabinet was dragged in front of the balcony."

"Any neighbors hear anything?" Caldwell asked him.

"No, sir. Must've used some kind of suppressor."

Lloyd and Epps stepped out onto the narrow balcony, examined the property below them, Jackson Square, and the view toward Chartres Street and Saint Louis Cathedral.

"Definitely lines up," Epps said.

"Yep," Lloyd agreed.

They returned to the living space. Caldwell was engaged in an intense conversation with another agent, then he walked over to them. "We got a neighbor four doors down who said she saw a guy in the hallway carrying a large black bag toward the stairwell, right about the time the shooting took place. She thinks he had a beard and was wearing a dark-knit cap, but she can't be sure. We're going to have someone work with her to get a sketch."

"It's Gerlach. I know it," Lloyd said.

FORTY-SIX

Returning to the heart of DC, Natalie ditched the stolen Civic in a city lot. She hoped she could eventually get it back to Gloria in Boonsboro. She took all the cash Gloria had in her wallet—sixty-seven dollars—and then left the purse in the driver's seat. Using the credit card again was too risky. After running away from the police station, and stealing a car and purse, Natalie was unsure what that now meant for her. Was she a wanted criminal? Would the police be actively looking for her? She was unsure what her abductors, who were pretending to be federal agents, told that police officer before she bolted.

For now Natalie decided it was best to stay underground. Although she had some cash stuck in her desk drawer at *PowerPlay* that she often used to pitch in for staff lunch orders, she wasn't comfortable going back there yet. Her office was one of the first places the police would look for her. She didn't want to pull her boss into this deal just yet, either, but she definitely needed help getting some answers. Finding a pay phone outside a convenience store, she quickly dialed Sam's cell number and listened to it ring, praying that he would simply answer and tell her he was okay. She glanced at herself wearing the dark-blue cap pulled low on her head in the reflection of the store window. The phone rang four times and went to voice mail. She listened to the sweet sound of Sam's voice on the greeting.

When the line beeped, she left a quick message. "Sam, it's Natalie. I'm okay. I hope you are, too. I don't have my phone. I don't have much. But I will keep trying to get in touch with you. I love you."

She hung up, not sure what else to say or who else might be listening. She didn't want to give away her location or any other detailed information that might somehow hurt him or her. If he listened, Sam would at least know she was safe—although she desperately wanted to know the same in return.

Natalie dialed the number for Benoltz & Associates. The front receptionist answered—a pleasant woman named Mary she'd met at a firm dinner last month.

"I need to speak with David ASAP," Natalie said.

"May I ask who is calling?" Mary said.

"Please just tell him it's about Sam."

"Sam Callahan?"

"Yes."

"Please hold."

Natalie's right foot bounced up and down nervously, her eyes on the small parking lot in front of the convenience store. A few seconds later, David Benoltz was on the line with her.

"Who is this?" David said, already sounding concerned.

"David, it's Natalie."

She heard David exhale. "Natalie, thank God. I've been trying to find you."

"Have you heard from Sam?" she asked.

David said, "No, I was going to ask you the same thing."

"Is he still in Mexico City?"

"I don't know. Something happened in Mexico City. One of our clients was shot and killed when he was with Sam. I don't know any details, but Sam did not feel safe and was hiding out. I haven't heard from him since late yesterday afternoon. He was trying to meet up with a guy I know who lives down there, but I haven't heard back from either one of them."

"Someone abducted me last night."

"What? Are you okay?"

"I'm okay now. I got away a couple of hours ago."

"Who was it?" he asked.

"I don't know yet. But they specifically referred to Sam, so I believe the two events are somehow connected."

David cursed. "Where are you?"

She was not comfortable telling anyone that yet. "I'm safe."

"Natalie, let me come get you," David insisted. "I can keep you safe."

A Metropolitan Police patrol car pulled into the small parking lot and sent a shiver up her spine. She spun around, hid her face from the parking lot. Out of the corner of her eye, she noticed two uniformed officers get out, glance over in her direction. David was calling her name repeatedly in her ear, with growing concern.

"I've got to go," she whispered, and hung up.

She didn't turn around, just started walking up the sidewalk and away from the convenience store. She waited to hear if one of the police officers would say something after her. No words came. Natalie turned a street corner, started running.

FORTY-SEVEN

Tommy pecked away on his keyboard with so much intensity that his fingers were starting to cramp. The direct message to warn Sam that had penetrated his secure system had sent him into a paranoid spiral. He was working all five screens at once, peeling the layers of the onion back, one after another, finding no comfort in what he was beginning to discover. Someone had been inside his system for the past two days, unbeknownst to Tommy, before Sam had ever pulled him into the mix, and had controlled *everything*. Someone had been playing Oz with him and manipulating everything he'd been viewing on his screens from behind a curtain. No one had ever hacked him like this before—Tommy didn't even believe it was possible. Had he gotten lazy? He didn't believe so. But how did someone do it? Who was he? He hadn't been able to find that information yet. If the hacker was so good that he'd been able to infiltrate his system, Tommy knew it would be a challenge to ever uncover his true identity.

On one computer screen, he continued to monitor news out of New Orleans. There'd been reports of a shooting in Jackson Square. Two were wounded but okay. No mention of any deaths. No mention of Sam Callahan or Ethan Edwards. Sam had survived. Tommy had made the right call. The warning had saved Sam's life. Even in all the panic of being hacked, Tommy was relieved he'd picked up the phone. Otherwise, Sam would likely be dead.

While he worked intently to search for threads to somehow identify the person who had hacked him, Tommy was also diligently putting up new firewalls and rebuilding his entire network from scratch. He was completely vulnerable at the moment, and that was an awful feeling. He had to rebuild his fortress—and as swiftly as possible. It was no small task after spending so many years doing it the first time, which left him with a dire feeling. How had someone found his way to the inside? Was someone smarter than he was?

Tommy refused to believe that. There had to be a different explanation.

A programmed alert popped up on his first computer screen.

Tommy spun around in his office chair, leaned in close toward the screen. The name *Natalie Foster* had a hit on one of the hundreds of networks he was currently monitoring. Tommy scanned through the list. Surprisingly, the alert came from a channel belonging to a rogue division of the CIA. Tommy typed into his keyboard, finding an audio file—a phone call. Why would the CIA be monitoring a phone call mentioning Natalie? Muting the heavy metal that filled the room, he quickly pulled the audio file up and clicked Play. He listened closely to a brief phone exchange between two men. No names for the contacts, only random phone numbers on the screen. The audio file was full of static, crackling, and distortion. The phone call was brief. Tommy rewound it and enhanced it as much as possible to make out the conversation, turning up the volume to its fullest.

Caller one: *"She's . . . [static] . . . gone, sir . . ."*

Caller two: *"Who?"*

Caller one: *"The girl . . . [static] . . . Natalie Foster . . . [static] . . ."*

Caller two: *"What do you mean . . . [static] . . . dead?"*

Caller one: *". . . [static] . . . yes . . . [static] . . . big mistake."*

That was it. Tommy stared at the screen. Had he heard right? He could feel his heartbeat pounding away inside his chest. He wasn't sure what to do.

A sudden pounding on his front door jarred him out of the moment. More pounding followed a few seconds later, followed by a deep and threatening voice.

"Open up! Police!"

Police? Tommy pecked onto his keyboard, brought up a live video feed from directly above his apartment door. A tiny undetectable camera pointed down at the face of a hulk of a man, maybe forty, with black hair, black goatee, and black leather jacket. Two smaller but equally intimidating men stood behind him. They didn't look like police. More like Russian mobsters. No way would Tommy open the door. He cursed. He had to get out of there. Although he had heavy-duty locks on the door, they wouldn't hold forever.

Looking back at the screen showing the audio file, he quickly assessed what tracks he needed to cover before he bolted. He logged in to Leia's Lounge, a path he'd once again secured by reconfiguring his system, and opened a new video box. He clicked a button that said Record and stared into the video camera above one of his computer monitors.

The pounding grew even louder outside the door.

"Sam, I'm going off the grid. We've been hacked. As a matter of fact, I think we've been watched the past two days. I'm not sure by whom yet. Someone is outside my door claiming to be the police, but it sure as hell isn't the police. I'll try to find a way to connect with you as soon as I land somewhere secure. One more thing." Tommy swallowed, wasn't sure how to put this in the right words. "I'm attaching an audio file. I don't know what to make of it. But I feel like I have to get it to you just in case something happens to me. I don't know, man. I'm sorry. I'll see you on the other side. I hope. Peace out."

Tommy heard his wooden door crack—sounded like the Hulk was trying to knock it down. He clicked off the recording, attached the audio file, and then hit Send. On another computer screen, Tommy pulled up an option he never thought he'd need to use. It was an image of the Hiroshima bombing with the big-ass cloud in the sky. He clicked on the image, typed in a password, and then everything immediately shut down in the room. All the computer screens went black. All the lights went out in the apartment. Tommy knew within seconds that his entire system would be wiped clean, as if it never existed.

The apartment door was about to come down. In the darkness, Tommy jumped out of his swivel chair and raced into the small bathroom. He pulled away a thick rug from the tile floor, revealing a small built-in wooden trapdoor—just big enough for him to slip through. He pried it open with a bony finger and then pulled it fully open. It was dark inside the hole in the floor. Tommy knew that two feet down was another matching trapdoor. He reached down into the hole, felt for a bolt lock, and twisted the metal knob. The second matching door swung open into another dark room—a storage closet behind the arcade directly below his apartment. Something no one else but Tommy knew about since he'd installed it himself.

He heard the apartment door splinter completely apart a second later. The boys were inside his unit. He could hear muttering.

Tommy dropped into the floor feetfirst. His shoes went through the ceiling of the storage closet. He reached around with his toes until he felt a metal shelf against the wall. Catching his balance, he carefully lowered himself all the way out of his own bathroom. With a hand, he pulled the small door closed. The thick rug in his bathroom was attached to the door in the floor in a way that would allow it to slide back into place, hiding the trapdoor from any visitors.

As Tommy climbed down the metal shelf in the storage closet, he could hear heavy steps directly above him. One of the guys was inside his bathroom. Tommy watched the ceiling, waited. A second later, the footsteps left the bathroom. Tommy exhaled. They hadn't discovered the trapdoor. He quickly exited the closet into a private back hallway behind the arcade. Moments later, he found a door to a back alley and disappeared into the city.

FORTY-EIGHT

Sam sat on cracked concrete, hidden between two crumbling tombs in the back corner of Saint Louis Cemetery No. 1, seven blocks from Jackson Square. It was as good a place as any to catch his breath, get his bearings, and think about his next move. The cemetery was a giant maze of wall vaults and oversize tombs—with a hundred different creepy hideaways. Sitting there, sweating profusely, his heart was still racing. While most others peeled off to safety after only a block or two, Sam had sprinted for more than five blocks. After all, he was the target.

That was a daunting thought. Someone had taken sniper shots at him.

He could still feel the cold sensation of a bullet buzzing right by him, feel the weight of the impact as it hit his backpack. Who was the shooter? From where was he shooting? Although his brain was flooded with questions, Sam's adrenaline was running so hot that it was difficult to process answers. Had he been set up by the black-haired woman in the gray coat? He shook his head. That didn't make any sense. She could've had him shot dead when he was meeting with her in Mexico City. Instead, she sent him on a wild-goose chase in search of what appeared to be his long-lost father—all apparently because two lawyers wanted out after a corrupt Mexican oil deal involving two dirty politicians and a crazy oilman.

Sam ran a hand over his sweaty, bald head. He'd lost his ball cap while running. He closed his eyes, took a deep breath, and exhaled slowly. If it wasn't for Tommy's phone call, he'd be dead right now. How had Tommy known?

Sam pulled his cell phone out of his pocket, logged in to Leia's Lounge. Once inside, he was surprised to find a video message from Tommy waiting for him. The second time in the past hour that Tommy had broken his own rules in order to communicate with him. Sam pushed Play and watched a frantic-looking Tommy on his phone screen. *They'd been hacked? Past two days? Someone outside his door?* Sam cursed but then perked up when Tommy mentioned something about an audio file. Below the video message, he found an attached audio message. Sam pressed Play and listened closely. Two men, talking about Natalie? When he heard the word *dead*, Sam felt a surge of bile in his stomach. He listened to the recording again. Then a third time. The man definitely said the word *dead*.

Sam felt light-headed, like he might pass out.

He couldn't hold it back. He leaned over, vomited on the concrete. This couldn't be real. Those words couldn't be true. Not now.

He refused to believe it. Not after everything they'd been through. Not after last week.

July 2
Eight days ago

Sam picked Natalie up at her apartment. She was dressed casual, as he'd requested. Blue jeans, gray Saint Louis Cardinals T-shirt, running shoes. Her thick, straight brown hair in a ponytail. Just a touch of makeup in all the right places. Sam marveled at this woman who could look so beautiful without even trying. He wore something similar: jeans, T-shirt, running shoes.

"Where are we going?" Natalie asked for the fifth time.

"I told you, it's a surprise," he said, grinning.

He'd returned from Denver a week ago. The time with Pastor Isaiah had been such a sweet salve for such a deeply wounded soul. Alisha had helped him pack on five pounds with her home-cooked meals, which Sam sorely needed—he'd lost quite a bit of weight after his mother's death. Healthy again for the first time in many months, both physically and spiritually, he was ready to get right with Natalie. Although Natalie was thrilled about the date, she was curious about wearing something casual.

He drove her in his black Jeep Wrangler, a used car he'd purchased with part of his signing bonus with Benoltz & Associates. It was a warm DC evening, and they had the top down as they eased through the city streets. Sam kept her distracted by asking all kinds of questions about her work. She seemed happy that he was engaged with her life, as it had been many months since they'd had such a conversation.

When Sam pulled into the batting cages, the place where it had all begun for them, Natalie looked over at him and smiled wide.

"For real?" she asked.

He returned the smile. "What? Are you scared?"

She laughed out loud. "Have you not learned your lesson yet?"

"I guess not. I'm a glutton for punishment."

"That's the truth."

He shrugged. "I just thought we could do something light and fun. I know it's been very heavy between us the past few months."

Natalie seemed very pleased. They collected bats and batting helmets. Sam had reserved the same batting cage they'd used their first night together—although he was certainly glad to not have a crowd watching them tonight. They stepped into the cage and did a little stretching and warming up with the bats.

"Okay," Natalie said. "So what are the stakes?"

"Stakes?"

Natalie frowned. "Well, we're not just here to goof around, are we?"

He laughed. "Is everything a competition with you?"

"Dang right. So who gets what when I win?"

"It's a surprise."

She frowned again. "Enough with the surprises already!"

"You trust me?" he asked.

Her eyes narrowed. "I think so."

"Okay, good. Punch that red button, and let's get this party started."

He stepped outside of the batting cage. Natalie pushed the button and got herself situated at the makeshift home plate, took a few more practice swings as the machine warmed up in the distance. A few seconds later, baseballs started whizzing her way at seventy miles per hour. She swung the bat like a professional, started cracking them back up the middle. He loved watching her swing, so smooth and effortless. There was a reason she'd gotten a softball scholarship to Missouri. She hit nine out of ten balls into the far-off net, but she was seriously frustrated about the one ball she fouled off the end of her bat.

"You left me an opening, Ms. Foster," Sam teased.

"Shut up!" she said, pouting, stepping out of the cage.

He laughed, entered the batting cage, and pushed the button. He got himself in position and waited for the fastballs. When they came, he pounded them back up the middle, one after another, determined to beat her this time around. When he got to seven straight hits, Natalie started to razz him a bit, with, "Hey, batter, batter! Swing, batter!" But it didn't work. Sam nailed number eight back up the middle. Then number nine. Natalie got very loud for the last pitch. But he was dead set with focus. Number ten cracked off the bat and flew into the net.

Sam spun around, held the bat up over his head, and yelled, "Victory!"

Natalie gave him a menacing glare. "I hate you!"

"Sore loser," he said, again poking at her.

She frowned. "Fine, you win. What do you want?"

He stepped out of the cage, stood right in front of her.

"I want you, Natalie," he said, with firm eyes.

She stared at him, seemed to sense that he was no longer joking around. "You have me, Sam. You know that."

He shook his head. "No, I want you *forever.*"

Sam slowly lowered himself to one knee, stuck his hand inside his blue-jeans pocket. Natalie covered her mouth with a hand, stunned at the sudden turn of events. Sam pulled a diamond ring out of his pocket, held it up for her to see.

"Will you marry me, Natalie Foster?"

Her mouth dropped open. "That's my mother's wedding ring."

"Your dad gave it to me two days ago."

"You went to see my dad?"

"Of course. You think I'd be on one knee right now without asking Thomas Foster for his blessing? I'm not crazy. Well, not entirely. He offered me the ring."

"I can't believe it!" Natalie exclaimed. "Yes, of course, I'll marry you."

He slid the ring on her finger, and they embraced. In that moment, Sam did not feel panicked. He felt at peace. Pastor Isaiah had said it best. Sam was at a crossroads. He could choose to put the shackles on again and remain in his emotional prison—a place of misery that strangely felt safe. Or he could walk out of the prison cell and finally close the door behind him.

Sam was slamming the damn door shut.

FORTY-NINE

Natalie stood behind a tree, watching the faces of the people walking up and down the sidewalks around the Lincoln Memorial and Reflecting Pool. This was her stomping ground, where she jogged during her lunch hour nearly every day, so she knew who fit in and who stood out. Already hating her life on the run, she wasn't sure how Sam had gotten through it all last November.

Right on time, a woman in her midthirties with short brown hair, wearing a dark-blue trench coat, sat on a bench across the water from Natalie's perch. Natalie took a moment to scan left and right, again looking for any watching eyes. When she found none, she left her hiding spot, walked around the Reflecting Pool, and quickly approached the woman. Her name was Michelle Blair, a good friend of Natalie's who also happened to be a special agent with the FBI. They'd struck up a friendship during Natalie's first year in DC, right after Natalie had graduated with honors from the University of Missouri School of Journalism and taken the job with *PowerPlay*. Natalie was doing an investigative piece about a new police program and met Michelle as a potential source. They'd bonded in many ways. Michelle was tough, just like Natalie, with two older brothers, and she had also lost her mother when she was just a teenager.

"You okay?" Michelle asked, looking genuinely concerned.

"Not really. I appreciate you meeting me."

"Of course."

"Did you find out anything?" Natalie asked, eyes alert.

"The white van was rented yesterday morning by a man named Curtis Self." She pulled a piece of white paper out of her trench-coat pocket, handed it to Natalie. "This is a copy of his driver's license. He look familiar?"

Natalie took the piece of paper. She'd asked Michelle to run a check on the license plate she'd memorized of the white van that was used in her abduction. Curtis Self was the van's driver—bald, square glasses, and beard. *Abe.* It was definitely the same guy.

"It's him," Natalie acknowledged.

Michelle sighed. "I was afraid you were going to say that."

Natalie looked over at her friend. "Why?"

"He's CIA."

Natalie was shocked. "This guy is CIA?"

Michelle nodded. "Been with the Agency for ten years. Special Operations Group."

"What division is that?"

"Special Activities Division. Covert operations. Underground stuff that's way above my pay grade, where I could get flagged if I try to dig around too much."

Natalie stared at the face on the paper. "I can't believe it. These guys really are CIA? I thought they were just pretending to be agents when they showed up at the police station. The CIA can grab innocent people right off the streets and hold them captive?"

"I can't answer that. The CIA plays by its own rules."

Natalie's mind was spinning. "What do they want with Sam?"

"I don't know. But I have some news there, too."

Natalie looked over at Michelle. "What? Is he okay?"

"I can't say for sure. Apparently, we're looking for him right now."

"The FBI? Why?"

Michelle shook her head. "There's an assassin we're currently tracking in the States. Alger Gerlach, also called the Gray Wolf."

"I've read about him," Natalie interjected.

"I'm sure you have. He's on every most-wanted list around the globe."

"What does that have to do with Sam?" Natalie asked, her brow furrowed.

"Sam is his current target."

Natalie was stunned. If news of the CIA being behind her abduction was a left jab, the news of a famous assassin hunting down Sam was the right cross.

Natalie shook her head. "But . . . Sam is in Mexico right now."

"Not anymore," Michelle responded.

"How do you know?"

"We have security video from just an hour ago showing him in New Orleans, where we think he just barely survived an assassination attempt by the Gray Wolf."

That was the knockout uppercut. *Assassination attempt?* Natalie was reeling. "Do you know where Sam is now?"

"We don't. But we're on an all-out manhunt. I'm afraid someone wants Sam dead, badly enough to bring in a million-dollar international assassin to do the job. So we have agents everywhere looking for both Sam and the Gray Wolf."

Natalie stood on wobbly legs, because she couldn't sit any longer. "What the hell is going on, Michelle? The CIA kidnapped me, and I know for a fact it has to do with Sam. Now you're telling me that Sam just barely missed being killed? What's the connection?"

"I don't know," Michelle admitted. "The CIA angle is brand-new to us. It could just be a rogue agent. We can't be sure it's an official Agency operation."

"I have to get to Sam."

"I think you should come in with me. Let us protect you. Tell your story officially. And let us work on solving it. This is what we do."

Natalie shook her head. "I can't do that. I'd go crazy. You already know what I know—there's nothing else to say. I'll take my chances."

Michelle didn't seem to like her response. "Natalie, this is crazy! You're in real danger. You're just a reporter, not an FBI agent. You're going to get yourself killed trying to save Sam on your own."

Natalie was already thinking ahead, developing a plan.

"Thanks for your help, Michelle. I appreciate it."

"Natalie?"

But Natalie was on the move, away from the bench. She heard Michelle call out her name one last time, with grave concern, but Natalie was gone.

FIFTY

The Gray Wolf slipped onto a bar stool at the Old Absinthe House, a two-hundred-year-old saloon on Bourbon Street. Gone were the beard and knit cap. Gerlach was now clean shaven and bald, wearing a loose-fitting purple silk shirt, khaki shorts, and flip-flops. Nearing the lunch hour, the saloon was full and bustling with crowd noise. He ordered the Absinthe House Frappe, the saloon's signature cocktail, from the attractive blonde female bartender. A TV was on above the bar, a local channel showing news of a shooting in Jackson Square. Gerlach was still seething about his unsuccessful attempt at taking out his target.

"Crazy, huh?" the blonde bartender mentioned, sliding his cocktail in front of him.

"What's that?" Gerlach asked, practicing a touch of Cajun accent.

She nodded toward the TV screen. "Shooting in Jackson Square."

"Oh, yeah. Crazy. What's wrong with people?"

"I know! This world has gone to hell."

"At least no one was killed," Gerlach mentioned, only slightly amusing himself.

"You want something to eat?" she asked him.

He eyeballed a menu. "What's your favorite?"

"The jambalaya."

"I'll take that," he said, smiling and winking at her.

"Coming right up."

A few minutes later, a man of fortysomething slid onto an empty stool next to Gerlach. He was bald on top and wore the thickest pair of glasses. His shirt was a short-sleeve red polo, and his shorts were light blue. He also wore white tennis shoes with white socks that were pulled up to the knees. A pocket protector would've completed the look.

"What happened?" Gerlach asked, not even looking at the guy, his thick German accent returning. They were huddled close together. Closer than Gerlach liked, but it was loud in the place, and this brief public exchange was necessary. Gerlach was not interested in meeting in private with his client. He didn't trust him. For good reason.

"What do you mean?" the guy replied. "You missed."

"He was warned," Gerlach growled under his breath. "Someone alerted him at the last second, and he took off running."

"You can't hit a moving target? I thought you were the best."

It took all of Gerlach's will to not reach over and break the guy's neck. But he knew he couldn't do that. The nerd knew it, too, which was why he was acting so brash and bold. He took a big swig of his cocktail, calmed himself down. The blonde bartender returned, took an order from the nerd, slid his drink in front of him. The two men sat quietly for a few minutes.

"What does he want me to do?" Gerlach finally asked.

"Finish the job," the nerd said resolutely.

Rising from the stool, the nerd pulled an envelope out of his pocket, set it on the copper-topped wooden bar next to Gerlach's cocktail glass, and headed for the door.

Gerlach again seethed. He deserved more respect. He took the white envelope, opened it, found details inside of his target's last location—a time stamp of only ten minutes ago. The bartender slipped a plate of jambalaya in front of him. It smelled incredible. He really liked this city. He stuffed the envelope in his back pocket, decided he would at least enjoy his meal before resuming his hunt on foot.

"You mind changing the station?" he asked the bartender.

FIFTY-ONE

Sam was on the move again, determined to find Rich Hebbard. If he remained still for too long, he'd do nothing but dwell on Natalie, and that would completely suffocate him. He refused to believe what he'd heard in the choppy phone-call recording. Natalie was *not* dead. No way, nohow. He wouldn't accept it unless he confirmed it with his own eyes. Not with everything they'd been through the past couple of years. Not with their engagement just last week. Not with their whole future waiting ahead of them. She would fight and stay alive. He said a prayer, put it out of his mind, determined to not linger on these thoughts any longer, and then bolted out of his hiding place in the old cemetery.

According to Tommy's research, Tom Hawkins had an ex-wife who still lived in the city. They'd been divorced for four years. Hawkins's ex-wife had gone back to her maiden name: Teresa Pearsons. If Tommy's info was accurate, Teresa now owned and managed a small thrift store on Frenchmen Street. He was headed there now.

Sam cautiously made his way across town. He darted mostly through alleys, staying off highly trafficked streets and as far away from people as possible. He'd done this before; he could do it again. Off the grid. In the shadows. With the phone recording of Natalie fresh in his mind, he felt an even stronger resolve to attack this thing head-on and get out of it alive. He navigated the dozen blocks to Frenchmen Street before he finally slipped inside a pink one-story building that housed Restoration Thrift. There were currently six shoppers inside the small store. Five women, one man. None of them felt like a threat. Two college-age female clerks were working. He grabbed a men's dark-green military-style jacket off a rack, found a brown-knit beanie that fit him, and moved to the checkout counter. One of the clerks came over to help him. Claire, according to her name tag, had short black hair with a dash of purple in it.

"Find everything you need?" Claire asked, arranging his items.

"Yes, thanks. Is Teresa here?"

"She's in the back office."

"Can you tell her I need to speak with her?"

She looked up. "Sure. Whom shall I say is asking?"

"Ethan. I know her ex-husband."

He paid for the new items with cash from the roll Tommy had left for him, and then Claire stepped through a curtain into a hallway. Sam took a moment to slip on his new jacket and beanie, hoping it would give him an extra layer of anonymity. He'd been wondering if the shooter was Desperado—the same man from Mexico City. Had he somehow followed him across the border? Or did Sam now have someone else trying to take him out?

A few seconds later, a lady of fortysomething stepped out. Blonde hair, casual black summer dress, sandals, kind smile. "Can I help you?" she said to Sam.

"Teresa?" Sam asked.

"Yes. What can I do for you?"

"Ethan Edwards. Can we talk in private?"

She looked at him with concern but offered a hand toward the hallway. Sam stepped through the curtain into a hallway lined with boxes stuffed with clothes and other items. Teresa led him into a small back office with a wooden desk. He sat in a metal folding chair while she moved behind the desk and sat in a cheap office chair.

"This is about my ex-husband?" Teresa asked.

"Sort of. I'm actually looking for Rich Hebbard."

"Oh, sorry, but I haven't spoken with Rich in probably more than a year. I honestly don't have much to do with Tom anymore. I only see him here and there if one of the kids comes home to visit, which is maybe twice a year. I assume you tried their office?"

"Yes, neither one of them were at work."

He didn't mention that *nothing* was inside the office.

"Not surprised," Teresa replied. "Those two guys always liked to play much more than they liked to work. One of the reasons we got divorced. Tom was completely irresponsible with our money. Rich used to own a house over off Governor Nicholls. Not sure if he still does."

"Yes, I've been by there, too. Anywhere else you can think of that I might find him?"

She shook her head. "No, I'm sorry I can't be more help."

"That's okay. Thanks for your time."

He stood, shook her hand.

"How is Tom?" she asked him.

He shrugged. "Tom is Tom, you know what I mean?"

She rolled her eyes. "Yes, I'm afraid I do."

Sam did not have the heart to tell her that her ex-husband was now dead, at the hands of a ruthless assassin who was probably working for a corrupt Mexican politician. At least Tom died trying to do the right thing, or so it seemed.

"Thanks again," Sam said, turned to leave.

"Wait a second," Teresa said, stopping him. "Tom and Rich used to go to a lake house over in Saint Tammany Parish near Honey Island Swamp. A real dump of a place, according to my son."

"Can you get an address?"

"Sure. Just a second."

FIFTY-TWO

The cab ride took him forty minutes outside the city on I-10, where they crossed over Lake Pontchartrain and into Saint Tammany Parish. Sam tossed an extra twenty-dollar bill over the front seat and asked the old mellow driver wearing the black beret to keep his eyes on the rearview mirror for him, alert him if he felt they were being followed. The driver seemed just fine with that as he hummed along to his soft reggae music. Teresa had given him the address for Hebbard and Hawkins's swamp cabin—at least that's what her son called it. It was apparently way off the beaten path and somewhere deep into swamp country. Sam silently prayed that Hebbard would be hiding out there.

If not, he wasn't sure where to look next.

On the ride over, he logged in to Leia's Lounge. Tommy was still nowhere to be found. No new messages awaited Sam. No answer on the other end. Sam felt a heavy knot develop in his stomach. He hoped his friend was okay. They were dealing with sinister people who clearly had every intent to stop the truth from ever getting out. Sam wasn't sure how he'd live with himself if he'd pulled Tommy into this mess, only to get Tommy killed. Tommy had mentioned in his message earlier that someone was trying to get inside his apartment. Tommy was maybe the least physically imposing person that Sam knew, although the guy more than made up for it in being outstandingly clever. His whole life had been set up through the lens of paranoia and conspiracy, so Sam felt there was no way Tommy didn't have an escape plan. If Tommy Kucher was still breathing, he was busy getting himself reestablished online somewhere else—it was just a matter of time and opportunity.

Once within Saint Tammany Parish, the cab driver followed his GPS through a half dozen small towns until the paved roads eventually turned into dirt ones and the towns thinned out. Gray clouds had moved in over southeast Louisiana, and Sam watched raindrops begin to hit the windshield of the cab. The old driver followed a very long and windy dirt road for a full mile, not passing another car or house the entire drive, until he took one more left, drove down another dirt road, and they finally pulled to a stop in front of an isolated green block of a house with a white front porch. Sam noticed that the back of the house was sitting right on the edge of the murky river water. He did not spot another vehicle parked anywhere. If he was hoping to find someone, that was not a good sign.

"You want me to wait?" the cab driver asked.

"Yeah, that'd be great, thanks."

"Yes, sir. Take your time."

The driver turned the jazz up a notch, eased down into his seat, and closed his eyes.

Sam got out, looked around. Thick Spanish moss hung from the cypress trees. It looked spooky as hell. He could hear a chorus of what he thought must be swamp insects singing. Getting wet from perspiration just standing there, he walked over to the green house and under the covering of the front porch, where he looked into a dirt-stained window beside the white front door. He could make out a small living room and a room that looked like a kitchen in the back of the house. Sam guessed there were maybe two bedrooms on the other side. He did not see any movement, but he did notice that several lights were currently on inside the cabin.

He knocked on the front door, waited. He heard nothing. He put his hand on the doorknob, twisted. The front door was unlocked. This didn't necessarily strike him as unusual. The cabin was out in the middle of nowhere, so no reason to lock the doors. If a thief was willing to come all the way out there, he could simply walk right in and grab whatever he wanted, with no people around to hear anything, anyway.

Sam stepped inside, shut the door behind him.

"Hello? Anyone home?"

No response. He eased down a tattered-brown carpeted hallway. The first door led to a clean bathroom and shower. The second door was a bedroom with a neatly made bed and dresser. He searched the small closet. A few jackets were hanging; there were rubber boots on the floor. He moved farther down the hallway to the third door and found a near-matching bedroom—another closet full of jackets, pants, and boots. It didn't look like anyone had been sleeping in either of the beds. Not a good sign.

Sam returned to the living room. A flat-screen TV sat on top of a low cabinet. A plaid couch and two leather recliners. Framed on the wall was a creepy picture of a large, dark figure sloshing through a swamp entitled *Honey Island Swamp Monster*. Sam shook his head. As if being out there in the middle of a swamp with alligators wasn't scary enough, he thought. In the corner near the kitchen, he found a small rolltop desk with a computer sitting on top of it, the screen currently black. He stepped inside the tiny kitchen. On the counter, he found copies of *Field & Stream*, *Florida Sportsman* magazine, and *In-Fisherman*. The subscription labels all showed they belonged to Rich Hebbard and were current editions. Hebbard had recently been inside the cabin. But just how recently?

Sam noticed a red light blinking on the coffeemaker and brown liquid still inside the glass container. He walked over, put a hand on the glass. Warm. Sitting next to the coffeemaker, Sam found a green coffee mug half-full. Someone had used the coffeemaker that very morning. But was that someone still there?

Behind the kitchen was a door that led to an enclosed porch that housed several white wooden rocking chairs. The porch hovered directly over the swamp water. Sam stepped out onto the porch, turned, and nearly had a heart attack. A ten-foot stuffed alligator with its jaws wide open glared at him from the back corner. He walked up to it, touched it, and shook his head. Next to the alligator, he found a large collection of fishing poles and gear, all neatly organized. Peering outside of the porch, Sam spotted a small wooden dock with a fishing boat still tied up. Was there a second boat? Could someone be out there right now fishing in these waters? He highly doubted Hebbard would resort to fishing under his current circumstances—although men had done stranger things.

Sam returned to the main cabin, feeling restless. He still hadn't found *anything* to lead him to Hebbard. He walked over to the desktop computer. He jiggled the mouse, and the computer screen sprang to life in front of him. Sam cocked his head, surprised. The computer was not powered down, as he would've expected if someone had left the cabin after a visit. A guest likely would not have used the computer. With Tom Hawkins dead in Mexico City, that left only Rich Hebbard. That was his hope. Sam sat in the desk chair, stared at the computer screen. A security box was already up and asking for a password. He sighed. Where was Tommy when he needed him? Sam scrolled through his mental file on Rich Hebbard and began to take random guesses.

Hebbard's birth date? No.

Kids' names? No.

Ex-wife's name? No.

Archie Manning? No.

Sam leaned back in the chair, feeling defeated. The box on the screen told him he had only three more attempts before the computer would lock down for twenty minutes. He didn't have the luxury of sitting around all day and typing guesses into a computer. He again thought of his baby picture sitting on Hebbard's office shelf. Sam typed in his own birth date, pressed Enter. The screen suddenly loaded. The password worked. His jaw dropped wide-open. He'd never met the man, and yet Hebbard was using his birth date as his password? He cursed out loud. What the hell? He really didn't have time to sort through the emotions of this all right now. With Natalie still hanging out there somewhere—and Tommy also on the run—Sam knew he couldn't get bogged down thinking too much about his own daddy issues. There'd be time for that later—*if* he lived.

He squinted at the screen, which showed the normal icons for more than a dozen file folders, along with a web browser and e-mail. Sam searched through the file names. Random ones like *Wilcox, Harbors Deal, Acton Oil, Cannons–Forger Merger, Nasix Oil, Burner Petroleum*. He quickly went through each folder, clicking open Word documents, Excel files, PDFs, and so on. They all looked like standard client files. He found nothing in any of the folders that interested him or that he felt was somehow tied to his current situation. He did a quick search on the entirety of the computer, typing in all the names that were connected to the conspiracy. No mention of Arnstead Petroleum or Lex Hester. Nothing on Francisco Zapata or a Mexican government oil auction. Nothing tied to Senator Liddell of Alabama. He was coming up empty-handed.

Sam clicked on the e-mail icon. When it loaded, Sam searched for the attached address: Swampman52@gmail.com. He thought it must be one of Hebbard's personal e-mail accounts—except it was an account that Tommy hadn't mentioned. Could he have somehow missed it? Sam shook his head. No way. Tommy missed *nothing*. However, Sam scanned through dozens of e-mails, finding Hebbard's name listed throughout. The account indeed belonged to him. Most of the e-mails looked like random spam from various hunting, fishing, and golf websites, along with a few personal exchanges with perhaps some friends.

Then Sam paused, stared hard at the screen. An e-mail exchange near the top, from only four hours ago, grabbed his rapt attention. On the other end was this address: LiddellM77@gmail.com. Senator Mark Liddell? Was it Liddell's personal e-mail account? It had to be him!

He quickly read the exchange. The first e-mail came from Hebbard's account at 10:32 a.m., and the exchange between the two men went back and forth over a five-minute period.

Swampman52: Everything has blown up. I can't find Tom. I think he's dead. And now they're coming at me. What do you want me to do?

LiddellM77: How fast can you get to DC?

Swampman52: I can go to the airport right now.

LiddellM77: If you get here, I can protect you.

Swampman52: What about the feds?

LiddellM77: No. Let me handle it.

Swampman52: On my way.

Sam sat back in the chair. He'd found Rich Hebbard. Had the man been sitting in this very chair when he'd sent the e-mail to Liddell? If that was the case, Sam had missed Hebbard by only a few hours. He checked the time on his phone and thought Hebbard might already be in the air, on his way to DC to meet with Senator Liddell—to find some *protection*. Hebbard had a head start. Sam at least knew where to go next to find him. He felt a sudden burst of adrenaline. He had to return to the New Orleans airport ASAP.

Sam heard the car horn wail outside and turned sharply. It wasn't a few quick beeps, either, as if the driver was simply tired of waiting and giving him notice. The horn sounded as if the driver was keeping his hand pressed down fully for close to fifteen seconds now. Sam got up, walked to the front of the cabin. Then the noise stopped. He peered out a window. That was odd. He couldn't see the driver inside the car through the windshield. Where was he? Had the old driver laid on the horn and then jumped out of the car?

Panic surged through Sam.

FIFTY-THREE

The first shot punctured the window and clipped Sam in his right arm. The only thing that kept him from being hit square in the head was Sam's escape instinct kicking in and causing him to begin moving. The wound in his arm shocked him but not enough to slow him down. He bolted through the cabin for the back porch. The second shot nearly knocked the beanie right off the top of his head. Grabbing the screen door to the back porch, he flung it open. The next two shots splintered the door frame but missed him. He wasn't sure from where the sniper was shooting, but Sam knew he had to keep moving. Sam dashed toward the screened-in wall on the right side of the back porch. He'd spotted it earlier—the screen had a big gash in it just above the wooden railing. Diving headfirst, he held out both fists in front of him, plunging himself forcefully through the screen, splitting it wide open, before landing in shallow, muddy river water on the outside.

He scrambled to his feet, sloshed forward through the water, looking for the first thick cypress tree he could find. Diving behind a tree again, he pressed his back up against it, completely hidden. He waited a few seconds before peering around the opposite side, could see a shadow by the hole in the screen on the back porch. The assassin was inside the cabin. Sam had tucked away when three more shots punctured the tree. His breathing was heavy, and he could tell he was already bleeding badly down his arm. He could see blood dripping out onto his fingertips. Blocking out the pain, he listened. He knew the guy inside had a choice. He could either climb out through the same screen hole as Sam did and drop into the swamp water. Or he could make a run after Sam by going back out the front door of the cabin.

When Sam didn't immediately hear any noise from the back porch, he knew the assassin had chosen to make his way back around the front. Sam had to keep moving. Pressing off the tree, he carved a path deeper into the marshland, sloshing through the shallow swamp water, away from the cabin. He was loud, moving about in the water, as there was no way to hide the splashing of his steps, until he found a muddy path up the bank onto drier land. Crossing through several more tree sections, he dropped behind one again, where he was nearly swallowed up by the thick Spanish moss, hiding him from view. He peered around the tree, looking for signs of movement, and saw nothing. Where was the guy?

Sam was developing a plan in his mind. His only hope was to lure the killer far enough away from the cabin, then somehow circle his way back to the car. Thinking about the cab driver, he cursed to himself. The man was probably already dead.

Pushing away moss, he looked for a path farther into the marshland. Then he stepped out from the tree and sprinted as quietly as he could toward the next tree line. Mud splashed up in his face as he dove behind a tree. Rain came down now, creating a welcome noise buffer, as the heavy drops pounded the swamp water all around him.

Peering around the tree, Sam finally put eyes on the shooter fifty feet behind him, slowly making his way through the marshland. The man, bald and clean shaven, was about his size and dressed in all black: black pants, long-sleeve shirt, and work boots. A black rifle hung on a thick strap over his shoulder. He looked to be in his forties. Sam didn't recognize him, as he wasn't one of the guys who had chased after him in Mexico City. Who the hell was he? Was he the same guy that had taken shots at him in Jackson Square? He had a stone-cold look about him as he held the handgun with a long silencer attached to the end—not that the assassin needed to hide the sound of his gunshots out here in the middle of nowhere. The guy was cutting a slow path about thirty feet to Sam's right, so he was not coming straight at him. Sam had done enough to create some room away from where he'd originated. Could he get back without being detected? To get that opportunity, he would need to wait until the very last second.

Sam grimaced again, feeling biting pain shoot up and down his right arm. He needed to get some pressure on the bullet wound, cut off the blood flow. Staying very still, he watched the man begin to level up with him, still thirty feet off to his right, carefully moving in and out of swamp trees. The guy would stop, listen, and then point the gun in different directions. Sam practically held his breath, slowly scooted around his current tree to stay blocked from view. Looking around again, he watched, knowing he had to choose the perfect moment. The assassin would stop hunting at some point and make his return to the cabin. Sam needed him at the farthest distance possible.

The assassin made it about twenty feet beyond him when Sam decided to make a run for freedom. His survival was going to be determined by who could run through swamp water the fastest, although Sam was at the disadvantage of maybe having to evade bullets in the process. He counted down in his mind, begged God for a miracle, and pushed himself off the wet tree. Sloshing through mud, he kept his head ducked low, circling in and out of trees. He didn't have the luxury of stopping to look or listen to see the progress of his hunter. He just had to keep running no matter what and hold nothing back.

Spotting the cabin a hundred feet ahead of him, he slipped in the mud, fell face-first into swamp water, and saw something long and dark slither off to his right. He cursed, quickly got back up, raced forward, his shoes trudging through the marshland until he finally made his way into the clearing beside the cabin. No other vehicles were parked there except the cab. How did the assassin make it to the cabin? He rushed around to the front, toward the cab driver's door. He pulled it open and found the driver slumped over in the seat, a bullet hole in his head. The assassin must've taken him out from a distance, which explained the driver falling forward onto the car horn for several seconds.

Sam yanked him out of the seat and onto the ground. He jumped into the driver's seat, found the key in the ignition. The cab rumbled to life. Sam shifted into reverse and hit the gas pedal. He slammed the brakes, shifted into drive, stomped the gas pedal again. That's when the man appeared in the opening directly behind him. Sam watched his mirror before ducking as low as possible in the driver's seat. The back of the cab was then littered with bullets. They shattered the back window and went all the way through to puncture the windshield. Sam peered up just enough to keep from driving straight into a cypress tree as the dirt road weaved left in front of him. He kept his foot to the floor, the car racing ahead.

When he didn't hear another explosion inside the car, Sam figured he was far enough away that the man had stopped shooting. He eased up, checked the rearview mirror, couldn't see anything but dirt road behind him. He'd put enough space between himself and the man. About a half mile up the long dirt road, he came upon a dark-gray minivan parked along the edge. He slowed as he approached, wondering if more assassins were inside the vehicle. He ducked low in his seat, looking for any movement, hoping the guy was working alone. He didn't spot anyone else.

Sam didn't have time to search the van, to see if he could find some kind of identification. The man would likely be running up the road behind him. Sam had to keep going, although he knew he would have a much better chance of making it out of there if the assassin didn't have a vehicle. He backed the cab up, angled it toward the front of the van. The cab raced forward and hit the minivan's front left, crumpling metal and plastic. The minivan jolted backward, skidded off the edge of the road, and slid into muddy water. Sam backed up again, shifted into drive, stomped the gas again. More metal crunched, and this time the minivan pitched even deeper into swamp water beside the dirt road. Sam made sure to hit the brakes on the cab before he also got stuck in the muddy water.

He examined the damage. Both of the van's front tires were sunk in at least four feet of brown water, and the front frame of the van was crunched up around the left wheel. He doubted the assassin would have any chance of using the vehicle now. It would take him at least some serious effort—by then, Sam would be gone.

He pulled the cab back onto the road and hit the gas.

He checked the rearview mirror, thought he could see the shadow of a runner in the distance. Sam quickly disappeared when the dirt road made another twist to the left. He exhaled, stared at his muddy face in the mirror. When he felt safe enough, he stopped the car on the side of the road, took off his jacket, and examined his bloody arm. It looked like the bullet had gone straight through the edge of his triceps. It hurt like hell and was bleeding profusely. He managed to tear a sleeve off his jacket and carefully wrapped it around his arm, right above the bloody hole. He used his teeth and did his best to tie it into the tightest knot possible, hopefully cutting off the flow of blood. First chance he got, he would clean it up and doctor himself, but not before getting as far away from there as possible.

As he drove on, Sam said a prayer for the cab driver.

FIFTY-FOUR

Grabbing a quick lunch at a table inside Muriel's Jackson Square, Lloyd and Epps reviewed a stack of eyewitness testimonies from the sniper shooting earlier that day. Most accounts were from people who recalled only chaos—although there were two who did mention seeing a young man in his midtwenties who seemed to have a head start on everyone else. Lloyd assumed it was Callahan, who still eluded them in spite of the FBI upping the velocity of its search. Dozens more FBI agents had been summoned from satellite offices in Alexandria, Shreveport, Baton Rouge, and Monroe. They were basically going door-to-door within a ten-block radius, flashing Callahan's photo at everyone, and searching every security video they could find. Callahan was hiding out somewhere. They would find him.

Simultaneously, they were hunting the Gray Wolf. They'd found another security video right outside the Pontalba buildings that showed a brief glimpse of the same man that had been identified earlier by the apartment neighbor—beard, knit cap, carrying a large black bag. They knew he walked north of Jackson Square, but that's where the trail went cold. The assassin was still loose in the city, and everyone within his vicinity was at serious risk. Lloyd knew that Gerlach was prone to kill randomly while completing a job. That concerned him the most.

All of New Orleans was in harm's way, so they decided that local police had to be notified. So far, they'd managed to keep this away from the media. However, it was just a matter of time. No cop was going to keep word of a famous assassin being on the streets private. Someone would eventually tell a brother or a cousin or a drinking buddy. It would blow up from there.

Lloyd scooped up a bite of his blackened Mississippi catfish, stuffed it in his mouth. "Still nothing back from Krieger on the woman in the video?"

Epps shook his head. "Not yet."

The video they had of Callahan running in Jackson Square showed him sitting down for several minutes with an unidentified black-haired woman who wore thick sunglasses and a gray trench coat. It looked to Lloyd like she had initiated the meeting, and at first, Callahan was resistant to speak with her. Who was she? Had she been used in the assassination effort? They couldn't be sure. When the shooting happened, she bolted away as quickly as Callahan, although she was clearly not the target. Still, she did not have the look of a person who expected the sniper to start shooting. She seemed genuinely alarmed and just as panicked as the others. They did not spot her anywhere in the other security videos they'd secured over the past couple of hours. Krieger was running her image through their facial-recognition program.

Epps was eating shrimp Creole and kept smacking his lips, while saying, "Damn, this is good, Chief." When his cell phone rang, Epps wiped his mouth on a cloth napkin, pressed the phone to his ear. He had a quick conversation with someone on the other end, then said, "Send us everything you got ASAP." Epps hung up.

"What?" Lloyd asked.

"Natalie Foster has been found. *And* lost again."

"Where?"

"She showed up at a police station in Boonsboro, Maryland, a few hours ago. She claimed to have been abducted by several men in a white van last night and then held captive in a warehouse nearby. Somehow, she escaped this morning, ran straight to the police."

"You said lost again?"

Epps nodded. "According to the officer, she was waiting in a conference room while they reviewed her case. Then two men claiming to be CIA agents showed up to get her."

Lloyd nearly spit out a bite of his roasted new potatoes. "What? CIA?"

"That's what the officer said. Claimed they showed him official ID."

"So the CIA has Natalie Foster?"

Epps shook his head. "She took off out the back, stole a car belonging to the office administrator there, and fled town. The officer said the agents also took off after her."

"He get names of the CIA agents?"

"No, sir. He didn't write anything down."

Lloyd sighed. "What the hell is going on? Nothing adds up."

"Agreed."

"I'm going to call Markson over at the CIA. See if I can get anything."

"You trust him?"

"I don't trust any of those guys. But if there's a chance they can shed some light on this, it's worth a try. And Markson owes me."

Lloyd finished off his catfish, stared out the front window, putting the pieces of the puzzle together in his mind. A random rookie attorney. An infamous German assassin. A political reporter. And now the CIA? What was the thread that tied it all together? Again, something didn't sit right. It hadn't from the very first moment he'd heard the Gray Wolf was paying a visit. Lloyd was beginning to fear it would be too late for Callahan or Foster before they finally discovered the connecting thread.

Hell, it might be too late already.

FIFTY-FIVE

On his way back to New Orleans, Sam pulled into a Walgreens parking lot in the small town of Slidell, just on the edge of Saint Tammany Parish. He parked off to the side, away from the front doors, did his best to wipe at least some of the mud from his face with his mud-covered jacket. It didn't do too much good. At least the mud all over his body helped to mask some of the sticky blood that had run down his arm and onto his hand.

The rain had stopped. The humidity was stifling.

He entered the doors of Walgreens, smiled at the young guy behind the counter, as if it was no big deal that he looked absolutely filthy. The clerk didn't seem to mind—maybe with all the fishing and swamps nearby, plenty of folks came in looking like a fresh mud pit and smelling like dead crawfish. Sam circled the rows and found the section for medical supplies in the back. He grabbed a handful of items, including a bottle of rubbing alcohol, and headed back up to the front. After paying the clerk, he asked about the restroom. The clerk pointed to the opposite corner of the store.

Sam locked himself inside the men's restroom. He took a few minutes to wash his face and hands clean in the sink with hot, soapy water. He very slowly untied the jacket sleeve he'd used to cut off the blood flow to his arm. The jacket material stuck to his skin and stung as he tore it away from the bullet hole. He was no longer bleeding badly. The jacket sleeve had at least helped with that. Sam unscrewed the cap from the bottle of rubbing alcohol. He leaned over the sink, poured the entire contents of the bottle over the bullet hole in his arm. He yelped quietly, wanting to scream, but he bit down on his bottom lip instead. When the bottle was empty, he used a stack of paper towels to clean it all up. Because he couldn't go to a hospital right then, he had to do whatever he could to avoid infection.

Placing a thick pad of gauze on top of the wound, which he could now see was on both sides of his triceps, he stuck two large bandages on top of the gauze and capped it all off by wrapping his arm in white medical tape to secure everything in place. He needed this bandage to go the distance. He'd prefer not to lose use of his arm in the process—although if something happened to Natalie, he couldn't care less about his arm.

He left Walgreens and found a Walmart farther up the road. He was less insecure about how he looked now that he'd cleaned himself. He still had the muddy clothes to deal with. He ducked inside the store and quickly picked out a new pair of jeans, new running shoes, new gray T-shirt, and a black Saints cap. He paid for the items, along with some granola bars and Gatorade at the counter. He returned to the cab, which he'd parked at the far end of the parking lot, dropped back inside, and quickly changed into the new clothes.

He took a moment to again log in to Leia's Lounge. He sighed, frowned. Still no sign of Tommy. With each passing failed attempt to reconnect, Sam was growing more fearful that something had happened to his friend. He was also having more and more trouble suppressing his growing angst about Natalie. Getting shot had toyed with his emotions. Every few seconds, he allowed panic to creep into his mind, and it would damn near suck the air right out of his chest.

He started the cab, pulled out of the parking lot.

He eased into traffic on I-10 and made his way back across Lake Pontchartrain.

It was time to go back to DC.

Time to end this already.

FIFTY-SIX

Ethan Edwards booked a last-second flight to DC.

Sam's newest alias would allow him to board an American Airlines nonstop flight in thirty minutes. Then a quick two and a half hours to DC. He'd be on the ground by seven this evening. Which meant he'd have just over two hours to find Rich Hebbard and deliver him—assuming the original conditions still applied. He had no choice but to proceed as if they did. He'd find Hebbard, somehow turn him over, and once again be reunited with Natalie. That was the plan, although nothing so far had gone according to plan. Would they let him walk away at that point? He highly doubted it. He'd have to sort that out when he got there.

Using the alias again made Sam worry about Tommy. He knew he would've been dead already if Tommy had not repeatedly worked his magic on Sam's behalf. The guy owed him nothing but always came through for him in the clutch. He could only hope that Tommy had saved some magic for himself, since he'd gone completely AWOL. Sam again tried to contact Tommy, to no avail.

Sam tucked away in an airport bar near his gate, ordered a beer. Three flat screens were above the bar, two of them showing sports. The other showed CNN and Wolf Blitzer. Sam was sipping his beer and casually monitoring the TVs when something came across CNN that grabbed his attention. Footage of Jackson Square in New Orleans. A male reporter was holding a microphone and standing right next to yellow police tape. Sam could see the statue of Andrew Jackson in the distance behind the reporter. The TV was muted, but he could see the words popping up on a closed-caption ticker at the bottom. The reporter was talking about a sniper shooting in New Orleans earlier in the day. Two people were in the hospital with non-life-threatening injuries. The FBI was involved.

Then the story took a sudden dramatic turn. Wolf Blitzer said CNN sources had identified the FBI's primary suspect in the shooting: Alger Gerlach, known as the legendary Gray Wolf, a German assassin wanted around the globe. There were more than a dozen prominent kills attached to his name, although no one was certain how many were legitimate and how many were myth. Blitzer went on to read about some of the noteworthy kills. An Italian prime minister. A French minister of foreign affairs. The Greek finance minister. And so forth. CNN cut away to archived news footage during the times of the deaths. All tied to Gerlach. According to CNN sources, the FBI strongly believed he'd pulled the trigger in Jackson Square. They also believed he could still be in the city, armed and extremely dangerous. Four pictures of Gerlach popped up on the screen, splitting it into squares. He looked different in each picture. Some with dark hair, some with light, some with facial hair, some without.

Sam stared wide-eyed at the TV screen. The fourth picture snagged his full attention, the one with Gerlach clean shaven and bald. Sam was certain it was the same man who had been hunting him through the swamp just an hour and a half ago. Why in the world was an international assassin coming after him? Wolf Blitzer was talking about how the Gray Wolf was known to command up to $5 million per job. Who would do that? Francisco Zapata? Zapata had likely sent other guys after Sam in Mexico City. But would Zapata put up *that* kind of money to come after him? Was it Lex Hester, the crazy millionaire oilman? Hester certainly had the necessary cash. Sam had been speculating that Hester was the man behind luring him into this sinister hunt for Natalie. So while the money made sense, nothing else about it did. If Lex Hester was behind Rich Hebbard's disappearance, he could have had Sam killed way back at El Ángel when Sam was first meeting with the black-haired woman in Mexico City. What perplexed Sam the most was the thought that it would likely take *a lot* of advance coordination to hire someone like Gerlach. He was not likely a guy who could be rounded up in twenty-four hours. Whoever hired the Gray Wolf must have been planning it for weeks. How was that even possible?

Sam shook his head, quickly finished his beer.

He noticed people starting to board at his gate. He dropped cash down on the bar top, pulled the Saints cap even lower on his head, and hustled over to the boarding line. He could not get out of this city fast enough. Two encounters with a famous assassin were plenty for him. He did not want the third time to be the charm.

FIFTY-SEVEN

The cab dropped Natalie in front of the Avalon Theatre.

She'd already been by Tommy's apartment, the address of which she'd found through a police source. The door had been jimmied open, and she found it completely ransacked. No sign of Tommy. That left a bad taste in her mouth. Could Tommy already be involved? Sam had mentioned a couple of times that Tommy liked to meet him at the historic theater—a movie house that was the oldest in the city and regularly showed classic films, including some of his favorite old Westerns. Natalie knew she was grasping at straws, but she had to keep searching for him. With what looked like powerful players at every turn, including government agencies, she needed to go outside her own network for help—the kind of help that only a guy like Tommy could provide. Assuming he was still alive.

The theater was situated in a classic old brick building in the middle of a commercial strip along Connecticut Avenue. Natalie had been there once a few years ago for a showing of *My Fair Lady* with Audrey Hepburn. She quickly pushed through the doors, stepping inside a small café in the front of the theater. Several people were sitting at small tables, eating, some working on laptops or reading their tablets. None of them were Tommy. She approached a man with a mustache who was working the café counter.

"Have you seen a young man of maybe twenty?" she asked quietly. "Could have spiky hair of various colors. Lots of earrings, maybe even a nose ring. Lots of tattoos. Goes by Tommy?"

The mustache man shook his head. "Sorry."

Natalie sighed, turned around, and examined the faces in the café again. She stepped back out in the lobby, wondered if she should go check inside the actual theaters. That seemed like a stretch since Tommy would've had to purchase a ticket at the café counter to go to a movie. Frustrated, she headed back toward the front door, wondering where she would look next. Before she got there, a young guy wearing a theater uniform and carrying a broom and a dustpan stopped her. He had long brown hair in a ponytail and looked to be in his early twenties.

"Hey, lady," he said. "I know Tommy."

"You do?"

"Yeah, he comes in here all the time. Cool guy. He in trouble?"

"Not with me. But he'll be in big trouble if I can't find him ASAP."

"Who are you?"

She studied him. He knew something. "A friend, I swear."

"Tommy doesn't have many friends. I'm certain he would've mentioned you. Can I get a name?"

"Natalie. Why?"

"Wait here."

Natalie watched as the guy walked around a corner and disappeared. She wondered if he had a way to contact Tommy. Two minutes later, he returned.

"Upstairs theater, inside the projector room."

She felt her adrenaline spike as she hustled up the stairs, down a hallway, and then found a door marked PROJECTOR ROOM. Natalie walked into a dark room where a projector was shooting its bright beam through an opening into the upstairs theater. Turning the corner, she came face-to-face with Tommy, his black hoodie pulled up over his head.

"Natalie!" Tommy exclaimed.

They exchanged a brief hug.

"I thought you were dead," Tommy said, shaking his head.

"Why?"

"We knew about your kidnapping. Earlier today, I intercepted a recording of a phone call about you, where one of the men on the recording implied that you were already dead."

"You said *we*? Who is *we*?"

"Me and Sam."

"Is Sam okay?"

"I don't know. My apartment got raided a few hours ago. Several guys came looking for me. I'm just now getting to a place where I can get back online securely." She noticed an open laptop sitting on the carpet in the corner of the room.

"Where is Sam?" she asked.

"The last time we talked, several hours ago, he was in New Orleans."

This confirmed information that Natalie already knew from speaking with Michelle, her FBI friend. "Why is he in New Orleans? What's going on?"

Tommy had her sit next to him on the carpet, brought his laptop up for both of them to see the screen. He gave her a quick rundown about what had happened to Sam during his client meeting with Tom Hawkins upon arriving in Mexico City yesterday. The assassins, the car chase, the federal police building, the mysterious black-haired woman, Rich Hebbard, Francisco Zapata, Lex Hester, and Senator Mark Liddell. He told her about Sam's trip through the drug tunnel and across the US border. He showed her photos of several of the key players and all the information he'd been able to transfer out before putting a stick of dynamite to his old system.

It was a hell of a lot for Natalie to take in all at once.

Tommy said, "Sam has been playing their game, trying desperately to find this Hebbard guy, so he can save you."

"He doesn't know I'm alive?"

"No. The last thing I sent him before bolting my apartment was the phone recording that implied you were dead."

"Can you contact him?"

Tommy shook his head. "I just tried a few seconds ago. No answer."

Natalie cursed. "None of this makes sense. Not when you put what you just told me together with what I found out a short while ago about the CIA."

"CIA?" Tommy asked.

She nodded. "The guys who grabbed me in the parking garage and held me in the warehouse overnight were CIA agents."

Tommy cursed. "Shadow Shepherd," he said, out of the blue.

"Shadow what?"

"I think we've been played from the very beginning on this, Natalie. Someone was in my system before Sam ever even contacted me yesterday. I don't know how they did it. It was someone incredibly skilled— even better than me, I'll admit. I'm convinced they've been controlling and manipulating all of my information. *Everything* I've been feeding Sam to try to help him. I don't really know what's up or down anymore. I'm just now beginning to sort it all out now that I'm free and clear from them."

"What do you mean, Shadow Shepherd?" Natalie asked.

"Something I just now found online, somehow connected to Sam, with a direct thread to what looks like some kind of covert CIA operation."

"What kind of operation?"

"I have no idea. I got blocked right after finding it. That's what I've been working on right now, trying to find another passageway inside, but *nothing* is working so far."

"You think the CIA has been manipulating your system?"

He shook his head. "I can't say for sure."

Natalie ran her hands through her hair, exhaled. "What do we do? We've got to find Sam. Do we go to New Orleans?"

Tommy heard a beep come from his laptop. He stared down at it, cursed again—although it seemed to her like a happy curse.

"What?" she asked.

Tommy smiled wide. "We don't have to go to New Orleans. Sam's coming to us."

FIFTY-EIGHT

Sam slept hard on the plane. Once the flight lifted off the ground, he sank low into his window seat in the very back. His mind was flooded with so many overwhelming emotions—Natalie, Tommy, his real father—that it basically shut completely down on him. He didn't want to think about it anymore. He'd also downed a handful of painkillers at the airport bar earlier to help dull the throbbing ache in his arm. The pills seemed to be working. His head was bobbing within minutes.

He closed his eyes, sank away, and barely stirred the entire flight.

His dreams were vivid. The last time he was with Natalie, the night before his trip to Mexico City, and their parting kiss. Suddenly, she was wearing a simple white dress, barefoot, and standing on the beach beside him, the waves pushing up onto shore just a few feet away. He wore a loose-fitting white button-down, untucked, with cream-colored slacks. Pastor Isaiah was there, too, standing before them, a Bible in his hands, and Sam realized they were getting married. Before he could say "I do," Natalie suddenly turned, let go of his hand, and started walking out into the ocean waves. She kept looking back over her shoulder, like Sam should somehow stop her, but he couldn't move. His legs felt stuck. The waves were up to her waist now, as she continued to wade out even deeper. Sam began to panic. Yet he still couldn't do *anything*. The water rose to her neck. Natalie gave him one last longing look, her eyes full of tears, her face terrified. He begged her to stop, but she didn't. He was screaming her name at the top of his lungs when the water overtook her.

Sam woke with a start, his breath short, covered in sweat.

"Sorry to wake you, sir," the female flight attendant said. "But we've arrived in DC."

"Okay, thanks."

He quickly got to his feet, wiped the sweat from his face, tried to catch his breath. He looked up ahead and noticed almost everyone else was already off the plane. He hustled forward into the back of the line near the cockpit, and then exited the plane into the gate tunnel. Once again, he felt the nerves creep in as he considered the possibility that imposing men would be standing at the foot of the gate, waiting to grab him.

Stepping out into the clearing of the terminal, his eyes carefully bouncing in every direction, he didn't notice anyone staring back at him. He walked briskly down the concourse, intent to grab a cab and get out of the airport as soon as possible. When he turned a corner, someone slipped in right beside him, almost shoulder to shoulder, startling him. Black hoodie pulled up over his head, sunglasses, reeking of cigarettes. *Tommy!*

"Don't look at me, Sam," Tommy urgently whispered, eyes straight ahead. "Just keep walking. Follow me outside."

Feeling a wave of incredible relief push through him, Sam wanted to grab his friend and give him a huge hug, but he resisted the urge and did as he was told. Tommy surely had a reason for his instructions. Sam wondered if others were around them that Tommy somehow knew about. Without another word, he followed Tommy as they pushed through glass doors to the outside, crossed a walkway, and then entered one of the attached parking garages. Halfway down one row of cars, they came upon Tommy's small black Kia Soul hatchback. Sam glanced behind them, made sure no one was following.

He finally turned to Tommy, grabbed him by the shoulders. "You're okay!"

"I am," Tommy replied, grinning ear to ear. "So is someone else."

Sam turned around. The back door of the Kia suddenly flew open, and Natalie was standing there in front of him, like a vision. Was he still dreaming? He scooped her up in his arms, ignoring the sharp pain exploding in his arm, pulling her in so close to him he thought he might actually crush her. She squeezed him tightly in return, kissed him on the lips. He held her face tenderly in his hands, tears already dripping down their cheeks.

"You're alive," he exclaimed, out of breath.

"So are you. Thank God."

"All right, all right, enough of the mush," Tommy interjected, pulling open the driver's door. "If we all want to *stay* alive, we've got to go right now."

FIFTY-NINE

Tommy booked a room at an airport hotel under an alias. Sam knew the guy probably had twenty different sets of names and IDs at his disposal. They huddled inside a room on the sixth floor that overlooked the Potomac. Sam moved to the window, pulled the curtains back. The sun was setting on the most powerful city in the world. He could see the Capitol Building over the water in the distance. He could hardly believe he'd somehow made it back to DC—after everything he'd been through the past two days—*and* he already had Natalie right beside him. They could hardly stop embracing long enough to even talk. Still, Sam knew this wasn't finished yet. They had to figure out what to do from here.

He still had to find Rich Hebbard.

They quickly ordered burgers from room service. Tommy sat at the desk with his face stuck in his laptop, his fingers moving at warp speed. Pacing the room, Natalie shared every detail she knew about her abduction and escape. She talked about meeting with her FBI source a few hours ago, who informed her that her captors were actually CIA agents. Sam was impressed with her survival skills and street instincts. He wasn't the only one who could find his way out of a real mess.

The food arrived. Sam finished his in five bites and took his turn to fill them in on everything that had happened to him since his last communication with Tommy. The only thing Sam didn't mention was the possibility that Hebbard might be his real father. He still couldn't say those words out loud. They felt stuck in his throat. He needed final confirmation—something still felt off about it. Until Sam could put his finger on it, he just wanted to keep the information to himself. He hated lying to Natalie—especially after everything they'd been through—but he rationalized it as his way of protecting their relationship from further emotional pain.

Had they not been through enough already?

When he finished, Sam could tell Natalie had switched into reporter mode. She snagged a notepad off the hotel desk and was scribbling furiously.

She turned to Tommy. "So who sent you the message to warn Sam in Jackson Square?"

Tommy didn't take his eyes off the screen. "I don't know. I can't find *any* angle or connection. Because I had to wipe my system clean, I can't even go back and try to retrace the path to me. Even if I could, I don't think I'd find anything."

Sam again walked to the window. It was now 8:30 p.m. and dark outside.

"You sure no one ever mentioned Shadow Shepherd?" Tommy asked Sam for the second time in the past few minutes. His friend had told Sam about finding the name and what looked like a direct connection to Sam through what he called a rogue CIA network.

"Nothing," Sam repeated. "I've never heard of Shadow Shepherd."

Natalie walked up to him, gently touching his wounded arm. "You really should go to the hospital and get this looked at."

He gave her a quick smile. "I'm fine, I promise. It can wait."

She didn't look pleased. "You have to stop getting shot already. Twice in one year is more than enough for me."

"I'll try my best."

A cell phone on the table buzzed—a burner phone Tommy had picked up earlier for Natalie. She raced over to it, stared at the message.

"It's her," Natalie confirmed. "She can meet me in twenty minutes."

"I'll go with you," Sam said.

"No, you stay here," Natalie countered. "Work with Tommy. I'll be back in under an hour. She won't talk to me if you're there, anyway."

"I'm not letting you out of my sight again, Natalie."

"I'll be fine," she insisted, taking his hand in hers. "I can take care of myself. Did you not hear how I climbed out of a bathroom ceiling, stole a car, and got away from two CIA agents? You're not the only badass here, babe. Plus, this is a friend—*not* someone trying to kill me. Believe me, your time is much better spent here than playing bodyguard for me."

SIXTY

Sam stared down at the Potomac below. Across the way, DC was lit up in marvelous lights. The Capitol Building glowed the brightest, which Sam considered ironic with the level of corruption among many of the elected men and women who worked there. People they were all supposed to trust. He thought about Senator Mark Liddell, the man who had supposedly helped to coordinate the shady back-room oil deal between Lex Hester and Francisco Zapata—a crooked deal that had somehow eroded and pushed both Hawkins and Hebbard to seek government asylum. An act that had put Natalie in jeopardy, almost killed Tommy, and sent Sam on a desperate run. He shook his head. Once again, this great city had smacked him directly in the face with a nefarious act of power and greed.

They weren't out of the woods yet.

He checked the time again. Natalie had been gone only twenty minutes, but he was already anxious. He knew it was an important meeting where they hoped to get some answers, but it was difficult letting her out of his sight.

He turned to Tommy. "Sorry they wrecked your apartment, buddy."

Tommy glanced up from his laptop, shrugged. "No worries. Probably time for me to move on, anyway—set up a new shop somewhere else. I was already thinking I should become more mobile. My world is getting more complex and dangerous every day. I shouldn't stay in one place too long anymore. Governments are catching up. Hell, they should be since they're now pouring billions into hacking and antihacking efforts. The CIA even paid one of the boys I used to work with a million dollars to join their team. That traitor sold out and took the money."

"You ever think of taking the money?" Sam asked.

Tommy frowned. "What am I going to do with a million dollars, Duke? Nah, you won't ever see me make that turn."

It was actually comforting to hear Tommy say that. "Any luck yet with Shadow Shepherd?"

Tommy shook his head in frustration. "No, man, they've got so many roadblocks and redirects around this thing. Whatever info is behind that wall is *very* valuable to them. And whoever is hiding it knows their way around the block." Something popped up on Tommy's screen and grabbed his attention. "Sam, come check this out."

Sam moved in behind Tommy, stared at the laptop screen. They'd been monitoring Hebbard's personal e-mail that Sam had discovered while at the swamp cabin earlier that day. Two hours ago, Hebbard had sent a new e-mail within the same strand to the address they thought belonged to Liddell: I'm here. Waiting for instructions.

A reply had just arrived.

LiddellM77: Phoenix Park Hotel. The Congressional Suite. 15 Minutes.

There was an immediate reply from Hebbard.

Swampman52: Headed that way.

Sam read it twice. He'd have both Hebbard *and* Liddell together in the same room. If he left now, he could be there around the same time that Hebbard arrived.

Tommy looked up at him. "What're you going to do?"

Sam considered it for only a second.

Was Rich Hebbard *really* his father?

It was time to go get the damn truth—on all fronts—once and for all.

"I'm going to join their little party."

SIXTY-ONE

"Where is he?" Lloyd asked Krieger.

"Phoenix Park Hotel. Next to Union Station."

"We got his room?"

"No, sir. But we got men in the lobby."

"How many men?"

"Two. Nelson and Ford."

Lloyd cursed, pivoted to Epps. "Get twenty more men over there in a hurry."

"Yes sir," Epps replied, pulling out his phone.

The FBI jet had landed just a few minutes ago. A couple of agents whisked him and Epps away in a hurry inside the back of a black Tahoe. Agent Krieger was waiting on them in the backseat of the vehicle. There was a clear sense of urgency within the group. A private jet had flown out of New Orleans before them—a Gulfstream G450 that could hold sixteen passengers—and yet only *one* passenger was listed on the manifest. A passenger with a name and paperwork that didn't register as a real person in any of their systems, but someone who matched one of the descriptions of Alger Gerlach. It was a late discovery, and Lloyd already felt behind on it, but it was a potential break nonetheless. They believed the Gray Wolf was also back in DC.

"We know who booked the private plane?" Lloyd asked Krieger.

"A group called Grafton. That's all I can find, sir. No other details."

"*You* can't find anything else?" Lloyd asked, surprised.

Krieger sighed, shook his head, looking defeated. "It's a cover, boss. That's for damn sure."

"CIA?" Lloyd asked Krieger directly.

Krieger gave him a stunned look. "I don't . . . I don't know. The Agency is quite capable." His forehead wrinkled up. "You think the CIA is flying Alger Gerlach around?"

"I'm open to anything at this point."

Lloyd had finally talked with Agent Markson, his insider source at the CIA, although it took several frustrating hours to coordinate the call. Markson made sure that Lloyd jumped through a half dozen irritating hoops until he was certain Lloyd was on a secure phone. Even once they were on the line, Markson was still overtly paranoid about their conversation. However, he owed Lloyd, and Lloyd was looking to cash in that full check. Markson said he wasn't sure what was really going on—everything was *way* underground. Markson admitted that a covert operation might be ongoing involving Sam Callahan and Natalie Foster. He couldn't pinpoint what department was running lead or any of the agents involved. Markson didn't know anything about the Gray Wolf, other than what had come across the news. *And* he wasn't going to travel any lengths to find out—he didn't owe Lloyd that much.

Before hanging up, Markson added one last thing, in a dramatic whisper. "Listen, Spencer, this is *way* above my pay grade. And certainly above yours, too, so be careful. Don't go around asking too many questions, if you know what's good for you."

The Tahoe sped through traffic into DC proper.

SIXTY-TWO

Natalie entered Café Berlin, two blocks from the Hart Senate Office Building, a German café that was on the ground floor of several joined-together townhomes. She grabbed a table in the back corner, away from the busy sidewalk patio, where she could have her back to the wall and watch every face that entered the room. Candace Velasco had been Senator Liddell's chief of staff for the past three years. She was tough and didn't take crap from *anyone* in DC. She'd been a good source when Natalie had been working on a story last year involving an opposing senator. They'd hit it off and had met for coffee a couple of times in the past year. Although Natalie was unsure how Candace would respond when her own boss was the target of her questions. She'd have to carefully walk the line.

A tall redhead of forty with fierce gray eyes, Candace arrived on time as usual, making her way toward Natalie in the back corner. She wore a dark suit, heels, and moved like she was eager to get on to the next meeting. They shared a quick hug, sat opposite each other.

"You want a drink?" Natalie asked.

"Don't have time, hon. I've got to get back."

"I appreciate you coming last minute."

"You said it was an emergency. What're you cooking up?"

Natalie nodded. "You know a guy named Rich Hebbard?"

She decided to just come right out with it. Candace always appreciated her being direct. Natalie knew there was no reason to beat around the bush. Candace was savvy. She understood the necessary relationship between reporters and politicians in the DC game.

Candace shook her head. "No, who is he?"

Natalie was surprised. "An oil attorney out of New Orleans."

"Never heard of him," Candace said, eyes firm. "Why're you asking me?"

"Hebbard has been working on an oil deal involving Senator Liddell."

Candace frowned. "Not true. Where'd you get that?"

Natalie studied the older woman. "You're telling me that Liddell doesn't know Rich Hebbard?"

"I'm not saying he doesn't know the guy. I can't account for every single person Liddell knows. I'm just saying he hasn't been involved with him during the past three years. Not since I've been leading his staff."

"What about Lex Hester?"

Candace again shook her head. "Don't know that name, either."

"Francisco Zapata?"

Another frustrated shake of the head. "Nope. Sorry, but you're batting zero for three. Never heard of *any* of them. Liddell has had nothing to do with those names, unless it was way before my time with him." Candace frowned again, this time with more irritation. "Are we going to play the name game all night, Natalie, or are we going to get around to the point of this meeting? I still have important business back at the office tonight. I'm doing you a favor by sitting here."

Natalie pressed. "You're telling me Liddell hasn't made multiple trips to Mexico City in the past year to privately meet with Zapata?"

"I've been with Liddell almost every day for the past three years. If he'd made trips to Mexico City, I sure as hell would know about it. I'm his damn chief of staff. I basically know every time Liddell goes to the bathroom, brushes his teeth, or tries to sneak a shot of whiskey in the morning."

Natalie was confused. None of this made sense. She thought about Liddell's personal e-mail exchange with Hebbard earlier that day. "There's no chance that Liddell could operate outside of you? Personal travel, personal phones, or a personal e-mail address?"

Candace sighed. "I control *everything* he does. Liddell usually doesn't scratch his ass without me scheduling it for him. I highly doubt he has a private phone or e-mail that I don't know about. Look, I know how to do my job and protect my boss, so I'm going to ask you one more time, why the hell am I here?"

"Someone is trying to implicate Liddell in a story. I'm just gathering facts."

Candace immediately went into protective mode. "Who? Someone on Hansel's staff? You can't trust them."

"Not them. I can't say."

Candace softened. "Listen, your source is feeding you lies. You know I've always shot straight with you. Don't go writing anything without talking to me first. I can show you his travel records. I can give you his complete calendar. I can vouch for nearly every second of that man's life the past thirty-six months."

Natalie nodded. "Thanks, Candace."

"I've got to get back."

She watched as Candace walked out of the café. Natalie was stunned. They had so much information connecting Liddell with Zapata and Hebbard. They had hotel records, photos, and of course, they had today's personal e-mail exchange with Hebbard. Yet she believed Candace. Natalie had become quite an expert at reading people's faces. She'd even had professional training in that area. In this town, you had to be an expert to be good at her job, as DC was the single largest collection of the greatest liars in the world.

Candace Velasco was telling her the truth.

SIXTY-THREE

Gerlach was furious. From the beginning, it was clear he hadn't been given all the cards. Someone else was playing dealer, and that didn't sit well. If something like this had happened in the past, he would have made sure a client paid for it with his life. This was a different situation altogether. He should never have taken this job. It was a mistake. But his own ego pushed him into it. Feeling exposed, Gerlach's instinct was to bolt town; however, his brazen pride had kept him in the game. His target had proved to be a worthy adversary. Twice now he'd somehow evaded Gerlach's reach. That was damn near unheard of. Gerlach had *never* left a job unfinished—that made him the best in the game. His 100 percent completion was what had put tens of millions of dollars into more than a dozen secret offshore bank accounts. That was what allowed him a free pass inside some of the most ruthless countries in the world. He couldn't walk away now.

Gerlach stood in front of the mirror of his hotel bathroom. He was bare chested but wore khaki pants and cheap brown loafers. Staring at himself, he carefully placed the blond toupee on his bald head, situated it just right. The adhesive would seal it in place. He'd already lightened the eyebrows. A thin mustache matched the toupee. Turning around, he pulled a short-sleeve white button-down shirt off a hanger, sliding it on over his arms. He buttoned it halfway up and tucked it into the pants. He grabbed a rolled-up bath towel and stuck it down inside the shirt before buttoning it to the top. He patted his new paunch. He easily looked thirty pounds heavier. The gold horn-rimmed glasses were last.

He studied himself in the mirror, felt satisfied.

He walked into the bedroom, found the silver case on the dresser. Opening it, he took out the black gun and silencer, screwed them together, and shoved the weapon into a small holster on the flat of his back, beneath the khaki pants. The handgun was a strategic move. He wanted to be up close and personal to ensure he finished the job. No more shooting from a distance. Not with this target and his uncanny ability to somehow evade a sniper shot. Gerlach was not concerned with witnesses. He could strip the entire costume within seconds and disappear. He lifted the camera and strap from the dresser, draped the device around his neck.

Another peek in the dresser mirror. Bob the Tourist.

Gerlach checked his watch. Darkening the lights, he moved to the hallway. At the elevators, he was joined by a young mom with her two small boys. The boys stared up at him. He gave them a wink and a smile, pretended to take their pictures with the bulky camera. They smiled shyly back at him.

"Cute kids," he told the mom, who grinned and said thanks.

They rode down to the lobby together. Gerlach let the family out first, then moved into the corridor behind them. He spotted one federal agent at the front check-in desk, hounding a hotel staffer, another by the front door, watching hotel guests as they came in and out. The agents were anything but inconspicuous. Gerlach walked right past the agent at the main glass doors without a second blink, got nothing from the man in return. They were such amateurs compared to him. Gerlach couldn't fault them—he was the very best.

It was time to finish the job.

SIXTY-FOUR

The cab dropped Sam a block away from the Phoenix Park Hotel. He walked to the street corner, his heart already in his throat. Not because he was afraid for his life. After all, inside this hotel room was just a politician and an old lawyer. However, after everything Sam had discovered the past two days, his nerves had more to do with finally coming face-to-face with a man who, by all accounts, was indeed his *real* father. He felt his hands trembling, both with angst and anger. If the man in fact knew Sam existed, where the hell had he been Sam's whole life? A life that had been filled with so much deeply scarring pain, both physical and emotional. Standing there, Sam couldn't help but reflect on every tumultuous foster-care situation he'd somehow survived—like a barrage of bad movie scenes spinning on a reel through his mind. Every swing of an angry fist. Every cigarette burn to the arms and legs. Every bruise in the name of discipline. Every angry word spit in his direction, telling him he was worthless garbage.

He felt overwhelmed by the moment.

Sam had already been through many of these same emotions with his mom. He'd somehow survived that and found healing. But there was a soft spot with her from the beginning. He wasn't sure why—maybe because he knew his mother had also endured a painful life. They were on equal footing. Something felt very different with his father. The pain felt more intense, and the wound ran even deeper. He'd never wanted to take a swing at his mother, no matter how angry he was with her in the beginning. Sam knew it might take everything within him to not immediately aggressively unload on his father as soon as Sam walked inside the hotel suite. Standing there, he wanted nothing more than to crush the man's nose with the full velocity that twenty-six years of pain could muster.

He took a deep breath, exhaled. He glanced up North Capitol Street, where he could see the glow of the Capitol Building a few blocks away. He thought about Senator Liddell, wondered what he was about to walk in on. Sam understood that this moment was more complex than just an angry abandoned son who was meeting his long-lost father for the first time. This moment was all wrapped in a political conspiracy that reached the height of power and corruption, where innocent people were being killed. He had to control his emotions.

Sam would need to keep his boxing gloves in the closet for now.

He stepped across the street toward the green awning at the main entrance of the Phoenix Park Hotel. Several people were out and about on the sidewalks—it was a busy area, with Union Station and the National Postal Museum nearby. His heart began beating faster with each step closer to the front doors. The two men should be inside the hotel suite by now. He was within sixty seconds of standing outside their door.

Sam felt him before he saw him. It was a strange sensation, but part of the odd way his mind always worked. The man walked out from the shadows. Sam could immediately feel all of the man's focus directly on him. Sam stopped walking, looked straight over at the guy. Twenty feet away. At first, Sam thought maybe he was wrong. It was just a normal-looking guy in a white shirt, glasses, camera hanging around his neck. Then Sam locked in on the eyes behind the glasses, and he knew his instinct was right. He'd seen those eyes before—just a few hours ago, while tucked under a cypress tree behind a thick curtain of Spanish moss.

The Gray Wolf.

Panic gripped him. Sam knew he had to react first, or it was over. As if in slow motion, he saw Gerlach reach around to his back. Sam turned, jumped off the sidewalk, darted into the busy street. A taxi swerved, honked its horn, barely missed crushing him. He never slowed. More cars swerved, honked, as he skirted the intersection. Sam broke into an all-out sprint straight toward the front of Union Station, where he knew he'd find a mass of people and potentially hundreds of places to get himself lost—if he could only get inside without a bullet hitting him in the back first. He skipped up on another sidewalk, threaded a group of people who were standing outside on the sidewalks around Columbus Circle.

Sam took his first chance to look back over his shoulder. The man in the white shirt was not far behind. Sam dashed forward again, causing people to turn and stare. But he couldn't slow down. He knew the Gray Wolf would kill him right out in the open. The assassin had already made that perfectly clear. The only safety for Sam was getting away completely.

Sam burst through the doors of Union Station's main entrance, hustled inside the massive main concourse. Union Station was packed with shoppers, diners, and travelers. Sam ran straight into the middle, his mind immediately sending him a dozen different maps with alternative escape paths. He circled through the crowd, raced toward a descending escalator. He pushed his way in front of some shoppers, drawing their ire and complaints, and hopped onto the descending escalator.

Another peek behind him. The Gray Wolf was still there. Fifty feet back but coming on strong. Sam shoved his way through more people as he hurried down the escalator without waiting. He reached the lower level and spilled out into the food court—another crowded area. Again, people began stopping and staring at the guy who was running like a crazy man. Sam heard more yelling from behind and knew that Gerlach was aggressively pushing his way through the same crowd.

Sam swiftly zigzagged across the entire food court, at one point hurdling a small child who stepped out in front of him. He never saw the custodian with the mop and bucket just ahead of him. His shoes hit the wet floor and flew out from beneath him. Sam fell hard, slid twenty feet, causing people to gasp all around him. Then he heard panicked screams.

Someone yelled, "He's got a gun!"

Sam turned back, spotted Gerlach stomping right toward him, gun in hand and pointed in his direction. Sam pushed off the floor, hustled forward. The first shot hit the floor a few inches behind him. Massive panic swiftly rippled through the crowd, as more screaming ensued, more chaos. With an active shooter now in play, everyone in the food court was making a mad dash for safety, for an exit, somewhere far away from the madman.

Sam found his way to a twisting stairwell, where groups of people were already ducking behind the short wall. He climbed the stairs four at a time, bounding over and around people, his head ducked low, his feet propelling him forward. As he found his way up, he could feel the assassin climbing up behind him. When Sam reached the top, a stone vase with a plant on a display stand exploded just a foot away from him, causing Sam to dive and hit the floor again. He quickly picked himself back up. The chaos had reached the main concourse, and a sea of shoppers and diners were scrambling about in all directions, many of them pushing each other down, their only care their own safety, more yelling and screaming.

Sam ran like hell, wondered if this was the end.

When he neared the main entrance of Union Station, a dozen men and women in dark windbreakers suddenly stormed in through the front doors, each of them with guns already drawn. Sam skidded to a stop a few feet away from them, stunned by their explosive entrance.

One of the larger men immediately tackled Sam to the ground, quickly followed up by two other men, creating a protective barrier over him.

"Stay down, Sam!" the big guy instructed.

More windbreakers entered Union Station, more guns drawn, and they quickly fanned out in all directions. Sam lost count at twenty federal agents. They were everywhere. He lay still on the floor, tried to peer behind him, looking for the face of Gerlach. He didn't see the assassin anywhere. He squinted, thought he caught a glimpse of white shirt and khaki pants in the far-off distance. The figure quickly disappeared with the blur of the crowd.

After spending a few minutes pinned to the floor, the big agent helped Sam to his feet. Another much older guy walked up to him.

"Sam Callahan?" he asked.

Sam nodded, still dizzy from the chase.

"Special Agent Spencer Lloyd."

SIXTY-FIVE

Agent Lloyd surveyed Union Station. His team had secured the entire concourse, and yet still no sign of the Gray Wolf. The assassin had simply evaporated into thin air—like a ghost. One moment right out in front of them, the next gone. Frustrated, Lloyd had just started to question Callahan when his phone buzzed in his pocket. He was prone to ignore it until he saw that it was a direct call from FBI Director Stone, his boss—everyone's boss. Lloyd thought it entirely strange to be receiving a phone call from the top man at such a crazy moment.

What the hell could Stone want?

He stepped away so that he could hear better, answered it. "Sir, Spencer here."

"You got Sam Callahan?" Stone barked.

Lloyd was surprised. "Yes, sir, we do."

"Let him go," Stone ordered.

"Sir?" Lloyd questioned.

"You heard me, Spencer. I said to let the kid go. Tell Callahan he should immediately proceed to the Congressional Suite at the Phoenix Park Hotel."

Lloyd was baffled. "But, sir, I don't understand. We're in the middle of absolute chaos here, with Gerlach still on the loose, and Sam Callahan is at the center of it all. He's key to my entire investigation."

"I'm not concerned with your understanding. Just obey my orders."

Lloyd wanted to argue but knew he couldn't. "Yes, sir."

Stone hung up. Lloyd stared over at Callahan.

Who the hell was this guy?

SIXTY-SIX

Sam sat on a bench inside the main concourse at Union Station, surrounded by six FBI agents. It had calmed down some—a swarm of FBI agents securing the area and now a massive police force also on hand. He licked his bottom lip, tasted blood. Other than his arm throbbing in pain beneath all the bandages, a bloody lip seemed to be the worst of it. He so desperately wanted to pull out his phone and call Natalie, but he was afraid with all the feds around, it might just lead to more trouble. He resisted the urge. He wasn't sure what was next. Hebbard and Liddell were currently in the hotel suite next door, and he was stuck there with the FBI. After such a long road the past two days, Sam was frustrated. He wanted a chance to finish this, to stand face-to-face with his real father. Would he ever get that chance?

The man who introduced himself as Special Agent Spencer Lloyd walked back up to him, a pained expression on his face. Looked like bad news. Sam braced for the impact.

Lloyd said, "I've been ordered to instruct you to proceed immediately to the Congressional Suite at the Phoenix Park Hotel."

Sam tried and failed to hide his surprise. "How do you know about the Congressional Suite?"

"I'm not at liberty to say."

Sam stood. "So . . . I can just leave?"

Lloyd nodded, again looking pissed about it.

Sam slowly began to walk toward the main doors, taking a couple of glances behind him along the way, wondering if this was all a bad joke and federal agents were about to tackle him again. No one did. He reached the outside, maneuvered through the crowds and police cars, and walked a block over until he was back in front of the green awning of the Phoenix Park Hotel. He peered up and down the sidewalk, making sure he was not about to get ambushed again. He had a dozen different theories bouncing through his head, one of which had the Gray Wolf somehow working with the FBI to have him killed. He dismissed that idea along with all of the others. He simply had no idea what was about to happen.

Sam entered the hotel, made his way to the elevators, and punched a button for the top floor. Seconds later, he stepped out into the hallway and found the door for the Congressional Suite. Inside, he was supposed to find a meeting between Hebbard and Liddell. Now, after the whole bizarre FBI deal, he wasn't so sure. He noticed the door to the suite was already cracked open. Should he knock? Was someone expecting him?

He cautiously opened the door and stepped inside, feeling an eerie calm. Whatever happened next, he'd at least reached the end of this journey. He'd survived two days that proved to be even more intense and treacherous that what he went through with McCallister and Redrock Security last fall.

He heard no noise coming from inside the suite. No talking. No TV. Nothing. Strangely quiet. Sam moved down a short hallway and then stepped out into a spacious living room. He stiffened, suddenly couldn't breathe. A half dozen familiar faces stared back at him from all corners of the living room, as if they were simply waiting for him to arrive. He was stunned. Standing to his left was Desperado, the assassin from the Four Seasons in Mexico City. Right next to him stood Tom

Hawkins, who was still wearing his Hawaiian shirt. Hawkins gave him a quick nod. With furrowed brow, Sam's eyes moved left to right. Sitting in a chair was Agent Mendoza from Mexico City's federal police building. A quick grin from Mendoza. On the end of the sofa sat Uncle Jerry, who gave him a quick two-finger salute. Right next to Uncle Jerry sat Teresa, Hawkins's ex-wife from New Orleans. The final member was the black-haired woman in the gray trench coat, who sat in another chair. She gave him a curt smile.

Sam felt like he was having an out-of-body experience.

After what felt like an eternity of silence, an older man finally stepped into the living room from a back bedroom. Sam blinked. The gray-bearded man. Marcus Pelini, formerly of the CIA, standing there right in front of Sam, wearing all black: black sport coat, black shirt, black slacks. Sam's mind was spinning off in all directions. He *had* in fact seen Pelini in New Orleans. It wasn't just a vision he'd made up in his own mind. The man *was* there. Why? Sam couldn't make sense of any of this. Tom Hawkins was dead. Sam had seen the man standing right beside Hawkins put a bullet into him, clear as day. Now, they were both standing next to each other like they were buddies? What the hell was going on?

Pelini moved to the middle of the living room, stood directly in front of Sam. "Good to see you, Sam," he said. "I'm glad you made it."

Sam opened his mouth, but no words came out. He didn't know what to say.

"We have a lot to talk about," Pelini continued. "Let's get started."

Pelini turned to the others, snapped his fingers. The cast of characters began making their way out of the hotel suite, but not before each one of them came up to Sam, shook his numb hand, patted him on the shoulder, and shared words like, "Good job, Sam." "Impressive." "Really nice work." "Hard to believe, but you actually did it."

When they were all gone, Pelini asked Sam to have a seat on the sofa. It was just the two of them now alone in the living room. Pelini walked over to a bar. "Can I get you some water, Sam? Coffee? Maybe something stronger?"

Sam slowly shook his head, dazed. He almost wanted to pinch himself to see if this was all real. He felt like he'd just fallen down a rabbit hole, like Alice in Wonderland. Pelini poured himself a glass of scotch and leaned against the fireplace.

"I'm sure this is very confusing," Pelini began, taking a sip.

"You got that right," Sam said, his first words.

"The people you saw in here all work for me."

Sam tilted his head. "CIA?"

Pelini nodded. "Correct."

"I thought you were retired?"

A quick grin. "You never fully retire from the Agency."

"But . . . why?"

"I'm going to be very direct with you—I think you at least deserve that. This group of agents is part of a deep-cover special unit that I lead. We are the best of the best. But we don't officially exist, if you know what I mean. You can't Google us. We're not on any CIA website. Not on any budget sheet. Only a small group of people inside the Agency with the highest level of clearance even know about us. Over the past two days, you've been an unwitting participant in one of the most clandestine but important operations I've ever led."

Sam's mind was clearing. "Shadow Shepherd," he stated.

Pelini seemed genuinely surprised at that mention and quoted, "If a man owns a hundred sheep, and one of them wanders away, will he not leave the ninety-nine on the hills and go to look for the one who wandered off?"

Sam recognized the quote as scripture. "You a priest, too?"

Pelini smiled. "No, but I'm impressed."

"I'm supposed to be the lost sheep?"

Pelini smiled again. "In many ways, yes, we all hope so."

Sam was getting pissed off at all the gray-bearded man's coy smiling. "I don't understand," he said. "What the hell are you even talking about?"

"Operation Shadow Shepherd was uniquely designed just for you, custom-fit to test your unique abilities to the absolute max. I already knew you were an incredibly gifted individual—you proved that to me in every way last fall. However, I had to go above and beyond to prove it to my boss. He needed to know exactly what you were capable of in the direst of situations, where we controlled *all* the variables."

"You're telling me this was all some sick game?"

"Not a game. More like an assignment, if you will."

"An assignment for what?"

"We want you to join us. We need an outsider like you for a critical mission."

Sam's jaw dropped open, like Pelini had just used a foreign language. "I think I will have that drink, after all."

Pelini poured a glass of scotch, handed it to him. Sam stood, downed it in one gulp, and began to slowly pace the room. "So you're telling me all of this was not real? It was just a test? The entire story about a corrupt back-room Mexican oil deal gone bad between Francisco Zapata and Lex Hester? The connection to Senator Liddell and Hebbard and Hawkins? All concocted? All orchestrated by you?"

Pelini nodded. "Correct. Senator Liddell exists, of course—we needed to use an actual politician to make it believable. But all of the other characters were fabricated."

"How is that even possible? We found all kinds of information out there. There are pictures, articles, travel records, you name it."

"All created and planted by us," Pelini confirmed.

Sam thought of Tommy and what he'd said about feeling like his system had been controlled and manipulated from the very beginning. "So *you* fed it all to Tommy."

"Brilliant kid, by the way. That was maybe our toughest challenge."

"You sent men to his apartment?"

Another nod. "Like I said, the kid is way too smart for his own good. We needed to shake things up for him, or the operation might have been blown early."

"But you kidnapped Natalie!" cried Sam, getting really pissed, taking an aggressive step toward Pelini. "How the hell could you do that to her?"

"We never harmed her," Pelini said, trying to reassure him. "Any scratches on Natalie were at her own doing. She's one tough girl. A few of my guys have the injuries to prove it."

"Does Liddell know you used him as a pawn in your game?"

"No, he doesn't. And he'll never know. We'll make sure of that."

Sam felt like his head was going to explode. The alcohol wasn't helping. He quickly ran every scene from the past two days through his mind. "I almost killed myself jumping from a hotel balcony," he declared, glaring hard at Pelini.

"But you didn't," Pelini countered, as if that should matter to Sam.

Sam sat on the sofa again, feeling nauseated.

Pelini jumped back in, using his most grandfatherly voice. "Look, Sam, you handled the past two days brilliantly. Just like I knew you would. You're more naturally gifted than any highly trained special agent I've ever had on my team in over thirty years of doing this job. I knew you'd make it through unscathed. I knew you'd succeed, even in the face of every obscene obstacle we put in your path. I just needed the opportunity to prove it to my boss—and to you."

Sam looked up at him with wild eyes. "Are you a lunatic, Marcus? You really think I'm going to join you and the CIA?"

"I understand your frustration."

"Frustration? Frustration is how you feel when someone cuts you off in traffic. What I'm feeling right now can't be described with words. If I had my way, I'd like nothing more than to put my hands around your neck and squeeze until your life is gone—just like you've done to me the past two days. That's how I feel."

Pelini didn't respond to that. He grabbed Sam's empty glass, refilled it, put it back on the coffee table in front of Sam. Sam picked it up, took another sip. More and more scenes flooded his mind.

"You're telling me the bullets were all fake?" Sam asked.

Pelini shook his head. "Some but not all. Intended to miss you at every turn, of course."

"Some of them came *very* close, Marcus."

"Yes, I know."

Sam almost didn't want to ask the next question, it pained him so much. "The whole entire story about Rich Hebbard being my real father—all fabricated and manipulated by you?"

"Yes," Pelini admitted.

Sam cursed, felt like throwing his glass at Pelini. "Damn, Marcus, that's cruel and cold. Even for someone like you."

Pelini sighed. "I'm sorry, Sam. We had to test every part of you. We needed to know the full scope of your physical, emotional, *and* mental makeup. We also knew we had to pull certain emotional strings to get you to fully engage in the operation. Natalie was, of course, part of that. Dangling your real father out there was the second part."

Sam could feel the brutal weight of disappointment collapse on top of him, like a tidal wave tearing him to pieces. Although he'd wanted to punch Rich Hebbard upon meeting him for the first time, Sam had still desperately wanted to meet him. He wanted to come face-to-face with his real father. The truth felt devastating.

"And the Gray Wolf?" Sam sighed, trying to occupy his mind with something else. "Gerlach wasn't a real assassin, either?"

Pelini exhaled. "Well, that's where things got a little tricky for me."

Sam stared at him. "Tricky?"

Pelini finished his glass of scotch. "Alger Gerlach is a real assassin. The best in the world, as a matter of fact. However, he was *not* part of my script for this operation. Gerlach was brought in unbeknownst to me as an outside player."

"Brought in by whom?"

"My boss."

Sam cursed, again stunned. "Wait, you're telling me that the CIA hired a notorious assassin to try to kill me?"

"Yes." Pelini moved to a brown leather chair, rested his elbows on his knees. He stared over at Sam. "Apparently, my boss didn't fully trust that I would pull out all the stops. He doubted that I would put you through the complete wringer without a safety net. And in order for this next mission to succeed, the one for which I'm recruiting you—an operation that is absolutely critical to the safety of America, mind you—my boss wanted to know that you were the real deal. Someone truly capable of the most extraordinary feats."

"And your boss figured the only way to know that is for me to go head-to-head with the most lethal assassin in the world?"

Pelini slowly nodded, sipped his scotch.

Sam shook his head. "Your boss sounds like a swell guy."

"Once we found out about Gerlach, I removed the remaining obstacles from our end. We knew Gerlach was more than enough challenge for you."

"Gee, thanks. That was really nice of you. So, you're the one who sent the message to Tommy to warn me inside Jackson Square?"

"Correct."

Sam put his elbows on his knees, face in hands. Again, he felt nauseated.

"You survived him, Sam," Pelini mentioned. "You beat the Gray Wolf."

Sam looked up. "You act like I should be happy about that. Like I should somehow be pleased with myself about all of this. Surviving your sick game. Outlasting an assassin on three separate occasions. Surviving a balcony fall, a car chase through Mexico City, running for my life through a drug tunnel while being hunted by cartel members, whom I highly doubt were on your payroll. Well, guess what? I'm pissed, Marcus! I didn't sign up for any of this. Hell, what I really want to do right now is turn you in to the police, get you and all your friends thrown in jail. But I know that is futile—you are the damn police! You guys can clearly do whatever the hell you want, even to an innocent civilian like me. What choice do I really have here?"

"I'm giving you a choice now."

"So, what, you actually think I'm going to sign up to help you with some super-secret CIA mission after all of this? Go serve my country simply because you say it's going to make America safer? Nice try, Marcus. If I really have a choice here, you can go screw yourself!"

Pelini didn't respond. He just let Sam sit there for a moment and stew.

Sam leaned back, stared out the balcony window. He could see the Capitol Building. Something dawned on him. "Why didn't your boss fully trust you?"

"What's that?"

"You said your boss wasn't sure you'd put me through the full wringer."

"They felt I was too close to the situation."

"Why? Because of our direct involvement last fall?"

Pelini shook his head. "No, other reasons."

"You don't strike me as an empathetic character. However, your boss was right. You warned me in Jackson Square. I'd be dead if you hadn't. So why'd you do it?"

Pelini seemed to consider his next words for a long moment. "Although Rich Hebbard was a made-up figure, I know your real father, Sam."

Sam's eyes narrowed in on Pelini. Was the man again playing games with him?

Pelini reached into his sport-coat pocket, pulled out a folded sheet of paper. He held it for a moment, almost like he was unsure what he wanted to do with it. Then he handed it over. Sam unfolded the paper, stared at it. A copy of laboratory results from a medical DNA-testing service. There was a chart with various letters and numbers in boxes under two columns, one for *Child* and the other for *Alleged Father*.

Sam's eyes settled in on three lines at the top.

Child: Samuel Weldon Callahan

Alleged Father: Marcus Eugene Pelini

Probability of Paternity: 99.9999%

Sam's eyes widened, his mouth parting. *What?* He read it all again. The man sitting across from him was his *real* father? Was that possible? He couldn't speak. He just kept staring a hole through the test results, the paper practically shaking in his fingers.

Pelini began to explain. "I met your mother in Denver in my early days with the Agency while on a training assignment there. We had a brief fling when I first arrived, until I found out she wasn't actually a college student like she'd claimed. She was much younger than that. By then, she was already pregnant. I tried to get her to terminate the pregnancy, even offered her money. Your mother refused—even after I told her she would *never* see me again. I was set to leave the following week on assignment in Turkey with no clear plans to return to the States."

Sam couldn't even look directly at the man; he just kept staring at the test results. "After all I've been through the past two days, how am I supposed to believe this is actually true? And not just another one of your sick ways to manipulate me?"

"We can go get a second test tomorrow, confirm it, if you want."

Sam stood on weak legs, walked over to the window. "Did my mother know it was you last fall? When you took her away from her facility?"

"Not at first, but she figured it out. I convinced her that it was for your own safety to never reveal my true identity. That my life with the CIA would only make your life hell, if you ever knew."

Sam again thought about his mom and the hours right before her death, where she'd wanted to share some hard truths about his past. He had a feeling he now knew what she was going to say. She was finally going to tell him the whole truth. He let out a deep breath, stared out at the city lights. He had so many questions; however, at the moment, he felt emotionally wrecked and unable to handle any more surprises or damaging truths.

"How much time do I have to decide?" Sam asked.

"Decide what?" Pelini asked. "About the second paternity test?"

"Whether or not to join you on this mission."

Pelini seemed pleased at his question. "I need to know by tomorrow."

Sam glanced over, frowned. "You can't be serious."

Pelini said, "We don't have the luxury of time here. You'll understand if you choose to join us. Until then, I can't tell you anything more."

"If I say no, I go back to my normal life? You never bother me again?"

"Correct."

Sam's eyes went back to the window, and he studied himself in the reflection. He was beat up to hell. His whole body had hurt from head to toe before this meeting. Now it was nearly indescribable how he felt. Like being dragged behind an eighteen-wheeler for two straight days, somehow surviving that brutal carnage, only to stand up in the road, dust himself off, and suddenly be swept away at the last moment by an F5 tornado.

"One more thing," Pelini added. "You can't tell a soul about this."

Sam turned, his eyes saying everything.

Pelini shook his head. "Not even Natalie."

SIXTY-SEVEN

Sam took a deep breath, collected himself. He was all tied up in emotional knots—way beyond anything he'd ever experienced in his life, which was saying quite a lot considering his arduous past. What came next for him only would make him feel much worse. He had no choice. Reaching up, he knocked on the hotel-room door, felt a lump in his throat the size of a baseball. Natalie yanked the door fully open, nearly tackled him to the carpet. They hadn't communicated since she'd left for her meeting with Liddell's chief of staff more than two hours ago. Tommy stood up from his laptop at the hotel desk, also looking quite pleased to see Sam safely return. There had clearly been some heightened tension in the room while they both waited for him.

"What happened?" Natalie cried, nearly out of breath. "I saw the shooting and the chaos at Union Station. Were you there?"

"Yes, but I'm okay now."

"I've been going crazy trying to reach you."

"Sorry, I lost my phone in the whole ordeal."

"Where have you been, Sam? That happened over an hour ago!"

"I'm so sorry." Sam pulled her out into the hotel hallway, nodded over to his left. Two imposing men in black suits stood ten feet down, waiting for them. Sam moved back inside the hotel room. "I've been with the FBI going over *everything*. The good news is the feds finally have the situation under control. We're all safe now."

He could see the tension release in her shoulders. She let out a deep breath, sat on the end of the bed. Sam still felt as wound up as ever, although he was trying to hide it. The two men in the hallway were not FBI, but CIA agents from Pelini's team. It was all part of his constructed cover story. The lies had begun. It sucked. He hated not being honest with Natalie, especially in this tender moment, but he had no choice. He would do everything he could to protect her. She could never know that Pelini was his real father. He still didn't want to believe it himself. Nor could she ever know the truth about the CIA being behind the hell they'd all been put through the past two days.

If Natalie knew the truth, there was no way she would *ever* let it go. If she even saw a crack of potential Agency corruption, she would relentlessly go after it. Sam knew, at least for the moment, he had to do whatever possible to fill those cracks and assure her safety—even from herself. At least, that's what he kept telling himself. Each lying word felt like a drop of acid on his tongue. Sam had yet to decide what to do with Pelini. He was still seething about what he'd been put through, completely overwhelmed by the shocking revelation that Pelini was his real father. Unable to process through it, he had so many questions that were still left unanswered.

At this point, he wasn't sure he wanted any answers. He wasn't sure he ever wanted to talk with Pelini again. He needed some space to think, to clear his head, to privately sort this all out. Pelini had served him up another intricately fabricated story to help Sam explain away the situation in detail over the past two days, as they knew Natalie following along was critical to moving forward—with whatever direction was next. Sam was skeptical. Natalie was not easily deceived. Pelini ensured Sam the story would be foolproof, from *all* angles—if Sam had not yet noticed, Pelini and his team were incredibly skilled at creating a believable mirage.

Sam said, "They want you both to go answer some questions."

"I'm not going *anywhere* with the FBI, dude," Tommy chimed in. "I'm glad we're safe and all. But I'm not letting those guys secretly implant microchips in my back."

Sam smiled, said, "Just be cool, Tommy. It'll be quick and easy. Otherwise, you'll make this a much bigger mess for all of us."

Tommy grunted, looking annoyed. "Fine. But only because it's you guys."

"What did the FBI tell you?" Natalie asked Sam.

"They have Rich Hebbard in custody. The feds picked him up an hour ago, before I ever got in to see him. Although Francisco Zapata wanted Hebbard dead, just like Hawkins—to cover up their lies and corruption—Lex Hester still very much wanted Hebbard alive. According to the FBI, Hester thought he could use Hebbard to blackmail Senator Liddell and still get what he wanted in Mexico. Hester is now missing. The FBI said he jumped on his private jet, crossed the ocean, and they're not yet sure where he landed. They're hunting him down, but they said it could take them a while. The man has the resources to live well off the map for the next twenty years, if he wants. The FBI is also working directly with Mexican authorities to locate Zapata, whom they believe disappeared today behind the protective walls of a drug cartel."

"I've been trying to reach someone at Arnstead. Every number sends me to the same automated company voice mail. It's weird," she said.

Sam shrugged.

"What about Senator Liddell?" Natalie asked.

"They're privately questioning Liddell at this very moment."

"I don't believe he was involved," Natalie insisted.

Sam tilted his head. "Candace tell you that?"

Natalie nodded. "She swears he doesn't even know Hebbard, Hester, or Zapata."

"You believe her?"

"I think she was telling me the truth."

Sam shrugged. "The FBI would tell me only so much, since it's an ongoing investigation. If Liddell is hiding something, the feds will find it. Then again, Liddell could indeed come out clean on this deal." Sam watched Natalie closely, to gauge her response. He knew this could take a lot of quick-handed shadowboxing. He was instructed to report back whatever areas Natalie focused in on so that Pelini and his team could course correct. He tried to shift gears. "The FBI connected Alger Gerlach straight to Zapata through a series of wire transfers that went from a Mexican bank into a numbered account in the Caymans. They haven't been able to find Gerlach yet. They believe he's already out of the country."

"Let's pray so," Natalie said. "What about the CIA guys who grabbed me?"

"They're not CIA, like we thought. They're private operatives from a group who worked directly for Hester, who somehow secured official CIA credentials for them. Hester hired out the most skilled people he could find, both for on the ground *and* behind computers. When the CIA discovered his infiltration, they began a covert investigation into the situation, something they called Shadow Shepherd."

Tommy spoke up with agreement. "That's exactly what I've been finding. *Everything* points back to Lex Hester."

Sam was amazed at how quickly Pelini's team could work over Tommy. Sam felt awful about it. Tommy deserved so much better—he deserved the truth. But Sam would protect Tommy just like he was protecting Natalie. Sam could already tell her mind was burning it up, as she stood and began to pace, clearly chewing on all the new information he was feeding her. By the end of this, Sam knew he'd likely have to pull on her emotional strings to get her to drop it. That tore him up inside.

"I still don't get it," Natalie said, shaking her head. "It doesn't add up for me. If Lex Hester hired such skilled people, with millions at his disposal, why would he still feel the need to pull you into the situation? Why not just go find Hebbard on his own?"

Sam was ready for this question. "He *was* going after Hebbard. The FBI said a crew of contract operatives were also on the hunt. However, Hester was willing to work every angle he could possibly find to get the job done quickly. The FBI said once Hester's team discovered I was the attorney directly involved with Hawkins—and they found out about my full backstory with last year's Redrock scandal—Hester pulled the trigger to also use me to find Hebbard. I wasn't his only pawn, either. Hebbard's son was also desperately trying to find his father. Apparently, Hebbard's son has a baby whom Hester's team kidnapped in North Carolina. Fortunately, he's safe now, too, along with the child." Sam shook his head. "Hester is a crazy man. He wasn't satisfied with his hundreds of millions. He was going after the billions in Mexico, at all costs. We all got swept up in his sinister scheme."

Natalie sat on the bed again. "Hester needs to pay big-time."

Sam tried to move it along. "The FBI is asking for all of us to lay low for a while, at least until they can find and apprehend Hester. The man is *very* dangerous and vindictive. They said we could greatly assist in their investigation by keeping this entire matter to ourselves, so as not to create even more hurdles for them to find this guy and bring him to justice. They've offered us the option of private FBI protection for the next few months, if we want."

"Uh, no, thanks," Tommy declared. "I'm good."

Natalie had a serious frown on her face. "They expect us to just keep our mouths shut? You can't be serious, Sam! Don't they know I have a duty and responsibility to seek out the truth and expose this corruption? Plus, the guy had me thrown into the back of a damn van by goons who stuck a black hood over my head. I'm not just going to *lay low* to make their jobs easier on them. I have a powerful voice that could help find the man."

Sam sighed. "Natalie, please."

She huffed. "Look at what they did to you! You've been shot!"

"Believe me, I know. And I also want Hester to pay." Sam knelt in front of her, his hand on her knee, eye to eye. He gave her his most sincere look, his voice calm and caring. Time to pull on the heartstrings. "Look, I just want to go back to our normal lives, okay? Haven't you and I been through enough already the past eight months? I don't want to be part of another dramatic news story. Last year was more than enough for me—it made my life a living hell for a while. Right now, the world knows *nothing* about our involvement. I'm begging you to keep it that way, Natalie. I just want us to move forward, get married, and start our brand-new life together. Isn't that what you want?"

Natalie exhaled, softened. "Yes, of course, I want that. It's just—"

"Please, I'm begging you, let it go. For me. Okay?"

He could tell it was taking everything within her to yank on the reins, but she finally relented. "Okay, I'll think about it. For you."

He smiled, took her face in his hands, kissed her, and she wrapped her arms around his neck. He pushed her back onto the bed, began kissing her more passionately.

Tommy sighed loudly. "Uh, hello? Am I even here? Am I invisible? Can anyone see me? I'd tell you two to go get a room, but then we're *already* in a room. Maybe I should just step outside."

Sam laughed, sat back up. "No need, Mav. Let's get this over with already. I want to go home."

SIXTY-EIGHT

Spencer Lloyd opened the door to his condo.

Pop was sitting in the beat-up recliner, wearing only a Red Sox sweat-shirt and boxer shorts, snoring away, the TV on with the volume near full blast. Lloyd was sure the neighbors just loved that. He'd received four com-plaints already from building management. Lloyd had begged his father to keep the volume at a reasonable level, but it was no use. The old man prob-ably couldn't even hear management banging on the door. Lloyd quickly found the remote in the crack of the recliner and turned down the volume. Then he picked a few broken potato-chip crumbs off the man's chest, stuck them in the open bag sitting in his father's lap, and set the bag on the cof-fee table—which was littered with empty bottles of Old Thumper beer. It looked like his dad had helped himself to the entire six-pack.

Lloyd plopped down on the sofa next to his father, overcome with fatigue. It had been a hell of a long day—traveling back and forth to New Orleans—and he still didn't have any of the answers he wanted. He was frustrated about that. Why the hell would Director Stone call him out of the blue and order the release of Sam Callahan? Especially with a known assassin still on the loose? Callahan was his primary target! He let out a deep sigh, eased back into the cushions. William Holden was on the TV screen. Lloyd recognized the film as the classic *The Bridge on the River Kwai*. Pop loved that movie and had practically worn a hole in the DVD.

Lloyd rubbed his face. He reached down, grabbed the bag of chips, and began munching. His phone rang. Agent Epps. He quickly answered it.

"You find out anything?" Lloyd asked Epps.

"Apparently Stone got a call directly from Barton, who personally asked him to pull us off Callahan."

Lloyd cursed. "You're kidding me?"

"Nope. My source is as solid as they get. There was more discussion there between the two men, but she couldn't give me any more details on it. She said Stone has been very closed-lipped about the entire deal."

Lloyd tried to put it together. Cliff Barton was the director of the CIA. Barton and Stone had a decent relationship. It was certainly not hostile, like relationships had been in the past between the two investigative heads. So Barton at the last moment called Stone, who agreed to step in and completely torpedo Lloyd's entire investigation—all without further explanation. What the hell was going on? Lloyd was a loyal servant not prone to step out of line or disregard marching orders from the top. But this sure as hell didn't sit well with him. He'd put his own men in the line of fire. It pissed him off. Whatever was going on had to be big enough for Stone to do something completely out of character.

"Anything on our boy Gerlach?" Lloyd asked Epps.

"Nothing. The ghost has vanished again."

"I bet Barton knows."

"What do you want to do?"

Lloyd thought about it for only a moment. "I want you to keep tabs on Callahan. I don't know what all is going on here, but I don't like it. I want to know where he goes next."

"Yes, sir."

"And, Mike, one more thing. Don't go through any official channels. Let's keep this off-line and only between us for now."

"You got it, Chief."

SIXTY-NINE

The black Lincoln sedan dropped Alger Gerlach on the isolated airstrip next to a waiting Gulfstream. He took a moment, studied his surroundings. There were no other cars around the plane. The hangar was a quarter mile to his left. Just the same, he kept his gun within easy reach. The job had been unorthodox from the beginning. Although Gerlach had sat down with some powerful leaders over the years, he never expected to find himself sitting across a café table in Atrani, overlooking the Tyrrhenian Sea in southwestern Italy, with the head of the CIA. The man was one of the most powerful investigative forces in the world. Gerlach was never even checked for weapons, which he had at the small of his back and his ankle, as if they knew he would never dare go for the kill. The head of the CIA was offering him a contract. Gerlach was one of the most-wanted assassins in the world; yet instead of arresting him, the CIA was offering him a job. The geopolitical world had shifted dramatically. An assassin like Gerlach was now more valuable as a free man than an arrested man. Even so, Gerlach knew he should never have accepted the job. He'd let the thrill of the prospect cloud his better judgment. He regretted that now.

He felt even more perplexed now that they were pulling him off, as if the job was complete; the rest of the money had already been wired to his numbered account.

Complete? Hardly. His target had slipped through his fingers three different times. That gnawed at him. Gerlach wasn't sure what to think. Either he was off his game, or the target was a tremendous player—the truth might be somewhere in the middle.

Gerlach stepped into the night. The Gulfstream's powerful engines were already humming. He took one last glance in both directions, then quickly walked over to the plane and climbed up the steps to the cabin. There were two pilots in the cockpit and no one else on the plane. Gerlach eased to the back and sat in one of the plush leather seats. He watched out the window as the black Lincoln disappeared up the road. A few seconds later, one of the pilots stepped out of the cockpit, shut the door to the plane, and returned to the cockpit. He never once looked back in Gerlach's direction, which was very wise of him.

The Gulfstream's engines hummed even louder, and the plane rocked forward.

Pulling the folded photo out of his pocket, Gerlach studied the face of his target: Sam Callahan. He shook his head, cursed. The plane sped forward and began to lift off the runway. Gerlach stared out the window and could see the brilliant white lights of DC below.

His eyes shifted back to the photo in his hands, his blood continuing to boil just below the surface. Gerlach knew this wasn't over yet.

SEVENTY

Natalie went for an early-morning jog.

It felt good to get out, get some fresh air, get the blood pumping. Sam was still asleep on the sofa in her living room, after being up for most of the night, pacing back and forth. Twice she'd found him sitting alone in the dark of the living room, in complete silence, no TV, just staring at the walls. He tried to reassure her, claiming he was just having a hard time shutting down after the past two days, asking her to go back to bed and not to worry, but Natalie wondered if there was something more to it. He'd been acting a bit strange ever since they left their interviews with the FBI last night. Unusually quiet, even for Sam. More reserved than she'd *ever* seen him, even through their personal struggles the past few years. She didn't want to push him on it. After all, he'd been pushed to his limits the past couple of days, way beyond anything she'd experienced. If he wanted to keep quiet and stare at the walls for a few days, she'd certainly give him the space to do it.

But still . . . something didn't feel quite right.

Natalie jogged up her street, past other colorful row houses. She checked over her shoulder a few times—a habit from the past two days. No one was back there, as far as she could tell. Just the same, she did a little zigzagging through the neighborhood. They'd declined the FBI's offer of private protection. Neither of them wanted to be followed around by the feds the next few months. If they could handle life after the Redrock Security episode last year, they could certainly handle life after the past couple of days. Sam seemed oddly reassured that an assassin was no longer going to appear out of nowhere and try to take him out.

A mile up the street, Natalie peeled away into a park with a playground and benches. She stopped, stretched, searched the park. She spotted Michelle Blair, her source with the FBI, sitting on a bench across the way. Natalie walked over and sat next to her. Michelle was wearing a black suit and heels.

"Thanks for coming," Natalie said.

"Sure, Natalie. I'm just glad to see you're okay."

"Thanks. Did you find anything?"

Michelle pressed her lips together. "Are you sure you want to know about this? I don't want to cause any problems for you and Sam. You've certainly got a good thing going there."

Natalie nodded. "I'm sure."

"Okay. You were right. They weren't FBI. The men you talked to last night were CIA."

Natalie tilted her head. "Why would they claim to be FBI?"

Michelle shrugged. "No idea. It's bizarre, because I do know that Director Stone personally gave them the authority to misrepresent themselves to you as the FBI."

Natalie sat back in the bench. "Does Sam know any of this?"

"I don't know."

"Okay, thanks, Michelle. I appreciate it."

"Sure. Good luck."

Natalie watched as Michelle walked away. Her head was spinning with new questions. So much of this didn't make sense, and yet Sam was very insistent that they just put it all behind them and move on with their lives. As a matter of fact, he'd talked more with her about

He was actually much angrier when he thought his real father was Rich Hebbard. Now that he knew it was actually Marcus Pelini, there was just a hollow hole inside his chest—especially with what his father had put him through, not once but now twice. Marcus Pelini had chosen his own son as a pawn, first with Lucas and Lisa McCallister last fall, and now a second time with his trip to Mexico City. What kind of man would do that? What kind of father would choose to put his own son in so much danger? Sam couldn't comprehend any of it. Nor could he comprehend how the gray-bearded man wanted Sam to sign up *voluntarily* for a third round.

Yet Sam was somehow drawn to him, like a dumb moth to a flame.

Inside every man is a boy who wants to know his father.

Even if that father is his adversary.

"What do you need from me, Sam?" David asked on the phone, stirring Sam away from his own thoughts.

"I might need some time off, if that's okay. Just to get my feet beneath me again."

"You got it. Take whatever time you need."

"Thanks, David. I'll call you soon."

Sam hung up, began to walk the sidewalks. He circled around the National World War II Memorial, headed toward the Reflecting Pool. It began to sprinkle. He watched the raindrops ripple in the water. The drops quickly became heavier. A few umbrellas sprang up. Most people out and about began to scatter for shelter. Sam just continued to walk, hands in pockets, farther up the sidewalk, the raindrops soaking him.

He found him waiting on a bench. Black trench coat with matching fedora.

Sam took one last deep breath, walked over, sat next to Marcus Pelini.

They sat in silence for a few seconds.

Then Sam turned, said, "I'm in."

ACKNOWLEDGMENTS

Writing this book has been an incredible journey. I'm so grateful to so many who supported and helped me take this important next step in my writing career. Please forgive me if I miss you below.

Readers, your enthusiasm for Sam Callahan drives this whole thing forward. Thank you for giving Sam a shot, for writing so many great reviews, sending me encouraging notes, and telling your family and friends. Let's keep the momentum rolling!

Thomas & Mercer, my wonderful publishing family, thank you so much for giving me the opportunity to continue to tell Sam Callahan stories. I've loved every minute of working with each member of this unbelievable team. What a blessing!

Liz Pearsons, you're an incredible editor who cares for me so well, in spite of the way I constantly inundate you with random e-mails. Thank you so much for your patience as you help me grow and learn as an author. You've made this last year an amazing experience for me, and I'm forever grateful. Go, Pack, Go!

Sarah Shaw, thank you for hand-holding a newbie like me through the publishing process with its many quirks and nuances. You do it with such grace and joy, and you never make me feel stupid, which I value the most!

Bryon Quertermous, you were like a master wizard in the way you helped me dig deeper into the story, smooth out plotlines, and develop characters. The book is so much better because it was placed in your craftsman hands. Thank you!

David Hale Smith, my agent, thank you for guiding me through each step of this journey so far, with wise thoughts about my writing choices, next steps, and words of encouragement at just the right time. I'm in such good hands because you're behind the steering wheel!

To my wonderfully supportive community of friends and family who have been an unbelievable source of encouragement to me: although there are way too many to individually name here, so many of you kept excitedly asking me, "When is the sequel coming out?" The enthusiastic twinkle in your eyes drove me to put the words down on the page.

To Nancy, my mother, whom I know prays over my writing every single day, and to Doug and Nancy, my in-laws, who steadily champion me forward. To every member of my family who always offers me a consistent voice of support, I'm so grateful to each of you.

To my girls, Anna, Madison, and Lexi, who are proud to have a daddy who writes books and who do their very best to give me the time and space to accomplish such a feat. You girls make me just as proud of you!

To Katie, my wife and my rock, the one who keeps our family ship safely in the waters, who helps keep my feet on steady ground, and who has personally sacrificed *so much* of herself these past couple of years so that I can fully chase this dream. I couldn't do any of this without you and wouldn't even want to try. Thank you!

ABOUT THE AUTHOR

Chad Zunker studied journalism at the University of Texas, where he was also on the football team. He's worked for some of the most powerful law firms in the country and has invented baby products that are now sold all over the world. He is the author of *The Tracker*, the first Sam Callahan novel; lives in Austin with his wife, Katie, and their three daughters; and is hard at work on the next novel in the Sam Callahan series. For more on the author and his writing, visit www.chadzunker.com.